THE DARKNESS IN THE LIGHT

"A gripping, heartbreaking, and enthralling suspense so vividly immersive that I was hooked from the first page. With crisp, powerful writing and two extremely compelling voices, Kalla draws you in to the remote, intriguing world of the Arctic and the tragic, inexplicable suicide clusters that have ravaged a small, tight-knit town. Kalla is a clever master of surprise, dropping subtle clues and expertly changing course, so you can't possibly look away until the mystery is solved. It's an absolute must-read from a remarkable talent."

SAMANTHA M. BAILEY,
USA Today and #1 nationally bestselling author of
Woman on the Edge

"Explores powerful themes in Kalla's signature page-turning style. With hairpin turns and shocking twists, readers will be captivated until the final page."

ROBYN HARDING,
bestselling author of *The Perfect Family*

"Kalla excels at atmosphere and introducing us to environments that are unique in the genre. He deftly weaves together intrigue and important questions about how we treat mental health and ourselves, and I couldn't put this down until I discovered how it all worked out. Fast-paced and complex, this is a must-read."

CATHERINE McKENZIE, bestselling author of
Six Weeks to Live and *I'll Never Tell*

"Kalla is unparalleled in his ability to create compelling characters that embody societal trauma and medical complexities. . . . Both heartbreaking and brave, this is a boldly written story that fans will love and new readers will devour."

AMBER COWIE,
author of *Last One Alive*

LOST IMMUNITY

"Kalla . . . has a knack for writing eerily prescient thrillers."

CBC Books

"Always there to hold up a mirror to society—his last book, *The Last High*, took on the opioid crisis—Kalla's new *Lost Immunity* book sits smack dab in the middle of what the world has been going through for the last year."

Vancouver Sun

THE LAST HIGH

"A thrilling, front-line drama about the opioid crisis."

KATHY REICHS

"Kalla has long had his stethoscope on the heartbeat of his times. . . . In his latest, the focus is on Vancouver's opioid crisis. . . . [A] lively story."

Toronto Star

"A riveting thriller. . . . This important, must-read book is not only well-researched and entirely realistic, it gives a human face to a devastating epidemic."

ROBYN HARDING,
bestselling author of *The Perfect Family*

"Kalla is terrific at building suspense as the case progresses, uncovering a web of dealers, sellers, and users."

Globe and Mail

"A sobering glimpse into the drug overdose crisis. . . . An entertaining, if slightly eerie read."

Vancouver Sun

"If you want an engrossing, edge-of-your-seat thriller that combines good detective work, corruption, savage criminal practices, a dark, seamy portrait of a large Canadian city, and a hard-hitting lesson on the medical and emotional effects of opioid drugs, then *The Last High* certainly fills that prescription."

Montreal Times

WE ALL FALL DOWN

"A fast-paced thriller with an historical overlay and a dash of romantic tension."

Vancouver Sun

"A tightly plotted thriller, energetic and completely believable."

Booklist

THE
DARKNESS
IN THE
LIGHT

A THRILLER

DANIEL KALLA

PUBLISHED BY SIMON & SCHUSTER

New York   London   Toronto   Sydney   New Delhi

SIMON &
SCHUSTER
CANADA

Simon & Schuster Canada
A Division of Simon & Schuster, Inc.
166 King Street East, Suite 300
Toronto, Ontario M5A 1J3

This Simon & Schuster Canada edition May 2022

SIMON & SCHUSTER CANADA and colophon are trademarks of Simon & Schuster, Inc.

For information about special discounts for bulk purchases, please contact Simon & Schuster Special Sales at 1-800-268-3216 or CustomerService@simonandschuster.ca.

Interior design by Yvonne Taylor

Manufactured in the United States of America

10 9 8 7 6 5 4 3 2 1

Library and Archives Canada Cataloguing in Publication
Title: The darkness in the light / Daniel Kalla.
Names: Kalla, Daniel, author.
Description: Simon & Schuster Canada edition.
Identifiers: Canadiana (print) 20210311053 | Canadiana (ebook) 20210311061 | ISBN 9781982191399 (softcover) | ISBN 9781982191405 (ebook)
Classification: LCC PS8621.A47 D37 2022 | DDC C813/.6—dc23

ISBN 978-1-9821-9139-9
ISBN 978-1-9821-9140-5 (ebook)

For my daughters, Chelsea and Ashley

THE
DARKNESS
IN THE
LIGHT

PART I

DAVID

CHAPTER 1

"I'm not trying to kill myself." Though his expression was flat, Nigel McGowan's color—at least how it appeared on my laptop screen—was whiter than the wall behind him.

How many times have I heard those words? Another patient had sworn the same to me only two days before, during my weekend on call for the Anchorage Regional Hospital. That patient had begged me to free him from his involuntary confinement in the ER. But the raw ligature burns around his neck—from where the noose had yanked the hook free from the ceiling at the last moment—were far more persuasive than any of his pleas.

"You're not suicidal," I said, focusing back on Nigel. "You just don't want to extend your life any longer than necessary. That right?"

"Exactly right, Dr. Spears," he said, as sweat beaded along his receding hairline.

Having seen the worrisome images of Nigel's swollen, red-and-black blistered foot and shin, I was surprised he was upright at all with such an overwhelming infection snaking up his leg and into his bloodstream. "All right, Nigel," I said. "Say I dove to the bottom of a swimming pool and decided not to extend my life by resurfacing. Wouldn't that make me suicidal?"

He crossed his arms and rested them on his bulging belly. "That's a silly comparison."

"Is it, though? You've had uncontrolled diabetes for years, and you still refuse to take insulin. It gave you a heart attack before your fortieth birthday. And now you've got an infection that, according to your own doctor, will cost you your leg—probably your life—unless you agree to go to hospital for intravenous antibiotics." I pointed at the screen. "Make no mistake, Nigel. You're killing yourself. You're just doing it slower than most."

"I'm of sound mind. And I don't want medications." His damp lip quivered. "It's my choice."

He was right. I had no legal grounds to certify Nigel and keep him involuntarily in hospital for treatment—unlike my patient who'd tried to hang himself—even though his life was in the same degree of jeopardy. That conundrum made my temples throb. "And in my example, Nigel, it would be within my rights to stay underwater until I drowned."

Nigel swiped the sweat from his brow with the back of his hand. "This isn't helping."

"Help?" I stared intently at his wan face. "Since when do you come to me for help?"

His image froze on the video chat screen momentarily, but his words were still clear. "What kind of psychiatrist talks like that?"

"I'll give you this, you're one of my most reliable patients. Over three years, and I don't think you've missed an appointment yet. But in that time, when have you ever taken my advice?"

"You mean your drugs, don't you?"

"No, Nigel. Advice. For years, I've been begging you to come join group therapy. To join any group at all."

"Group therapy?" He huffed. "For an agoraphobic?"

"You're not agoraphobic."

"I have a pathological fear of rejection."

"As we've discussed, that's not agoraphobia." Besides, technically, it was a single rejection he kept reliving. Six years after being dumped by his then boyfriend, he was still grieving the breakup of a relationship that had only lasted months. "Let's say you don't die, Nigel. How do you feel about living with only one leg?"

"I hardly ever leave my apartment anyway." But the quick flick of his eyes betrayed his anxiety.

"And then when you lose the other leg? You OK with not leaving your bed, either?"

He eyed me dolefully. "Where's your compassion, Dr. Spears?"

Nigel had a point. A casual observer might have assumed I was taunting my own patient. But I saw no other choice. Pity was the one card Nigel relied on. It gave him a sense of control. He used it to handcuff the few people in his life who still cared about him, including me. And I knew from previous experiences that sometimes only harsh boundaries—even the threat of abandonment—would motivate him to comply.

"Enough of this manipulative crap," I said. "I'm calling an ambulance and you're going to go to the hospital. Right now!"

"I won't go."

I held his gaze. "If you don't, Nigel, I'm firing you as a patient. And you and I will have no further contact. Ever."

His eyes went a bit wider. "You can't do that!"

"Yes, I can," I said. "Don't worry, though. I'll find you another psychiatrist. One who will be far more sympathetic to your plight. You can tell him or her all about how Gary abandoned you while the gangrene creeps up your leg."

His voice faltered. "Please, Dr. Spears . . ."

I stared back at him, not giving an inch. His life hung in the balance. "It's your call, Nigel."

His image froze again, for longer this time. When the screen came back to life, his chin hung low, but he was nodding.

"It's the right choice, Nigel." I offered a reassuring smile. "This is what we're going to do: I'm going to hang up now and call the ambulance. And I'll see you at the hospital later."

Before he could reply, I ended the videoconference with a click of the mouse, partly because I wanted to dispatch the ambulance right away but mainly because I didn't want to leave any wiggle room for him to renege.

I picked up the phone and dialed 9-1-1. The dispatcher confirmed an ambulance would be arriving at Nigel's apartment within minutes.

As I dictated the note into his electronic medical record, I reflected on the pros and cons of virtual medicine, which had become so prevalent, especially for us psychiatrists, in the post-COVID world. Had Nigel been in my office, he might have had time to tell me he'd changed his mind while waiting for the ambulance. Then again, if we had been sitting face-to-face, connecting with one another's physical presence, maybe it would've been much easier to convince him to go to the hospital in the first place.

It was the paradox of virtual medicine. Psychiatrists needed to see their patients. Visual cues were often more important to us than words. And the widespread availability of videoconferencing made remote consults possible. But while virtual care offered all the convenience in the world, it also lacked the immediacy and intimacy of a one-on-one session, missing all those intangibles that could never transcend the screen. One day, some brilliant neuroscientist was bound to identify the alternate hot spots in the cerebral cortex and various pheromones that respond to human proximity. More than likely, some researcher already had.

But an in-person visit wasn't an option for my next patient. She lived almost a thousand miles away, beyond the Arctic Circle, in the northernmost town in North America: Utqiagvik—formerly known as Barrow—Alaska. For Brianna O'Brien, like my other patients who lived in a town that was only accessible by air, virtual care was their sole option, apart from my biannual visits. I tried to get up there in the spring and again in late summer, and my trip for later next month was already booked.

I clicked the invitation icon on my laptop, and Brianna's head appeared, framed by reddish-blonde hair that extended beyond her shoulders. With her makeup-free, heart-shaped face and her grayish doe-eyes, Brianna looked closer to fifteen or sixteen than the twenty-two-year-old she was. She wore the same black T-shirt—emblazoned with the words "Fuck the Police!"—that I had seen at previous sessions, but I didn't recognize her backdrop, which looked to be the interior of a trailer or an RV. Usually, during our sessions, she sat in her small but always immaculate kitchen.

Brianna nodded her greeting, her mouth set in the ambiguous Mona Lisa smile that I'd come to expect from her.

"Hi, Brianna. Where are you?"

"At a friend's."

"Where's Nevaeh?" Usually by now, her adorable four-year-old daughter would have popped into the frame and peppered me with rapid-fire questions.

"With my aunt."

Her inquisitive child resembled my Ali, in looks and personality, when my daughter had been about the same age. Nevaeh's absence only reinforced how I much I was missing Ali this summer. My sixteen-year-old had chosen to stay in Seattle with her mom to attend an intense dance camp instead of spending the month of August with me in Anchorage. Or, at least, that was how my ex-wife had justified it.

"How are you doing today?" I asked.

She ran a hand through her hair, pulling away loose strands. "I'm OK."

I picked up on the hesitance in her tone. "You sure?"

"I still feel kind of . . . fuzzy, I guess."

"Since you started the new medication?"

"Maybe, yeah."

"That's normal. The side effects with Ketopram are always worst in the first month. And they're usually gone by the end of the second."

Brianna accepted my explanation with a twitch of her shoulders.

"And your appetite?" I asked.

Her screen flickered for a second or two. "It's OK," she said.

"And what about your thoughts, Brianna?"

Her gaze drifted away from the camera. "They're . . . quiet."

I found her choice of words curious. "Quiet how? Peaceful?"

"Calm, I guess."

"How are you sleeping?"

"Not great." She bit her lip and then added, "But I never really do."

"Some people get vivid dreams when they start taking Ketopram. Are you experiencing those?"

"Just one. But I keep having it."

I flashed an encouraging smile. "Can you elaborate?"

"It's a nightmare, not a dream."

"Can you describe it to me, Brianna?"

"Me and Nevaeh are in my car," she said softly. "She's in her booster seat in the back, playing on my phone. We're not moving. It's really gray outside, and I can't really see through the window. At first, I think I must be parked in a dense fog or something . . ."

I gave her a few moments to finish, but she only picked at a few more loose hairs. "But it's not fog?" I prompted.

She sunk lower in her seat. "That's when I see the drip coming from the corner of the driver's window. Then the window cracks, and freezing water gushes inside. And just then—when I realize we're underwater—I wake up."

"You mean like submerged? Under the sea?"

She nodded.

"How did you end up there?"

"Don't know."

"In this nightmare, you didn't deliberately drive into the water, did you?"

"No."

"Do you ever fantasize about harming yourself, Brianna?"

"Nevaeh was in the car, too!" Her voice cracked.

"How about without Nevaeh?" I asked softly.

She shook her head. "I'd never leave my daughter alone in the world."

Brianna had rarely been even this forthcoming with me in the four months since I'd started seeing her. I didn't want to stretch the bounds of her trust, so I didn't push further.

Her family doctor had been treating Brianna with various antidepressants on and off since he'd diagnosed her with a delayed postpartum depression. I recognized early on in our therapy that Brianna was still suffering from a major mood disorder. Since the antidepressants she had been taking hadn't worked, I'd switched her over to Ketopram the month before. The groundbreaking drug, which had only been on the market for the past two years, had proven effective on other patients with refractory depressions that failed to respond to other antidepressants. Including my own.

"How about your overall mood?" I asked. "Are you finding more enjoyment in things?"

"Maybe? I mean, you know, with Nevaeh and all."

I chuckled. "That kid is something."

"She's everything," Brianna said with a blank nod. "I'm crying a little less, too."

"So . . . progress, then?"

"Yeah, maybe."

Her tone was too unconvincing to leave be. "Is there something else, Brianna?"

She opened her mouth and then stopped, dismissing it with another shrug. "I can't remember the last time I laughed."

"Laughed?"

"A belly laugh, you know? Like when you can't stop giggling with your girlfriends. Used to do it all the time. Before the depression."

Brianna had a way of describing her depression as a single sudden event, like an earthquake hitting, instead of an evolving medical condition. I had probed before, trying to find a specific precipitant for her despondency beyond the postpartum hormones, but she inevitably would clam up.

There were still so many pieces of Brianna's life that were missing for me. Areas that remained taboo. I knew hardly anything about the father who abandoned her family when she was young or the oil field worker who'd fathered Nevaeh. In an earlier session, Brianna had blurted something about a man who'd taken advantage of her while she was still in high school. But she backtracked almost immediately, and I wasn't able to unearth any more details. I hadn't pushed too hard, aware it would take a lot of time and patience to get her to open up about any trauma.

With some patients, I could establish therapeutic intimacy in a single session—with others, it took years, if ever. Brianna and I were nowhere near that point. And in my experience, each patient required an individual approach to getting there. As much as Nigel often needed a strong hand, Brianna responded best to a softer approach. I'd seen how quickly the wrong line of inquiry or even a single question could shut her down for an entire session.

As we only had thirty minutes booked for this appointment, I used the remainder of our time to emphasize the nonpharmaceutical remedies that we'd discussed before to complement her medication, including exercise and sleep.

As the session was ending, Brianna bit her lip and viewed me with uncharacteristic inquisitiveness. "Will I ever get back to being me again, Dr. Spears?"

"You will. It'll take time. But you will."

"Time . . . Yeah, OK." She dug her fingers through her hair again as if sifting through sand. "Dr. Spears?"

"Yes?" I surreptitiously glanced at the clock at the bottom of my screen. It was five minutes past the hour, and I could see my next patient had already logged into the virtual waiting room.

"It's just that . . . there's . . . I don't know . . ."

I could see she was struggling to put something into words, but I was distracted by the time-warning light that was now flashing on my screen. So instead of trying to draw what she wanted to say out of her, I said, "Let's pick this up on Friday, all right, Brianna?"

Not once did I suspect those would be the last words I ever spoke to her.

CHAPTER 2

My phone pinged with another text from my friend, Javier Gutiér-rez. "Late night," it began. "Make mine a quadruple shot." I'd forgotten that it was my turn to pick up coffees, which was going to make me even later to meet him.

I stood at my sink and glanced at the pentagonal pink pill between my fingers. I understood that pharmaceutical companies designed their tablets with such distinct shapes for various purposes, including ease of swallowing and to promote absorption at certain levels in the gut. But I also knew it was mainly a marketing ploy to hook doctors and patients on the pill's unique look.

I popped the tablet in my mouth and washed it down with a quick gulp of water. I'd been taking the medication for over a year and a half, which made me one of the earlier Alaskans to start using Ketopram outside of the clinical trials. I no longer experienced any side effects, but the first month had been rough. The fatigue and heartburn hadn't bothered me nearly as much as the intense dreams. They weren't exactly nightmares, but they were far from pleasant, often centering around my dead parents, full of the imagery of loss and loneliness, such as the hospice bed on which my dad died. The kind of dream where you are thrilled to see a lost loved one but somehow know, even in the moment, that none of it is real.

I stuck the cap on the bottle and shoved it back inside the vanity, aware that even if all the side effects—including those melancholic dreams—had persisted, I would have continued to take the medication. It saved my life.

I pulled on my shoes and hurried out the door of my condo, onto the elevator, and out onto Fourth Avenue, where the sun was already high at eight in the morning and would remain so until well after midnight.

One of the things I appreciated most about living in Anchorage's downtown core was that I hardly ever needed to drive in the summertime. I could walk from my home to my office or even to the hospital in under twenty minutes, which alone would have made the move from our old house in the residential Hillside East neighborhood worthwhile. Besides, staying alone in that big empty house, surrounded by nothing but bittersweet memories of Beth and Ali, would never have been an option. I couldn't imagine a quicker path to insanity.

Jogging down Fourth Avenue, I was sweating by the time I reached Steeps, my favorite coffee shop. The heat was building, well into the seventies, and I had little doubt we were heading for another record high for late July. If only climate change deniers would come to Alaska, they wouldn't even have to go see our rapidly receding glaciers. The near tropical temperatures in Anchorage alone should be enough to convince them of the foolishness of their beliefs.

Nicky, the chatty barista whose arms and neck formed a tapestry of tattoos, predicted my order down to the extra shots for Javier and had me back on the road in minutes. The two large coffees slowed me down, but I only had two more blocks to go until I reached the staircase leading down to the beachside trail.

The Tony Knowles Coastal Trail was easily Anchorage's most

popular summer destination for tourists and locals alike. With good reason. The eleven-mile paved pathway hugged the city's western shore along the Cook Inlet. The trail offered stunning views of the downtown harbor, framed by the Chugach Mountain Range to the east. And on clear days like today, there were several spots to get a peek of North America's highest mountain, Denali, that floated ethereally two hundred miles to the north.

Javier and I often walked the trail. Occasionally, if we had time on the weekends, we would complete the whole eleven-mile route that ended in the massive oasis of nature within the city limits that was Kincaid Park. Today, we were squeezing our walk in before work, so we would likely have to turn around once we reached Earthquake Park. I wondered what the point of such a short walk would be, but Javier wouldn't have let me cancel. He liked to keep close tabs on me. Both as my friend and my psychiatrist.

Dressed in stylish active wear with a Yankees ball cap pulled tightly over his thatch of jet-black hair, Javier paced at the bottom of the staircase. Fifteen years older, leaner, and a good two inches taller than me, Javier resembled a character actor whose name I didn't know but who often showed up as a distinguished, Latino political leader or business executive in the thrillers I liked to watch. Fiercely proud of his roots as a third-generation Hispanic Alaskan, Javier sometimes jokingly referred to himself as a "native A-latin-skan."

"Morning, David." He greeted me with a short burst of his distinctive machine-gun laughter. "Guess I'm going to have to settle for an iced coffee this morning, huh?"

"Sorry, Javier, time got away from me," I said as I handed him the cup.

Javier uttered a satisfied sigh when he took the warm cup from my hand. "Shall we?" he asked as he set off down the shoreline trail at his usual rapid clip without waiting for a reply.

The breeze off the water brought a welcome coolness, which

helped explain why the pathway was so crowded with walkers, joggers, and cyclists on a weekday morning.

"So?" he asked as I caught up to him.

"So . . . ?"

"How are you, David?"

"Fine."

"How are you sleeping, eating, et cetera, et cetera?"

"All good, thanks."

He flashed an exasperated smile. "Spoken like a patient truly withholding."

"It's been eighteen months, Javier. I'm back to myself now. And besides, I'm not your patient anymore."

"Now you sound like one in full denial."

Technically, Javier was correct. I was still his patient. And since it had been less than two years since my hospitalization, he was required to complete a form for the state medical board every month attesting to my fitness to practice. I hadn't seen him in his office in almost a year, but our walks were a hybrid between two close friends catching up and a mental wellness check, even if they were skewed heavily toward the personal rather than the professional.

"If only the pool of psychiatrists were a little deeper in this town," I said with a roll of my eyes, "I wouldn't be trapped in this pointless cycle with you."

"What about dating?" Javier asked, ignoring my dig.

"What about it?"

"When are you going to start?"

"Who has time?"

"Two years since you and Beth split up, right?"

"Roughly, yeah." I had to bite my tongue not to point out that it had been just over twenty-seven months.

"I think you might've exceeded the statute of limitations on faithfulness. Especially since you weren't the one who left."

Beth might have been the one who had moved out, but I had

no doubt who was to blame. In retrospect, I'm not sure why she hung in as long as she did. Beth had been right when she told me that I had shut her out "like a stranger." My depression might have explained my mood, but it didn't excuse my attitude. I couldn't have been much colder or more irritable with her. After twenty years together, beginning as med school sweethearts, I owed her more. I regretted how I'd treated her. And I still missed her.

"Look at me, David." Javier clutched his chest. "Maria's been gone for just over six months, and I'm dating up a storm."

"You never really liked Maria in the first place."

"That's not true. Well . . . not entirely. She was more of a transitional wife."

"Have you nailed down the fourth one yet?"

Javier let off another burst of laughter. "No, but I'm auditioning like crazy."

"No doubt you'll find crazy, too."

A rollerblader whizzed past as the trail took us southwest along the mudflats of Kinik Arm, which offered a dramatic view of the mountains across the narrow passage.

Deliberately changing the subject, I said, "I admitted a guy on the weekend. He tried to hang himself."

"And?" Javier shrugged. For a psychiatrist, admitting a suicidal patient while on call was as routine as a surgeon hospitalizing someone with appendicitis.

"This guy was already on antidepressants," I continued. "In fact, Ketopram."

"You sure he was taking it properly?"

"Blood test showed his drug level to be therapeutic."

He shrugged. "Show me a drug that is a hundred percent effective against anything."

As much of an advocate as I was for Ketopram, Javier was more so. He was the reason Alaska was an early adopter and one of the leading consumers of the medication per capita anywhere in the world. He had gone to school with the scientist who created Ketopram by adding an extra ring or two—I could never keep the biochemistry straight—to the familiar molecule of serotonin reuptake inhibitor contained in drugs such as Prozac. Javier lectured to colleagues statewide on its benefits, for which he was paid handsomely by its parent company, Pierson Pharmaceuticals.

"Just thought you should know," I said. "Seeing how much stock you own in Pierson."

"I've been begging you to buy in for the past three years, David. The stock has gone through the roof." He held up his palms. "Then again you only have to support *one* ex-wife, and she has a decent-paying job."

I chuckled. "Unlike your harem."

"My *defunct* harem. Can I help it if I'm only attracted to projects?"

I felt my phone vibrate in my pocket, but since I wasn't on call, I ignored it. "That patient who tried to hang himself, Javier. He told me the dreams—visions as he called them—were driving him nuts. That he couldn't take it anymore."

"We both know those are only temporary, David. They always abate with time."

"He has been on Ketopram for over two months, though," I said. "Have you heard of any others?"

"Treatment failures on Ketopram?"

"Or suicide attempts?"

He looked out toward the water. "You know as well as I do that it's a risk for any antidepressant."

It was true. Patients were most vulnerable to suicide attempts in the early stages of treatment with antidepressants, when their energy and motivation had begun to improve but their mood was still depressed.

"So there have been others?" I asked.

"A couple of sporadic cases reported. Yes. Tragic, but nothing unexpected."

Javier stopped without warning. He pulled his phone out of his pocket and pointed it toward the clearing off the side of the pathway. That was when I noticed that a moose was lazily grazing on the long grass about fifteen feet from us. There was nothing unusual about sighting a moose along this trail, but this one was as majestic as I'd ever seen, standing at least six feet tall, not even counting his prominent antlers. He gazed in our direction as he chewed, without showing the least fear. The sight reminded me again what a unique city and state we lived in.

After taking several shots with his phone upright and sideways, Javier slipped it back into his pocket and resumed his brisk walking pace. "David, I don't want to get ahead of myself. But *la amiga* from last night . . ." He whistled. "She could be the next Mrs. Gutiérrez."

"Well, we know one thing for sure—she won't be the last."

That set off a longer burst of Javier's laughter. Once it passed, he asked, "How's Ali?"

"Good. Very good. She won't be spending August here, though."

Javier's face fell. "Why not?"

"Beth enrolled her in some intensive dance camp in Seattle that goes most of the summer."

"What a shame. The only reason I spend anytime with you the rest of the year is so I can see that delightful kid of yours in the summer."

"Tough." I chuckled. "At least we'll still get our annual father-daughter road trip at the end of August."

Two summers ago, months after Beth and I separated, Ali and I had flown to Hawaii together. I splurged on a spectacular resort on the Big Island, but it was Ali's first vacation without her mom, and she brooded for most of it. I wasn't in much better shape. Last year, though, we had had a lot more fun touring Provence, where Ali fell in love with French art and history, refusing to skip a museum or gallery anywhere we went.

"Where to this year?" Javier asked. "Machu Picchu? Petra? Or perhaps straight to Atlantis?"

"Even better," I said. "I'm flying to Seattle and renting a car. Ali and I are driving up to Vancouver and then east from there through the interior of British Columbia—absolutely spectacular terrain, if you haven't seen it—and over to the Canadian Rockies. I've already booked hotels in Banff, Lake Louise, and Jasper. Ali's going to love it!"

"It's not like you're going to suffer, either, David."

"I only hope I don't miss one of your weddings while I'm gone."

"Fifty-fifty." He smiled.

We reached Earthquake Park and turned back for downtown, lapsing into conversation on the way back that ranged in topics from his mother's gourmet cooking to local politics. Javier and I said our goodbyes at the base of the same staircase where we had met. Once alone, I stopped to check my phone. I'd missed two calls, both from Dr. Evan Harman, one of the three family doctors who practiced in Utqiagvik.

Despite the warmth of the sun, a chill spread through my chest, and my fingers went numb. I had to lean back against the railing of the staircase.

Evan and I shared care for several patients in the town, but somehow I knew he had to be calling about Brianna. And the news would not be good.

CHAPTER 3

I stared at the blank screen back at my desk, fighting off the dread while working up the nerve to call Evan back. Though he was based over seven hundred miles away in Utqiagvik, I'd come to know the rural family doctor relatively well over the past four years. We spoke at least once a month to review care plans on our patients. About a year and a half ago, we'd switched from phone calls to videoconferences, which had tipped our relationship into what felt like a friendship.

Everything about Evan struck me as casual, from the dark jeans and wrinkled polo shirts he wore to work, to his messy mop of dark hair that always looked at least a month overdue for a trim. I also respected him highly as a physician. Not only was he up-to-date and knowledgeable, but he stayed in close touch with his patients. His insights into small, day-to-day changes in their lives proved invaluable to me. And I had no doubt that our patients benefited from our collaboration.

But my fingers were trembling as I reached for the mouse and clicked the icon to initiate a video call. Moments later, Evan's rugged face, handsome despite the sunken eyes and acne-scarred cheeks, appeared on my screen. Normally, he would have answered with a warm greeting and, usually, a corny joke. But his expression was as deadpan as his tone when he said, "Hello, David."

"Sorry I missed your call, Evan."

"Brianna O'Brien is dead," he said, as if her surname were necessary.

Even though his words were confirmatory, my breath caught in my throat. "How?" I croaked.

"Carbon monoxide."

"Jesus . . ."

"It could have been worse, David."

I was speechless.

"Nevaeh was in the car, too," he continued.

"Is she . . . ?"

"She's all right. She's with her great-aunt and -uncle. But she was in the back seat of the car."

"What happened?" I croaked.

"Brianna was drinking last night. Sometime, after midnight, she must've carried Nevaeh in her sleep out to the garage. She put her in the booster seat, plugged her phone into the radio, and turned the engine on. She even placed a rock against the accelerator." He stopped to clear his throat. "Her playlist was still going when they found her."

The horrific vision filled my brain. I imagined Brianna gently lowering Nevaeh into the car so as not to wake her. I could see her kissing the girl's forehead, closing the door, and then climbing into the driver's seat. "How . . . how did Nevaeh get out?"

Evan squeezed his temples between his thumb and forefinger. "The cops assume Nevaeh woke up at some point. Must've been early on. Otherwise the carbon monoxide would've gotten to her pretty quickly. Maybe she tried to wake her mom, but between the alcohol and the fumes . . ." He shook his head. "Nevaeh shut the garage door behind her, and at some point wandered over to her great-aunt's house. By the time they found Brianna . . ." His voice cracked. "Apparently, she always taught Nevaeh to close doors behind her."

The idea that the four-year-old inadvertently sealed her mother's fate by doing just what she was taught broke my heart. My eyes misted over, and I leaned away from the camera to wipe them with the bend of my elbow. "Did she leave a note?"

"No."

"I had an appointment with her only three days ago," I said more to myself than my colleague.

Evan grimaced. "I saw her just yesterday. She never even hinted . . . She told me things were getting better."

Never trust the word of the actively suicidal! one of my favorite professors used to preach to us during training. It was a proven fact that those who were most determined to kill themselves were often the least forthcoming about their plans. But all I said was "She fooled us both, Evan."

"Goddamn her!" he moaned. "To include Nevaeh? How could she have not said anything?"

My mind darted back to my last session with Brianna, analyzing the details as if watching a movie in slow motion, while scouring it for verbal or nonverbal clues.

"Did she mention her dream to you?" I finally asked.

"Dream? As in one of those Ketopram dreams?"

"Yeah. A recurrent nightmare. About drowning in her submerged car." I swallowed. "In the dream, Nevaeh was in the car with her, too."

"Nothing like that. No."

"Brianna promised me she would never try anything. Especially not with Nevaeh." My gaze fell to the keyboard. "I believed her."

"I saw her yesterday, David! Just a handful of hours before she did it. If anyone is to blame . . ."

"You said it yourself, Evan. She was drinking. No note. It was probably a spontaneous decision." I didn't really believe that, but he looked as desperate for reassurance as he must have thought I was.

"Probably."

"Will you let me know if you find out anything else? Toxicology reports and that kind of stuff? And, of course, any updates on Nevaeh?"

"Will do." His voice was hollow.

"Evan, there are times when no one can predict suicide."

"I hope this was one of those times."

I prayed it was. "Let's talk again soon."

After I disconnected the call, I fought the overwhelming urge to call my ex-wife. Beth had seen me through the worst outcomes in my career. As a colleague and a natural empath, she had a way of putting events into perspective when I couldn't. She would've known how to numb the searing pain and angst.

Instead, I opened the last note I had written on Brianna's electronic chart. "Cautious and withholding today—not unusual for Brianna," my words read. "Revisit her use of the term 'quiet thoughts' at a future session. She still requires close surveillance," I had concluded, without an inkling of how fateful those words would prove.

Had Brianna already decided on what she was going to do? Was that what she had been struggling to tell me before I hurried to end our session?

CHAPTER 4

The week following crawled past in a cloud of regret and self-recrimination. Work was a blessing in that it allowed me to focus on something other than Brianna's suicide and the haunting thought that she had almost killed her daughter, too.

As I was already on call for psychiatry at the Anchorage Regional Hospital this morning, I decided to drop in on Nigel McGowan on the medical floor where he'd been admitted. His foot infection had evolved into gangrene, which required an urgent radiological procedure to stent a blocked artery in his leg and save the limb. I'd been told that he wouldn't have survived another day at home.

I wasn't expecting his gratitude, but if I had been, I would've been sorely disappointed.

"Are you happy?" Nigel demanded as I stepped into his room.

"Not especially," I said, noting the IV line that ran into his neck and the bulky bandaging that wrapped his foot and leg up until the point where his mid-thigh was covered by the top sheet. While his complexion was not robust, at least he wasn't ashen anymore. "They tell me you're doing better."

Nigel tapped the tubing near his neck. "This is the last thing I wanted."

"You were about to lose your leg, Nigel."

What neither of us mentioned was that he was not certified and therefore could have left the hospital anytime he chose. In other words, he was voluntarily accepting the medical care.

Nigel eyed me almost wistfully. "What's the point of prolonging the inevitable?"

"It doesn't have to be inevitable, Nigel."

"We both know that's not true," he mumbled.

"Maybe this ordeal will finally scare some sense into you?" I sat down on the edge of his bed, carefully avoiding his bandaged leg. "To get you to start actually managing your diabetes? Hell, who knows? Maybe you'll even consider addressing your mental health issues in a meaningful way, too?"

He considered what I had said for a few seconds. "Who would care if I did?"

"I would, Nigel."

His expression didn't budge, but the words seemed to have struck a chord with him. At least I wanted to believe they had. Maybe I even needed to at this point. "You gave yourself a chance by coming into the hospital," I continued. "Why not give yourself a chance to heal? To meaningfully heal."

He looked away. "This isn't what I wanted," he muttered, but with less conviction than before.

"I'll drop in again tomorrow," I said as I rose and headed for the door.

I went down to the Psychiatry Unit to do rounds on my admitted patients. My first stop was at the seclusion room of the man who had attempted to hang himself. Every psychiatric facility had one or more of these sparse suicide-proof spaces, where everything down to the metal toilet was bolted to the floor or the walls to try to ensure that the occupants didn't harm themselves. Some patients still found a way to do exactly that, despite all the precautions. Some people were so single-minded in their suicidality that nothing would stop them.

The rope burns around Anton Hayes's neck had faded over the past week, but his mood remained as volatile as ever. The husky oil rig worker had been put back inside the seclusion room the evening before after he tried to break out of the locked unit by stealing a medical student's pass card.

Anton lay on his back on the mattress on the floor. He made no attempt to get up when I entered the room, so I knelt beside him, close enough to get a whiff of his stale body odor.

"How are you doing today, Anton?"

"Not too bad. Locked in a rubber room. Can barely keep my pajamas up without a draw string." He raised his eyebrows. "Eh, first world problems and all."

"You know that's for your own safety," I said. "Why did you try to bolt from the unit last night?"

Anton rolled away from me to face the wall. "Do you have any idea what it feels like to be imprisoned on a psych ward?"

I did, albeit briefly. But instead, I asked, "Do you know what it feels like to lose a loved one to suicide?" *Or to be the psychiatrist responsible for a patient who takes her own life?*

"The wife died last year," Anton said. "Rest of the family is scattered all over the Southwest. Most of my friends, too. Haven't heard from any of them in ages. I think they'd cope."

"You've been off Ketopram for over a week now. Have the nightmares subsided?"

"No more dreams."

"Must be a relief."

He rolled back to face me, his eyes seething. "I didn't try to off myself just because of a few fucking bad dreams."

I sensed silence was my best approach.

"My life is shit, Dr. Spears," he finally said. "I have nobody up here. Or anywhere. And I can't even find decent work these days. That rope would've done me and the world a favor. If only the fucking hook had held. Those nightmares . . ." He rolled away again. "They were just the final straw."

"It might feel like that now, Anton. It might even *be* like that right now. Doesn't mean you can't and won't change your circumstances."

"Sure, easy," he scoffed.

I didn't have the energy to try to convince him. Besides, it would've been futile at this point. "We're upping the dose of your citalopram today," I told him, citing the more established antidepressant I'd switched him to from Ketopram. "I'll see you again tomorrow."

Anton didn't acknowledge my comment, so I straightened and headed for the door, tapping at the bulletproof window for the security guard to let me out. As I stepped out into the hallway, I realized Anton wouldn't be released from the room anytime soon. Ketopram was the third antidepressant he had failed on or, more accurately, that had failed him. It was going to take a careful cocktail of medications, nonpharmacological interventions, and possibly electroconvulsive therapy to yank him out of his self-destructive despair, if anything could.

Sitting down at the computer at the back of the nursing station to chart my note, I reflected on the fine line that existed between the hopelessness caused by the neurochemical imbalance of a major depression versus the understandable despondence brought on by the cruel twists of fate. Hard as we psychiatrists sometimes liked to try, we couldn't medicate away all anguish.

A familiar voice came from over my shoulder. "Let me buy you a coffee, David. I know a quaint little vending machine on the third floor."

I looked over to see Javier. He wore one of his expensive slim-fitting suits—tan, today—with the requisite white collared shirt and brown leather accessories. If I'd been in a better mood, I might have checked his shoes to see if they were Gucci or Prada. "Tempting as that is," I said, "I have a consult waiting for me in the ER."

He eyed me with uncharacteristic seriousness. "I need to talk to you, David. As your department head."

I considered Javier many things—a close friend, a mentor, and even, reluctantly, as my psychiatrist—but apart from during our annual hospital reappointment interviews, I never thought of him as my boss. And I couldn't remember another time when he'd ever asked to speak to me in such an official capacity.

"Sure, we can talk," I said. "But save your quarters, I'm all coffeed out today."

We left the unit and headed to his office at the far end of the floor. We sat across from each other at Javier's desk, which was sleek and white and matched the rest of the room's trendy furnishings.

"Rough week, huh?" he said.

"You figure?"

Javier tapped his chin with interlocked fingers. "Do you know how many patients I've lost to suicide?"

"No."

"Me neither. Not specifically, anyway. There are a few I think about all the time. And others I don't even remember. It's the nature of the beast, David."

His remark wasn't meant to be cavalier or condescending. Not all suicides were preventable, and most psychiatrists expected to lose some patients that way over the course of their careers. But that didn't curb my irritation. "You can save this speech for your junior residents, Javier."

"Oh, I will. I really put the gravitas into the 'nature of the beast' thing. It kills with them." He let out a short staccato chuckle. Then his expression turned serious again. "They're concerned about you on the unit, David."

"The nurses?"

"And the other psychiatrists."

I glanced down at my fidgeting hands. "Why?"

"You've admitted nine patients this week and haven't discharged one."

I rolled my eyes. "You dragged me here to discuss my patients' lengths of stay?"

"You have some of the shortest lengths of stay in the whole department. Or you used to, anyway, before . . ."

"I lost my nerve?"

"It's only been a week. And I'm trying not to read too much into this."

"Then don't."

Javier offered me a sad smile. "Our service has never been busier. All that post-traumatic stress and depression following the pandemic . . . it never ends. The unit is bursting at the seams."

"Tell me something I don't know."

"You can't protect everyone from themselves by locking them in hospital."

I didn't need to hear from Javier how Brianna's suicide had affected my practice. The idea of letting any patient go home who might be even remotely at risk to him- or herself—even the ones whose safety I would've bet my own life on—had paralyzed me. I kept finding excuses to hold patients within the unit's locked confines.

"Message received, Chief," I said.

I began to rise from my chair, but his words stopped me. "What exactly are you blaming yourself for, David?"

"Brianna was trying to tell me, Javier."

"When was that? Right after she reassured you that she would never try anything?"

"It's often what they don't say that matters more."

Javier held up his hand. "We're not mind readers, David."

"I should've spent longer with her during our last session. Gone overtime. She had something more to tell me. Something important."

His hand fell to the desk. "It's easy to spot the warning signs in retrospect. Even easier to invent them."

Eager to change the subject, I said, "Brianna was the second one in the same week, David."

"Second what?"

"Second patient to attempt suicide before or after telling me about their Ketopram dreams."

"This again, David? Really?"

"It's a bit of a coincidence, isn't it?"

"Precisely." He sighed. "Coincidence. The rate of suicide is no higher on Ketopram than any other antidepressant. Studies suggest it may even be lower. And there are already tens of thousands of patients who are taking it. We would know if it were otherwise by now."

"It's a two-year-old drug, Javier. A toddler, in pharmaceutical terms. You know those kinds of associations can sometimes take years to establish."

Javier's eyes locked onto mine. "Do I need to remind you that this particular 'toddler' saved your life?"

CHAPTER 5

A second week passed after Brianna's death. And then another. I wanted to believe I was doing better. And in some senses, I was. I'd stopped trying to "lock the entire mental health population of Alaska in hospital," as Javier had put it during our most recent walk.

But while I was outwardly holding it together, I could feel the darkness from the winter before last creeping back around the edges of my life. My sleep was poor, and my appetite worse. I was grieving someone I'd only known through a video lens. Truth was, after four months of counseling Brianna, I'd hardly known her at all. But her death weighed on my shoulders like a heavy chain, especially knowing she had almost taken her daughter with her. My conversation with Brianna's aunt had only accentuated the guilt.

I had had mixed feelings when her aunt, Kerry McDougal, reached out to me on the day of Brianna's funeral service, the week before. I wanted to know how the family was coping, especially Nevaeh, but I also dreaded the answers. Kerry had not been comfortable with the idea of videoconferencing, so we spoke by phone.

After stiff and awkward introductions, I inquired about Nevaeh.

"No damage from the fumes. Not physically, anyway." Kerry's smoker's rasp was raw with emotion. "She got out just in time."

"And emotionally?" I asked.

"The poor little thing is confused. Doesn't understand where her mom's gone. Keeps looking for her everywhere. She ran away yesterday. My husband, Gus, found Nevaeh back at the door to their old house, a few blocks over."

How could a four-year-old begin to understand? "What will happen to Nevaeh now?"

"Taylor, the social worker, is trying to hunt down Nevaeh's dad, Dylan. Wherever he slunk off to." She stopped to emit a wet cough. "Gus and I will take her in though. Like we did her mom. We're the only family Nevaeh knows."

"What about Brianna's dad?" Brianna had spoken to me of her mom's untimely death, but she never mentioned her father.

"That useless deadbeat," Kerry snorted. "My little sister—Bree's mom, Jeanne—passed when Bree was only twelve. Heroin overdose. The dad had abandoned them long before. That mean bastard, he preferred the bottle over the needle."

"Brianna didn't talk about him."

"Can you blame her?"

"Was he abusive?"

"When he was drinking, sure. I saw the bruises that son of a bitch left on my sister. And the night he gave Jeanne a couple black eyes . . . Well, Gus beat the hell out of him that night, he did."

"Do you think Brianna's dad might have abused her, too?"

"Bree never said so. Neither did my sister. Besides, he took off when Bree was just a preschooler. I think he saved the beatings for Jeanne."

"Brianna once alluded to a man who might have been taking advantage of her," I said, trying to phrase it as delicately as I could. "But she wouldn't go into detail." I cleared my throat. "Did you ever suspect she might've been abused in her past?"

"You mean molested?" Kerry's voice cracked in surprise.

"Yes."

"This is the first I'm hearing of it," she said, her tone guarded.

"Maybe I misinterpreted what Brianna meant," I said, sensing I had upset her.

"My sister tried, in her way, but Bree never had real parents. Not until Gus and me took her in, anyway. We raised her from junior high on."

"I'm so sorry for your loss."

"I thought . . ." Kerry went quiet for a moment, as if composing herself. "I thought she was getting better."

"Me, too."

"You wouldn't've recognized her, Dr. Spears. Before Nevaeh. Not just before, either. Those first six or seven months after Nev was born, Bree was happy then, too. She used to have this spark. But then . . . she just got so glum. Nothing helped."

"Do you think that had anything to do with Nevaeh's dad leaving?"

"Nah. It happened before Dylan left. Not that it's any kind of excuse, but it's partly why he took off. Maybe I shouldn't be so hard on him. He tried for a while. Dylan was just a boy, really."

"But before . . . that night in the garage . . . you thought Brianna was getting better?"

"I did. Things improved this past spring for sure. Especially in the month or so right before she died." Kerry sniffled. "Bree was looking for work again, babysitting and stuff. But then . . ."

"Then what, Mrs. McDougal?"

"I almost called you the week she died. Wish I had."

"Can you tell me about that?"

"Brianna changed again."

"Changed how? Did her mood worsen?"

"Yeah. But . . . different from before."

I let the line go silent, waiting for her to continue when she was ready.

"She wouldn't talk about it," Kerry said. "Never said a word. But I could tell. Bree was scared, Dr. Spears."

"Do you have any idea of what?"

"Maybe she already knew what she was planning to do?"

I exhaled deeply and asked, "When was the last time you saw Brianna?"

"Two days before she did it. Bree called me. She was off. Kind of scatterbrained."

I couldn't believe Brianna had gone two full days before her suicide without reaching out to her closest living relative. That would have been unusual for someone planning to take her own life. Or maybe it spoke to the depth of her despair.

"What do you mean by scatterbrained, Mrs. McDougal?"

"She said something about having a lot going on. Things she had to sort out." Kerry's sniffle turned into a hacking cough. "I could tell Bree was really stressed. Never once did it occur to me that what she needed to sort out was . . ."

"You couldn't have known."

"I always prayed Bree wouldn't end up like her mom. I thought it would be different for that girl." Her voice dropped to a coarse whisper. "She used to have such a spark to her."

I shook off the dismal memory of that conversation and clicked the icon to launch my next virtual appointment on my laptop. Moments later, Amka Obed's round face appeared on the screen, and her piercing brown eyes stared back at me with distracting intensity.

"Hi, Amka."

"Hi, Doctor," she said, consistent with her habit of never calling me by name.

It wasn't as if she didn't know me. Amka had been the second patient I took on in Utqiagvik, over four years earlier. I was more familiar with the young woman than almost any other person in the town.

Amka was sitting, as usual, in her bedroom in the family home.

The walls were pink, and her childhood doll collection—a mixture of Disney princesses, Barbies, and Inuit dolls—was carefully lined along the shelf above her bed. As best I could tell, she never rearranged them. I still found it interesting how the dolls alternated exactly between Western and Indigenous ones.

"How have you been?" I asked.

"Bree's funeral was last week."

"I heard," I mumbled.

Amka and Brianna were the same age, twenty-two, and had grown up in town together. Amka had told me about her friend, years before I'd met Brianna. The two girls had been close. While Amka was Indigenous and didn't have a child of her own, there were parallels in their lives. The strongest, from my perspective, was that I'd diagnosed both with major depressions and started each on Ketopram. Amka had been on the medication for almost six months now, and her dosage seemed to be stable.

"The funeral must've been rough, huh?" I said.

"She was one of my best friends." Amka went quiet for a moment. "Kind of like with Uki, all over again."

Amka had come to me as a patient weeks after her older sister deliberately drowned herself in the frozen waters of the Chukchi Sea. Evan, Amka's family doctor, told me her parents had been terrified she might follow Uki's lead. While I never believed her to be at imminent risk of suicide, the grief from her sister's death had tipped Amka into a depression. But her symptoms weren't typical. She had gained over thirty pounds, and rather than sorrow, her depression manifested itself as irritability and impulsivity, including drug abuse, which had never been an issue before Uki's death. But four years later, I considered Amka a success story. She seemed to be thriving. She had broken up with her ex-boyfriend Rick—who had originally gotten her into cocaine—and she was working full-time at the local hardware store. She was also taking finance courses at Utqiagvik's community college, toward getting her business degree.

"What happened with Brianna . . ." I said. "It must've opened up some of the old wounds."

Hurt flickered across Amka's eyes, but she stared back without responding.

"It helps to talk about these things, Amka."

She shook her head.

"Are you angry with Brianna?" I asked. "Like you were with Uki?"

Her eyes darkened. "I saw Brianna that morning. The day she did it."

I bit back my surprise. "How did she seem to you, Amka?"

She paused for a moment. "Bree was Bree."

"No different?"

"She was in a hurry."

"You just ran into her?"

"We went for tea." Amka broke off the intense eye contact. "But she took off after like fifteen or twenty minutes. That was Bree. She had the spirit of a snow goose."

"Did she tell you why she had to go?"

She considered it a moment. "Right after we got our teas, Bree got a call. Said it had something to do with Nevaeh. Then she just bolted."

"Did she seem scared to you?"

Amka opened her mouth, but, appearing to change her mind, she shut it before a word came out.

"Amka?"

Her gaze was distant. "Bree didn't say goodbye. I do remember that."

"I'm sorry."

"At least Uki said goodbye."

"I'm sorry," I repeated, but this time I meant it as an apology. I was focusing on my need for answers about Brianna, rather than Amka's session. "How are you managing?"

"Managing?" she asked blankly.

"How is your sleep? Your appetite? Your mood? Do you think you've slipped at all since you found out about Brianna?"

Before Amka could answer, the door flew open behind her. A young man with a long ponytail and a wispy beard stuck his head into the bedroom. His small eyes scoured the room and, for a moment, landed on what must have been my image on her laptop. But his interest soon dissipated. "You coming, Amka?"

Her head whipped toward the door. "Out, Rick!" she snapped.

The door slammed shut, and Amka turned back to face me.

"I thought you two had broken up," I said.

Her cheeks reddened. "You were Bree's psychiatrist."

"I was."

"You keep asking if I noticed anything. What about you? Aren't you the one who's supposed to see the signs?"

I am.

Amka's criticism wasn't nearly as harsh as those that had been cycling inside my head, but hearing it come from a patient made me feel ashamed. "If there were signs, they were subtle," I said.

"And now she's dead."

"We're here to discuss how you're doing, Amka."

"How the fuck do you think I'm doing, Doctor?" She hopped up from her computer, so that only her bare midriff was visible on my screen.

Before I could get another word out, the video chat frame went black and Amka was gone.

CHAPTER 6

The next day, I didn't get back to my condominium until after nine p.m., exhausted after eight hours of office appointments followed by hospital consults. I would've loved to have come home to the company of a dog, but Beth had taken our adorable, hyper-shedding Samoyed, Toby, with her to Seattle. Between my schedule and Anchorage's unforgiving winters, the only pet suitable for me would have to be one that was self-sufficient alone indoors for long stretches of time, which would mean a cat. I'd always been a dog person, but as a psychiatrist, I'd seen the value any pet could have in improving mood, especially in those lonely patients who had adopted one at my urging. Aware that I now fit into that same sad category, I made a mental note to check with the local animal shelters to see if they had any reasonable feline candidates.

My thoughts drifted again to Brianna and, particularly, how hard her death had been on her friend. The recent session with Amka still troubled me, aware as I was of how much she appeared to have regressed since Brianna's death. And it concerned me to see Rick back in her life. He'd introduced Amka to Utqiagvik's drug scene. A trade that was thriving thanks to the steady stream of oil workers from Prudhoe Bay and other nearby drilling sites, who descended on the regional center on their weeks off with too much time and money on their hands. Amka probably would never have dabbled in coke or crystal meth, if not for Rick's influence. As long as he was back in her life, she would be at risk of relapsing.

Amka hadn't replied to the voicemail or the text I had left since she stormed out on me, virtually anyway, the day before. I'd even asked Evan about her when we were discussing another patient, but he hadn't seen her in over a week.

I stepped into the kitchen, but, not feeling particularly hungry, I strode past the fridge and went straight to the far cupboard that doubled as my liquor cabinet. I pulled down a bottle of the Macallan, my go-to single malt for everyday consumption. I eyeballed the fluid level and decided, with relief, that the bottle was still half-full. Since starting on Ketopram, I had allotted myself a maximum of one bottle every two weeks. And this one still had to last me another eight days.

I'd never been diagnosed with a drinking problem—though I appreciated from my practice just how many functional alcoholics had avoided the same label—but I did drink too much after Beth and Ali left. Alcoholism ran rampant in my mother's family. Three years earlier, Mom had died from it. Indirectly, at least. She had been sober for twenty years but relapsed out of grief and loneliness after Dad died from colon cancer. Less than four months after his death, my mother tripped and fell headfirst down the wooden staircase in her home while under the influence. She was awake when the paramedics reached her, but the blood thinners she was taking for an irregular heart rhythm did the fatal damage, and she died in hospital from an inoperable brain hemorrhage. Mom deserved a longer life and certainly a more dignified end. The double whammy of losing both my parents within months contributed to my depression and, indirectly, the dissolution of my marriage. It also made the bottle more appealing.

I poured two fingers of whiskey in a tumbler and headed out to the balcony. A light breeze drifted in from the west. The temperature felt ideal, somewhere in the mid-seventies. Judging by the height of the sun in the cloudless sky, anyone from the Lower Forty-Eight might have mistaken the time for somewhere in the early afternoon rather than almost nine thirty in the evening.

For a few blissful moments, my thoughts and worries went quiet. With so few tall buildings in Anchorage, the view from my balcony on the ninth and top floor was unobstructed, and I drank in the staggering vastness that encircled me. My gaze drifted eastward to the peaks of the Chugach Mountain Range, which loomed protectively over the city. It occurred to me that much of the summer had passed without me once hiking the range's scenic trails. No wonder my mood had been slipping.

Just as I settled into a near trance, my phone vibrated in my pocket. My heart warmed at the sight of my daughter's animated face on the video chat screen.

"Dad!" she said, as soon as I answered the call.

"Hi, Bean! How are you doing? How's Seattle?"

"I got it, Dad!" she cried.

"It?"

"The lead in our recital!"

I filled with pride. I considered raising my glass to toast her but then thought better of advertising to my daughter that I was drinking alone. "That's amazing! Tell me the day, and I'll book my flight!"

"Not till the end of the month, Dad. The very last Friday."

"What about our trip to the Rockies?"

Ali flushed. "Didn't Mom tell you?"

"No."

"I . . . I have to rehearse every day," she said in a smaller voice. "It's the lead, dad."

I swallowed back disappointment and forced a grin. "I know, Bean. It's huge! Thank God you inherited my lightness on my feet."

"As if! More like an elephant on rollerblades. Remember?"

I was touched she recalled the funny elephant meme I'd texted her as a visual metaphor for my lack of grace in skate skiing, which I'd taken up a few winters before. "What else is going on with you, Bean?"

"Everything, Dad. So busy with dance. I can't even think about starting junior year."

The idea that my daughter would be graduating high school in less than two years continued to astound me. My laptop screensaver was still set to the image of her snapped when Ali was only five years old, on our first trip to Disneyland. Wide-eyed with joy, she stood beside an actress dressed as Princess Jasmine.

"What's there to think about?" I asked.

"Um . . . like everything." Ali grimaced. "Not to mention my learner's permit."

"Oh, God. You behind the wheel? I already feel a little safer knowing I drive in Alaska, not Washington."

"Daaaad! Shut up!"

"If you want, we can practice driving when I come down there in a couple weeks."

The spark returned to her eyes. "You'll still come? Even if we don't do the trip?"

"Of course I will. We can do the Rockies next summer. Meantime, I'll hang out in Seattle with you. Maybe teach you a few of my moves on the floor?"

"It's a ballet, Dad. Not *Babar Goes Blading*!"

"Yeah, yeah." I chuckled. "Is your mom there?"

"Hang on." Ali's face disappeared, and all I saw was shifting images from the interior of the house as she navigated through the rooms. "Mom! It's Dad!"

As I waited, I felt indignation creep up the base of my neck like a heat rash.

Beth's face appeared on the screen, her lips pursed in a tight smile. The frown lines and the crow's-feet at the corners of her eyes were a bit more prominent. A few years earlier, when we were still together, Beth had been so horrified after her friends pressured her into trying Botox—which she said had turned her forehead "to plastic"—that she had forgone any further antiaging interventions and even stopped coloring her graying hair. I appreciated her naturally aging features. Besides, to me she would always be the same hazel-eyed girl with a ponytail braided like a rope and adorable freckles across the bridge of her nose. The one who marched up to me on the first day of anatomy lab and prophetically announced: "Looks like you and I are stuck as partners."

The fond memory didn't temper my rising anger though, and I had to clench my jaw to keep my voice in check. "Can Ali hear us?"

"No. She's gone back downstairs."

"What the fuck, Beth?"

Her expression was unapologetic. "This is the camp she really wanted."

"When were you planning to mention the recital? Or did you just assume I'd be happy to drive by myself to the Rockies?"

"I only heard today," she said coolly. "I thought the camp ended a week earlier. And I had no idea the recital was going to be such a big deal."

"It's a very big deal," I snapped.

"I meant for her, not you."

"You already cut my time short with her this summer."

"Not fair, David. You know this camp was Ali's idea. What she wanted."

I couldn't stop myself. "Just like moving to Seattle was her idea?"

The lines at the corners of her eyes deepened. "We're doing this again?"

"How would you feel if you lived two thousand miles away from your daughter and only got to see her once a month? And then if I canceled the one trip you had planned with her?"

"I didn't cancel this—"

"Christ, Beth! The summer is the only good chunk of time I get with her. She was supposed to be with me for all of August. And I already lost that." I took a slow, deep breath. "You have no idea how much I was looking forward to this trip."

Beth held my stare, but after a moment, her stony gaze gave way to a conciliatory nod. "You're right. I'm sorry, David."

More than her words, it was the empathy in her eyes that calmed me.

"The lead, David!" Beth broke into a smile that erased the last of my outrage. "The girl can really dance."

I sighed. "Guess she got my genes."

"Maybe you should watch our wedding video again. You might reconsider." Her smile gave way to a look of concern. "You look tired, David."

"I've been on call a lot this week."

"Nothing else?"

Beth had a knack for seeing right through me. Even through a four-inch video screen. "I had a tough case."

"What happened?"

"I lost a patient."

Instead of spouting the usual platitudes about how some suicides are unavoidable and how all psychiatrists lose patients, all she said was "That must really hurt."

"It does. Particularly this one."

"Why this one?"

"She was a young single mom. No previous attempts. Carbon monoxide poisoning."

Beth winced. "She must have been determined, huh?"

"The last time I saw her, I think she might have been trying to tell me." Suddenly self-conscious, I glanced away from the screen. "The worst part? She tried to take her four-year-old with her. Only blind luck saved the kid."

"Oh, God," Beth murmured.

"I'd just switched her over to Ketopram the month before. I thought she was making progress."

"She probably was. Besides, a medication change like that wouldn't be related. Not if she had been taking it as prescribed."

"She was getting those Ketopram nightmares, so I assume she must've been taking her meds faithfully." I paused. "In her case, they were more like premonitions of her and her child's death."

"Everything seems significant in retrospect. I've been there, David. We create relevance in the things they said that simply doesn't exist." Her tone was as reassuring as the warm smile that crossed her lips. "Wish I could give you a hug right now."

"Wish I could get one about now." I fought the urge to tell her just how much I missed her. How I would love for us to try again.

Before Beth could reply, Ali called out, sounding as if she were yelling from another room or possibly from downstairs. "Mom! Graham's here!"

Beth had never mentioned a Graham before, but it wasn't hard to piece together. Graham Blackburn had been a classmate of ours in med school. At the time, he had done a miserable job of concealing his crush on Beth or his jealousy of me for dating her. I hadn't seen Graham in years, but I'd heard from another classmate that he was an orthopedic surgeon in Seattle. I'd also been told he was recently divorced. "As in Graham Blackburn?" I asked.

Beth's cheeks reddened. "I've got to run, David. Can I call you tomorrow?"

"Not necessary," I said, but she ended the call so abruptly I wasn't sure she'd heard me.

"Fuck it!" I said to no one as I dropped the phone onto the side table and downed the rest of my scotch in one gulp. As I stood up to go refill my glass, the phone rang. I answered without even checking the screen, hoping it was Beth calling back.

"Dr. Spears?" a vaguely familiar voice asked. "David?"

"Yes."

"Hi, it's Taylor Holmes. From the North Pole."

"Oh, hello, Taylor," I said, wishing I hadn't answered, though it had nothing to do with the young social worker from Utqiagvik. I liked Taylor. She was always upbeat and helpful with the patients we comanaged. She had a practical, can-do approach to her work, but she was also realistic about the limitations of her role and the resources available in the remote town. And I appreciated her quirky, irreverent sense of humor.

"Sorry to bug you after hours," Taylor said. "You've probably got a lot going on in the big city."

"You might be the first person ever to call Anchorage a big city."

Taylor chuckled. "Everything's relative."

I wasn't in the mood for banter. "What's up, Taylor?"

"I was wondering if you'd spoken to Amka Obed lately."

Wariness wiped away my self-pity. "We had a virtual appointment yesterday afternoon. Why?"

"Can't seem to track her down. She didn't show up at my office yesterday."

"And that's unusual?"

"Not necessarily," Taylor said. "Except Amka was the one who made the appointment. She wanted my help on a school assignment."

"Oh."

"I couldn't reach her all day. I just dropped by her family's place on my way home from work. Her parents haven't seen her, either. They're a little worried."

As was I. "What time was she supposed to meet you yesterday?" I asked.

"Four thirty."

"Amka and I had our video conference session at three."

"And she didn't say where she was going after?"

"No." Even if I'd wanted to tell Taylor how abruptly the appointment ended, which I didn't, patient-doctor confidentiality would have prohibited me.

"K. Just thought I'd check with you," Taylor said. "Thanks for taking my call. Sorry to—"

"Listen, Taylor. Yesterday, during our appointment, her ex-boyfriend walked into her bedroom."

"Rick?" Taylor moaned. "Not that asshole! God, I hope she isn't back with him."

"He's deep in the local drug scene, isn't he?"

"His crew *is* the Utqiagvik drug scene. Bunch of dickheads. OK, that's not entirely fair. A lot of them are just troubled kids, really." She sighed. "The guy who runs them, though, Eddie . . ."

"You haven't spoken to Rick, then?"

"Nah. But he won't be too hard to find."

"You'll keep me posted?"

"Of course."

"I'm actually flying into Utqiagvik the day after tomorrow," I said. "It's been scheduled for months."

"Hopefully, Amka will have turned up by then," Taylor said.

I wasn't in a hopeful mood. Besides, Amka lived in a small town that was engulfed by nothing but tundra, ice, and water. *Where the hell could she have gone?* "Maybe I'll catch a flight tomorrow instead."

CHAPTER 7

"Would've been easier if I just grabbed a cab," I said, after I loaded my bag in the trunk of Javier's Tesla and climbed into the passenger seat. As usual, the interior was spotless and still gave off a hint of new car smell, a year after he'd bought it.

Javier glanced at me sidelong. "There's an old Spanish proverb: *Un verdadero amigo es aquel que entra cuando el resto del mundo se va.*"

When he didn't elaborate, I said, "A normal person would immediately translate that into English."

"A true friend is one who walks in when the rest of the world walks out."

"It's just a ride to the airport, Javier. You're not giving me a kidney."

He uttered his staccato laugh. "You didn't need a kidney. You needed a ride."

We both knew the ride had nothing to do with need or even convenience. Javier had called me last night soon after I got off the phone with Taylor. I didn't mention anything about my conversation with Beth or the orthopedic surgeon who had apparently replaced me in her life, but I did tell him I was flying to Utqiagvik in the morning. And after realizing he couldn't talk me out of going, he insisted on driving me to the airport. I'd already braced for another onslaught.

"You sure this is the right time for you to head to the Arctic?" Javier asked, as he pulled away from the curb.

"It's my scheduled time to go."

"Doesn't make it the right time."

I appreciated the concern in his tone. "I'm doing better, Javier," I lied.

"Maybe." He kept his eyes straight ahead. "But flying back to the village where she—where it happened . . . I don't see how that will help you."

"This has nothing to do with Brianna." I turned to look out the window. "I've got other patients I follow in that town. And one of them is missing."

"Missing?"

"Just for a day or two. She may well be with her sketchy boyfriend, but still . . ."

"You work for Search and Rescue now?"

Ignoring the dig, I stared out at the passing low-rise buildings that constituted downtown Anchorage. At six thirty a.m., there was practically no traffic on the quiet streets, and the car's electric motor emitted only a light hum. It gave the eerie effect that we were driving in a simulator. "I'm just trying do my job, Javier."

"As am I. Both as your doctor and your friend. This trip, now, will only increase your risk of relapsing."

"I know the signs. I can manage."

Javier smiled to himself. "How many times have you heard patients tell you the same?" When I didn't reply, he asked, "You haven't changed your dose of Ketopram, have you?"

"Nope. Same old twenty milligrams."

He nodded. "I was on call last weekend. I noticed you had taken three inpatients off Ketopram while you were the doctor of the week for the unit."

"One of them tried to hang himself while he was taking it, remember? Not sure about you, but I view that as a treatment failure."

"The other two weren't even suicidal. They had just started taking Ketopram after being admitted to hospital."

I thought of the two patients in question. One was a tiny woman who didn't seem to ever blink, and the other was so restless that I had to interview her while she paced the floor. "The first one wasn't sleeping because of her Ketopram nightmares. And the second was exhibiting early signs of mania."

Even in profile, his expression was pure skepticism. "So your decision had nothing to do with your recent professional experiences with the medication?"

"Maybe. I can't really say."

He considered it a moment. "Here's an English expression for you: a bad excuse is better than none."

"This isn't an attack on you, Javier. Why are you so defensive over this one drug?"

"Because it's the most effective antidepressant I've seen come to market in the past thirty years."

"Not because you're so invested in it? Literally."

"When it comes to that poor girl up north, I think you're confusing association with causation." Which was his scientific way of saying that just because two things happened at the same time, it didn't mean they were related. "The data would overwhelmingly suggest that her being on Ketopram was nothing more than an unfortunate coincidence."

I wasn't in the mood to argue. And besides, Javier had already turned off onto the airport road.

After he pulled up to the departure zone drop-off, he put the gear in park and turned to me with an intent look. "You'll call me if you need anything?" he asked.

"I won't need anything."

"But if you do . . ."

"I'll call you," I said, reaching for the door handle. "Thank you, Javier." I hoped he realized I meant for more than just the ride.

Once inside the airport, I whizzed through security, headed straight to my gate, and was settled in the window seat inside the 737 within fifteen minutes. As usual, the cabin was more than half-empty. It still surprised me that commercial jets flew in and out of a town as small as Utqiagvik, but it made more sense when I considered the over seven hundred miles distance from Anchorage. Also, with no road or sea access, except for a brief window for ships when the sea ice melts during the summer, the town is entirely reliant on those planes to transport not only people but all of its essential food and supplies as well.

We took off, and the plane cut smoothly through cloudless skies, offering a spectacular view of the ever-changing Alaskan landscape below—a potpourri of mountains, forests, rivers, and glaciers. Once we'd passed a few hundred miles north of Fairbanks, the tree line gave way to nothing but ice fields, lakes, and tundra. As we approached the northern tip of the continent, a blanket of clouds suddenly appeared, obscuring the view and turning our descent bumpy all the way down to the runway of the Wiley Post–Will Rogers Memorial Airport. I still found it ironic and slightly unnerving that the airport was named after two victims of a nearby fatal plane crash, one of whom was the legendary actor and humorist Will Rogers.

Icy air blasted my face as I deplaned down the rolling staircase onto the tarmac. I looked up to see snowflakes drifting lazily toward me. Even to an Alaskan like me, it was a surreal sight for mid-August. I wished I'd packed warmer clothes. I was so distracted by the weather that I didn't even notice the woman who was calling my name as she approached.

I didn't recognize Taylor. We had never met in person, even on my previous trips to town. Having only ever communicated with her via email and phone, I'd somehow pictured her as dark-haired and petite. Likely because she had a similar voice to my favorite social worker in Anchorage, who had long jet-black hair and was tiny despite her larger-than-life personality. But Taylor was as tall as me, with broad shoulders and short-cropped, blonde, spiky hair. She wore dark jeans and a loose flannel jacket. But she approached with light, graceful strides despite her tomboyish appearance.

She greeted me with an unexpected and warm hug.

"Good to meet you in person," I said. "You didn't need to pick me up."

She flashed an open-mouthed smile that revealed strong white teeth and lit her disconcertingly clear gray eyes. "Uber coverage can be hit-and-miss in Utqiagvik."

"There's no Uber up—"

"No." She laughed. "We only have couple of cabs. And most of the time, Larry doesn't feel like driving."

"Any word on Amka?" I asked as we walked toward the gravel parking lot.

"No, but I haven't had a chance to go see Rick since we chatted last night."

"I see." Despite the very rational explanation, the news still deflated me.

"Besides, I thought you might want to come with me to see him."

"Definitely," I said as I loaded my bag in the back of Taylor's truck, which was as high off the ground as any I'd ever climbed into.

We drove out of the lot and down the dirt road that led into town. I knew from previous visits that there were no paved roads in Utqiagvik, as the pavement wouldn't survive the relentless assault of a single winter. I'd been coming up to Utqiagvik biannually for the past four years—the first time being soon after the town voted to rename itself from Barrow to Utqiagvik, the exact meaning of

which the townsfolk apparently still argued about. Each time I vis-
ited, I was struck by its unapologetically spartan and hodgepodge
layout.

Utqiagvik hugged the muddy banks of the Chukchi Sea and was
divided into two major subdivisions, north and south, by side-by-
side lagoons that were frozen much of the year. The houses were all
rectangular or square, with simple slanting rooflines, and yet the
overall effect was totally incongruous due to the varying sizes, colors, siding, and even orientations of the buildings. The abandoned,
rusting trucks and cars we passed along the way, which had died
where they had last been parked, only compounded that impres-
sion. But despite the bleak architecture, I found the town's shoreline spectacular. I especially loved strolling the beach in late spring
when the endless ice flows still filled the expansive sea, forming, to
my eye, the epitome of desolate Arctic beauty.

Taylor drove us down the narrow road that bifurcated the
Lower and Upper Isatkoak Lagoons, heading north into the larger
and more residential Browerville subdivision, where the buildings
looked even more rickety to me.

"How long have you lived here?" I asked.

"Will be two years in September." Taylor shook her head, as if
she couldn't believe it herself.

"Where did you come from?"

"SoCal. At least, San Diego was my last gig. I've lived up and
down the West Coast."

"From Southern California to the Arctic, huh?"

She shrugged. "It's the natural progression."

"Did you know anyone here?"

"Not a soul."

"And you came on your own?"

"Absolutely. Why would I want to be pinned down in a dating mecca like this one? You haven't lived till you've Tinder-ed
Utqiagvik-style."

I chuckled. There was something infectious about her irreverent positivity. "Where are we going?" I asked.

"Rick's house."

The truck bounced along a narrower road, which felt even more potholed than the previous ones, and came to a stop at the far end of it, outside of a small, dilapidated house. The carcass of a rotting truck perched on the dirt out front constituted its only form of landscaping. We got out of the truck, and I followed Taylor up to the front door. I heard multiple dogs howling from somewhere nearby, but I couldn't see them.

After a few moments, the door opened and out stepped a stooped, gray-haired woman who barely reached the level of our upper chests. She extended her arms and Taylor bent forward to meet the hug. The woman nuzzled her upper lip and the base of her nose against Taylor's cheek.

"*Uvlulluataq*, Sonya," Taylor said as she straightened from the embrace.

"*Uvlulluataq*," the other woman repeated in a low cracking voice.

"Sonya, this is Dr. Spears."

"Hello, Doctor," Sonya said, without attempting to make eye contact.

"Can we speak to your grandson?" Taylor asked.

Sonya viewed her with sad eyes. "Not here."

"When did you last see Rick?"

"Two days," she said with disappointment. "He was supposed to fish with his cousins yesterday."

"He didn't tell you where he was going?"

"No."

"Where do you think he might be, Sonya?"

"Trouble." She sighed. "Ever since the accident, the boy always finds it."

Taylor glanced over to me. "I know where trouble lives in this town." She looked back to the shrunken woman. "I'll let you know as soon as I find him, Sonya."

Sonya nodded and turned back to the door without saying another word.

As we loaded back into the truck, I asked. "That greeting Sonya gave you . . ."

"Don't be calling it an 'Eskimo kiss,' city slicker."

"I wasn't going to." I could feel my neck heating.

"Just messing with you, David." She elbowed me gently in my upper arm. "The Inuit in Northern Alaska, especially here in Utqiagvik, are almost all of the Iñupiat tribe. And they call that form of a greeting a *kunik*."

"Interesting," I said, but I was more focused on why Amka's boyfriend was also missing. "Sonya mentioned an accident . . ."

"Rick's dad—Sonya's only child—fell through the ice seal-hunting when Rick was twelve or thirteen. He'd already lost his mom by then. His grandma was all he had left for family. And soon after his dad died, Rick got mixed up with the wrong crowd. Has been ever since."

"And you think you might know where Rick and Amka are?"

"Not for certain, no. But I do know what Sonya meant by trouble."

We drove five or six dusty blocks before Taylor pulled up to a much bigger house, although it looked to be in even worse shape than Sonya's. We got out of the car and I again followed Taylor up to the door.

After a minute or so, when no one responded to the first knock, Taylor banged on the door with the side of her fist. "Open up, Eddie!" she shouted.

Several more seconds passed, and then, without warning, the door flew open.

I froze at the sight of the man filling the doorway. The barrel of his rifle was leveled only inches from my face. I fought the urge to drop into a crouch and cover my head, but I held still, desperate not to give him an excuse to pull the trigger.

Tense seconds passed in silence. I slowly inched my gaze from the rifle to the man pointing it. He was fortyish with a widow's peak of thinning blond hair, a depigmented blotch of white skin across his left cheek, and a diamond stud in his right ear. His lip curled into a sneer, but he didn't say a word, and his noisy breaths filled the silence.

Out of the corner of my eye, I saw Taylor moving. I instinctively reached an arm to stop her, but it was too late. She lunged forward, grabbed the barrel, and jammed it downward. "What's wrong with you, Eddie?" she snapped. "You that keen to go back to jail?"

Eddie let the rifle dangle at his side, but he eyed her unrepentantly. "How the fuck am I expected to know who's at my door?" he asked with a trace of a southern twang, before glancing at me contemptuously. "'Specially when you show up with a fucking outsider like this one."

"Where's Rick?" Taylor demanded without bothering to introduce me.

"Not here."

Taylor folded her arms. "I didn't ask that, did I? Where is he?"

"No clue."

"How about Amka?" I spoke quietly, still shaken from having a firearm pointed at me for the first time in my life.

Eddie squinted at me for a long moment. "Probably with Rick. Hard to know with those two."

Taylor nodded at the rifle in his hand. "We'll need a little more than that if you don't want me to report you."

"I got a permit."

"Not to aim a gun at our heads, you sure as hell don't. That's threatening assault with a deadly weapon. Hard time, for sure."

Eddie snorted. "I don't know where that motherfucker is, but I'd like to find out, too."

"Why?"

"He owes me a shit ton of cash."

"For what?"

"Proceeds of a sale." Eddie's grin was somehow more menacing than his sneer.

"Did he stiff you on a drug trade?" Taylor asked.

"None of this is your business." Eddie pivoted back inside the house and slammed the door hard enough to send a gust of chilled air across our faces.

CHAPTER 8

One of the few buildings I had noticed on previous trips to Utqiagvik was the two-story police department headquarters with its prominent sign that read: NORTH SLOPE BOROUGH POLICE DEPARTMENT. It stood out for its blue glass and modern design, and especially the semicircular wall on one side. As I entered it for the first time, I breathed in a whiff of brewed coffee and saw that the bright, spacious office was just as appealing on the inside.

Taylor seemed familiar with the handful of staff present, exchanging friendly greetings with two uniformed officers and a hug with a heavyset man dressed in a blazer and jeans. When an officer ambled up to her with his police dog—a hulking shepherd—she stooped down to rub the animal behind his ears.

Within a few minutes of arriving, we were seated in the office of the police chief, Natan Bedard, a fiftyish Iñupiat man who had thoughtful brown eyes and graying hair, slicked back in a wave.

After introductions, Taylor said, "We can't find Amka Obed, Chief."

The chief's expression didn't change, but his eyes conveyed disappointment. "She back together with Rick Neakok?"

"Think so," Taylor said. "We can't find him either."

"Did you ask his grandma?"

"She hasn't seen him in days."

"Checks are coming," the chief sighed. "The boys are active again."

I glanced from Taylor to the chief. "Boys? Checks?"

"About this time every year, the local oil company, the Arctic Slope Regional Corp., sends dividend checks to most folks in town," the chief explained. "They'll be north of fifteen grand per person this year."

"And the boys are Eddie Snyder's crew," Taylor added.

"Plus, a few competitors," the chief said. "Check time is the harvest season for the local bootleggers and drug dealers."

I had almost forgotten that Utqiagvik was a dry town. Liquor sales were banned in the region, and a special permit was required to bring in any alcohol. I didn't have one, but no one had stopped me at the airport to check my bag and find the unopened bottle of scotch I was carrying.

The chief thumbed in the direction of the doorway, through which the dog could be seen sitting patiently beside a desk. "Lucky our boy Banjo's got a good nose for it. Confiscations doubled two years ago after we got him."

"We went by Eddie's, Chief, and got the expected warm welcome." Taylor rolled her eyes without mentioning the rifle. "Eddie's looking for Rick, too. Says he owes him money."

"Eddie wouldn't be my first go-to for a loan."

"I got the feeling Rick might've stiffed him on a deal."

"If that's true, then Rick might not want to hang around town." The chief frowned. "Good timing for him, I suppose."

"How so?" I asked.

"Up here, you've only got a three-month window where the roads are clear of ice and snow. And even still, you can barely make it to the nearest towns. Which aren't that near."

"Or fly to Anchorage or Fairbanks," Taylor pointed out. "And from there, go anywhere in the Lower Forty-Eight."

"We'll check the flight manifests." The chief clicked his tongue. "But I can't see Rick straying that far from home."

"True," Taylor said, brightening. "They're probably still somewhere in the North Slope Borough."

"Which extends how far exactly?" I asked.

"Oh, about the same landmass as Great Britain. And our officers here at NSB PD are responsible for policing every inch of it." The chief turned to Taylor. "So, aside from the obvious—namely, Rick—why are you worried about Amka?"

"She no-showed on me, Chief, which is unlike her. She hasn't been home for two days. And no one's heard from her since."

The chief nodded and turned to me. "And you're her psychiatrist, Dr. Spears?"

"Yes."

"You were also Brianna O'Brien's, weren't you?" I wondered how the chief knew that, and, as if reading my thoughts, he added, "Her aunt mentioned something about a psychiatrist from Anchorage."

I shifted in my seat. "Yes, I was."

"If I live to be a hundred, I'll never understand why she did it." He sighed. "With her own child in the back seat."

The reminder stung like a deep burn, but it also provided me the opening to pose the question I had been wondering about for weeks. "Did you get the toxicology report back on her?"

"We did," he said. "All she had on board was alcohol."

"What was her level?"

"In the high sixties."

I took some solace in the number. An alcohol level that number meant that a woman of Brianna's size would've been severely intoxicated at the time of her death. I so wanted to believe that her tragic decision to take her life and Nevaeh's had been motivated as much or more out of drunken impulse than premeditated planning. But I wasn't convinced.

The chief exhaled heavily. "Keep hoping I've seen my last one. And then, always, another call comes in." I assumed he was referring to suicides in general, but he didn't elaborate. Instead, he called out over our heads, "Hey, Kai!"

The man in the blazer, who looked more Polynesian than Inuit, stuck his head through the doorway. "What's up, Chief?"

"Taylor and Dr. Spears here are looking for Rick Neakok and Amka Obed."

Kai shrugged. "And?"

"They can't find them." The chief waved a finger from us to Kai and back. "I thought you—being the department's only detective— might be interested."

Kai grinned at Taylor. "I'd love to help, but I got my hands full tracking down the source of all that coke that's been circulating in town."

"Apparently, Rick screwed Eddie on some deal right before he went to ground," the chief said.

Kai stepped into the room, showing sudden interest. "That's some coincidence. Right when it's beginning to snow the fine stuff all over town, huh?"

The chief motioned from me to Kai. "Dr. Spears, meet Detective Tupou."

"Doc," Kai said with a brief nod, and then looked over to Taylor with another smile. "Let me do a little digging. And I'll get back to you with what I find out."

"You're a peach, Kai," Taylor said.

"Didn't you tell me I was a teddy bear last time?"

She laughed. "That, too."

Taylor and I thanked the two cops and headed back out to her truck.

It felt even colder than when we arrived, and more snowflakes fluttered down from the darkening skies. "I'll never get used to snow in August," Taylor said. "At least, I sure as hell hope I don't."

After we loaded back into the truck, I asked, "Is Kai Hawaiian?"

"His family's Tongan, I think. Believe it or not, there's a decent-sized Pacific Islander community up here. Tongans and Samoans, anyway."

"People from the tropics living in the Arctic. Snow falling in the summertime. The surprises never end in Utqiagvik."

"You're only scratching the surface." She laughed again and turned the ignition over. "Want me to drop you off at your hotel?"

"How about the medical clinic instead?"

"Why there?"

"I want to speak to Evan Harman."

"Oh, he's Amka's family doctor, isn't he?" She answered her own question with a confident nod. "Think I'll come in with you. It's good timing. Today is mainly an office day for me to catch up on emails, forms, and paperwork." She made a snoring sound. "I don't have my first on-site visit until two."

I would've preferred to speak to Evan alone to give us a chance to discuss Brianna. But Taylor had been so hospitable, and besides, her self-invitation wasn't posed as a question, so I didn't protest.

"What's the deal with Eddie?" I asked instead.

"Eddie's a piece of work. He's from the South. Florida, I think? Or maybe I just want him to be from there." She chuckled. "Drifted up here ages ago—like so many of them do—to work the oil fields in Prudhoe Bay. But he shattered his leg and ended up on long-term disability."

"Which isn't his only source of income?"

"Not even close. He runs the biggest drug ring in town. He's like a magnet for troubled youths."

"Like Rick?"

"Eddie's the closest thing we have to organized crime in Utqiagvik. Not that it's all that organized."

"Why isn't he locked up?"

"The cops have tried. Nothing sticks. Eddie keeps his own hands pretty clean. And when they do make a bust, the junior guys always take the fall."

"Junior like Rick?"

"Yeah, except the others would know better than to rip Eddie off."

We drove north back between the lagoons and headed down a road to the nondescript building at the far end, which housed the medical clinic.

Inside, a young Iñupiat receptionist—who had not been around on my previous visits—sat at the front desk. The friendly woman recognized my name and led us immediately into the private office at the back of the clinic. Evan walked in wearing a white lab coat over his wrinkled T-shirt. His eyes looked even more sunken and the acne scars deeper in person, but his beaming smile exuded confidence and charm that made those features fade from notice. "Hiya, Taylor. And good to see you again, David." He shook both of our hands, clamping mine with a forceful grip, before he dropped into the seat behind his desk. "What brings you two here?"

"We haven't found Amka," Taylor said, as we took our seats.

Evan sighed. "I spoke to her dad this morning. I've got to tell you, he's concerned."

"We're assuming she ran off with Rick," Taylor continued. "But no one has seen either of them."

"I was Rick's doctor after I first moved up here ten years ago," Evan said. "He was a likable kid. Always smiling. He worshipped his dad, too. Then, after the hunting accident . . . His poor grandmother did the best she could." He shrugged. "Anyway, I haven't been his doctor for a long while."

"But you're still Amka's?" Taylor asked.

"Yup."

"When was the last time you saw her?"

"She was in a week ago Tuesday." Before either Taylor or I could ask, Evan motioned to me. "I looked it up after you mentioned her during our last call."

"What did Amka see you about?" Taylor asked.

Evan's forehead furrowed. "I'm not sure I'm entitled to discuss that."

"Why not? I'm her social worker."

"Taylor knows we've been treating Amka for depression," I assured him.

Evan accepted the explanation with another shrug. "She came in for a refill of her Ketopram."

"She didn't mention anything about the dreams or other side effects?" I asked.

"No. Nothing. But . . ." He shook his head.

"What is it, Evan?"

"She wasn't at her best, for sure. She'd been doing so well up until then. With work and school. Obviously, Brianna's death hit her hard. They were close. Very close. Amka just seemed a bit lost. Maybe that's why she ended up back with Rick?"

"Probably," Taylor said.

The guilt crept over me again. If only I had taken an extra five or ten minutes at the end of my last session with Brianna, then maybe I wouldn't be left wondering if I could've prevented her pointless death and all the collateral damage it continued to inflict. "Amka told me she had tea with Brianna on the day of her suicide," I said.

Evan sat forward in his chair. "She never mentioned that to me. What else did Amka tell you?"

"Not much. She was kind of evasive. All she said was that that Brianna cut their get-together short after receiving a call."

"A call? From whom?"

"Amka never said. Only that it had something to do with Nevaeh. Then Brianna rushed off without saying goodbye."

Evan slumped back in his chair. "The poor girl. Such a tortured soul."

Taylor frowned at me. "Why did Brianna go meet Amka that morning if she was already planning to kill herself?"

"Why do it at all?" I wondered aloud.

I must have looked as glum as Evan did, because Taylor said, "Alaska has double the incidence of suicide as the national average. And the North Slope Borough has a rate that's triple the rest of the state. Especially in Brianna's age group. You heard the chief? Ut-qiagvik is literally the suicide capital of the US."

I appreciated her attempt to reassure us, but I wasn't swayed. "Doesn't mean it wasn't preventable."

Evan smiled his gratitude, too, but his eyes remained downcast. "Listen, I'm worried about Amka, too," he said. "And after what happened with Brianna . . . I'd love to help you find her."

CHAPTER 9

That evening, I followed Taylor into Evan's home. I wasn't feeling particularly hungry, but my stomach still rumbled at the gamey scent of cooked meat that greeted us at the doorway, reminding me I hadn't eaten since arriving in town.

Evan met us with a stemless glass of red wine in each hand.

"Ooh," Taylor said as she enthusiastically took the glass. "Nothing like the illegal stuff to get the night started."

Evan only smiled. "They haven't revoked my permit yet."

"Thanks," I said, accepting my glass. "Is it a hassle to bring wine into town?"

"Not too bad. I order it by the case from Anchorage or Fairbanks. Sometimes, the officers even deliver it to my door. There's got to be some perks to my job."

Taylor raised her glass to him. "It's not like there's a lineup of doctors competing to replace you."

"As if I'm replaceable, Taylor." Evan held her gaze for a moment, and I wondered if there was something between them.

Evan led us into the living room area, where a plush couch,

flanked by two cozy chairs with a cowhide rug between, faced an unlit fireplace. A cheese plate was resting on the glass coffee table, and I couldn't resist cutting a piece and layering it onto a cracker.

After we made ourselves comfortable, Evan asked us, "Any more leads?"

"Not really," Taylor said. "We spoke to Amka's dad this afternoon."

Evan lowered his glass. "And?"

"He wasn't much help."

As Evan and Taylor continued to discuss the search for Amka, my thoughts drifted back to our earlier visit to her parents' home. Amka's house had only existed for me as her pink bedroom with the doll collection above the bed that I had seen so often during our virtual sessions. But the main floor of her house was surprisingly sparse, with the only furniture in sight from the doorway being a basic square table and four matching chairs along with a small flat-screen TV that stood on the faded linoleum floor. It spoke to a degree of poverty that Amka had downplayed and that made me appreciate why she valued her doll collection so much.

Tonraq Obed, or "Tom," was lean and shorter than me, but his bone-straight posture and intense stare—which he had obviously passed on to Amka—gave him an intimidating presence. Or maybe it was the rifle that was slung over his shoulder as he opened the front door for us, dressed for a hunt.

"You didn't find my daughter?" Tom asked Taylor without inviting us inside.

"Not yet, Mr. Obed," Taylor said.

"The boy." His tone was calm, but the words still somehow conveyed disgust. "I'll find her myself."

Taylor nodded to the firearm. "With your rifle?"

"We still have to eat."

"Of course," she said contritely. "We've spoken to the police,

Mr. Obed. They're all looking for Amka, too. Someone will find her soon."

Tom looked beyond her without replying.

"In the past, when Amka was with Rick . . ." I said, unable to add what I really meant, which was *when she had been using drugs*. "Were there times when you couldn't locate her?"

"The boy's grandmother could always find her for me." Tom paused. "Not this time."

"Were there any places Rick and Amka used to go? Did they ever leave town?"

"To where?"

"Other towns in the North Slope," Taylor answered for me. "Wainwright, Nuiqsut, or even Prudhoe Bay?"

"They'd have to take a boat or a plane."

"Would they know anyone there?"

Tom considered it for a moment. "Amka has cousins—fishermen—in Nuiqsut. And the boy used to work on the rigs in Prudhoe Boy." He scoffed. "Back when he did real work."

"Do you think Mrs. Obed might have any ideas on other places to check?" I asked.

"Leave her out of this." He glared at me. "She's not well."

"We'll find them," Taylor repeated.

"I am not losing another daughter."

I couldn't imagine how stressful Amka's disappearance must have been for her parents after their older daughter's suicide. But before either of us could respond, Tom closed the door behind him and stepped out between us. "Would be better for the boy if you found them before I do."

Evan pulled me out of the memory when he hopped to his feet and announced, "Your moose is cooked." He laughed at his own pun.

"You mean caribou, right?" Taylor said.

"Yeah, but moose sounds better."

We followed him to a long pine dining table that could have sat twelve, where three place settings had been laid. He insisted we sit while he shuttled back and forth from the kitchen, stacking the table with more serving plates that were piled with roasted root vegetables, grilled asparagus, sautéed mushrooms, Caesar salad, and finally a steaming caribou roast. We filled our plates, and Taylor's was heaped the highest of all three of us.

Evan opened another bottle of cab franc and joined us at the table. Taylor let out an appreciative whistle as she dug her fork into the root vegetables. "The produce alone that's gone into this feast must've cost you an arm and a leg, Evan!" she said, and I realized she wasn't joking. On my previous visits, I'd seen the exorbitant prices at the general store, including a fourteen-dollar head of lettuce that made me do a double take.

"Money well spent." Evan smiled. "Especially when it takes a VIP visiting from the city to get you over here for dinner."

"What can I say? I'm the Beyoncé of the Arctic. Impossible to book." Taylor's flippant remark didn't conceal her embarrassment. I sensed tension between them, but I couldn't discern if it was over a past romance or if maybe Evan held unrequited feelings for her.

Evan turned to me and raised his glass. "Thank you for coming all the way up here, David. And for taking such good care of my patients."

I knew he hadn't intended the comment to be ironic, but in the light of Brianna's suicide and Amka's disappearance, it didn't feel like much of a compliment. I merely lifted my glass and accepted the toast.

Taylor hoisted her glass, too. "Where did you get this caribou, Evan? It's divine."

"One of my patients brought it in for me last week. They're so generous. Always sharing with me after a big hunt."

"They really are," Taylor said. "No matter how deprived they might be themselves, they're always willing to share."

"No matter what the haul is. Caribou, musk ox, seal, walrus, polar bear . . ."

"Polar bear?" I asked in surprise. "They eat bear up here?"

"Yup. Apparently, a properly butchered polar bear will provide over five hundred pounds of meat."

"What does it taste like?"

"It's kind of like pork, but a bit fatter and gamier," Evan said. "Anyway, it's the cook—not the meat—that makes this particular dish special. The secret is in the glaze. It's all about the strategic deployment of the Worcestershire sauce."

Taylor laughed. "Pompous much?"

"What can I say?" Evan held his hands up. "Mom raised me to revere the kitchen. And the woman has some killer recipes."

"Where did you grow up?" I asked.

"Indiana. South Bend. But I did my college and med school in Chicago."

"And you came up here right after finishing training?"

"I practiced in Indianapolis for a while."

"So what you brought to Utqiagvik?"

"The milder winters." He chuckled. "They're actually not that much worse than the Midwest."

"What was it, really?"

"Haven't you figured it out yet, David? Anyone who moves up here is running away from something."

Taylor nodded her agreement.

"What were you running from?" I asked.

Evan cut a piece of meat and stabbed it with his fork. "An unfulfilled life."

Taylor eyed him skeptically. "You're not gonna tell us you came up here to make a difference, are you?"

"Not at all," he said quietly. "I did it for entirely selfish reasons.

I wanted to feel relevant, you know? I wasn't experiencing that working at a walk-in clinic in Indianapolis."

"Not sure if you're making a difference or finding any relevance to your life up here." I raised my glass. "But you do cook a mean moose."

He grinned. "That's relevant enough for me tonight."

The meal was as good any as I'd had in weeks. And the light-hearted banter and three bottles of wine we shared helped distract me from my troubles. At least for a while.

I was feeling tipsy as we said our goodbyes. I had to watch my footing as we stepped outside, just before eleven p.m., under only slightly dusky skies, and headed to Taylor's truck. She dropped me off at my hotel, the Top of the World, the name of which still struck me as the height of irony.

Once I was inside my room, I flopped onto the bed and immediately broke a promise to myself by phoning Beth. The line rang through to her voicemail, but rather than leave a message, I disconnected and called her right back, with the same result. I hung up and fired off a text to her. "Say hi to Graham for me. Tell him I'm sorry I'm missing the med school reunion you two are enjoying in Seattle."

The moment I tapped the send icon, I was filled with regret, aware that I was acting as impulsively as one of my personality disordered patients. But I couldn't help myself. When I wasn't ruminating over Brianna's suicide or Amka's disappearance, my thoughts would inevitably focus on my ex-wife. The idea of Beth being with my med school rival drove me crazy. It wasn't just the mental image of the two of them having sex. It was almost worse to picture Graham sitting down to meals with my ex-wife and daughter, as though he had completely replaced me in a life in which I'd once felt so secure.

Tipsy and emotional as I was, the psychiatrist in me recognized that my bitterness and anger were, paradoxically, good signs. They meant I still felt something and had not retreated to the same point of utter disconnectedness I'd reached a year and half earlier, when nothing mattered anymore.

Back then, it had begun with the death of my parents, which came within months of one another. The grief hit me hard but not unexpectedly. I'd been close to both, especially Dad. But unlike the normal stages of mourning, mine persisted like the polar night. Beth made the diagnosis of a major depression long before I was willing to accept it. When I finally consented to treatment, none of the usual antidepressants would improve my mood. After months of existing like a functional zombie, I was on the verge of undergoing electroconvulsive therapy—to literally shock my brain out of its funk—when Javier recommended I try Ketopram.

If not for that intervention, I still wondered whether I would've even lasted long enough to get the electrodes attached to my scalp. That one evening in January—two days after Beth and Ali had departed for Seattle and a few months after I'd moved into my condo— still haunted me. I must have sat on the balcony for hours, courting hypothermia in only a light sweater while gazing into the darkness of the Anchorage winter. I kept imagining what the icy wind would feel like whistling past my face as I plummeted to the sidewalk. Would I be conscious for impact? What last thought might pass through my brain as it compacted with the pavement?

More than a will to live, I believed mental exhaustion and an absolute lack of energy had prevented me from getting out of my chair—at least, before the cops showed up—and hurling myself off the balcony. But within a week of being hospitalized and starting on Ketopram, my soul slowly began to resurface and replace the automaton I had become. Soon, the dark fantasies receded, too. And like the guy from that old hair replacement ad, who was not only the president of the company but also a client, I became a staunch personal champion for Ketopram.

The memories faded as fatigue from both the travel and the wine kicked in. I nodded off at some point, fully dressed on top of the bedsheet. My sleep was fitful, punctuated by a vivid nightmare in which I was convinced Beth and Ali had moved back to Anchorage, but I didn't have their contact info and couldn't reach them no matter how hard I tried.

I woke to the actual ringing of my phone. I patted around the comforter in the dark until I found the vibrating device. I blinked at the screen. The time read 3:54 a.m., but the caller's name didn't appear, just a series of random digits.

"Hello?" I answered, groggily.

"Doctor, it's me," a soft voice murmured.

"Amka!" I said, instantly awake. "Where are you?"

"Doesn't matter."

"Yes, it does! Everyone is worried sick about you."

"Tell them not to bother."

"Where are you?"

There was a long pause, during which all I could hear was her breathing over the line. "I need help, Doctor."

"Of course I'll help you. Just tell me to where to find you!"

"I . . . I can't."

"Sure you can. Is it Rick?"

"No. Not him." Her voice cracked. "Brianna understood."

The words sent a chill through me. "What did she understand?"

"What's it matter, Doctor?"

"It does, Amka!"

"Don't you get it? Can't you see? Nothing matters!"

Her voice had become uncharacteristically shrill, and I wondered if she might be wired on coke or crystal meth. "I'll come to you, Amka," I said, though I had no idea how I would reach her in the middle of the night. "Tell me where you are."

"I can't, Doctor . . ."

"Amka, yes you can. I will come get—"

But the line was already dead.

CHAPTER 10

"**H**ave you traced the call?" I asked as I stepped inside the chief's office, barely four hours after Amka had hung up on me, with Taylor hot on my heels. After I'd texted her about Amka's call, Taylor insisted on not only driving but also accompanying me into the police station this morning.

The chief glanced over to Kai, who shook his head. "Couldn't," the detective said.

"Why not?" I asked.

"You know what VPN and VOIP are?"

"Not really."

"VOIP is voice over internet calling," Taylor answered for him. "And VPN is a service to hide your internet's IP address."

"Nailed it." Kai flashed Taylor a thumbs-up, before turning back to me. "The phone Amka called you from had both technologies. So short of calling in the NSA, it makes it impossible to trace the call."

"Which makes the call that much more suspicious," I said.

"The phone, maybe," the chief said. "But not necessarily the call."

"I don't follow," I said.

"The technology is cheap and easy," Kai said. "Criminals love it. Especially drug dealers. She probably used Rick's phone to call you."

"She begged me for help," I said, struggling to control my frustration at their seeming lack of urgency.

"Did she say she had been abducted?" Kai asked. "Or that she was in danger?"

"Not in so many words. But she sounded distressed."

"We'll do everything we can to find her," the chief said. "But this call is a good sign. It means Amka is alive and well and has access to a phone and a Wi-Fi network."

"She didn't sound well."

"I meant physically."

"I didn't see her. For all I know she could've been bleeding or badly injured."

"You're a medical doctor, aren't you?" the chief asked pointedly. "Did she sound like she was in physical distress?"

"She sounded . . . wired."

"As in high?"

"Maybe."

"So not hurt then?"

"Probably not, no," I admitted. "But she was in distress. That, I'm sure of."

"We'll pressure the usual suspects, including Eddie and the others," Kai said.

"We'll turn over the town," the chief agreed. "But at this point, we still don't have a definite crime."

"She's a missing person," I said.

"Exactly. But we've got no proof she was taken against her will. At least, we now know she's alive and seemingly unharmed."

I was annoyed to see Taylor nodding in agreement. "That's not always the case with missing persons up here, David," she said. "Often, we never hear from them again."

"We've checked the local airports, too, Doc," Kai said. "Amka and Rick haven't appeared on any flight manifests in the past week leaving from here or any other nearby airport."

"They could've gone somewhere by boat," the chief said. "But the only way out of the North Slope Borough is by plane. And while there's no proof of a crime, it's not going to stop us doing everything we can to find her."

"OK, thanks," I said, and turned for the exit, craving fresh air.

Taylor caught up with me out front of the building. We climbed into her truck, and as soon as we back on the road, she said, "They care, David. They do. They just show it differently up here." She frowned. "Actually, more often than not, folks here don't show their feelings at all. No wonder the suicide rate is through the roof."

"I didn't mean to sound ungrateful, but someone better find Amka soon."

"They will. As vast as this region is, there aren't all that many places to hide."

"What if Eddie finds Rick and Amka before the cops do?"

"Then it will be Rick's problem, not Amka's."

"Are you sure?"

Her expression didn't falter, but she lowered her head slightly. "Not a hundred percent, no."

We drove in silence across town to Evan's medical clinic. There was no snow today, but the overcast skies had a ubiquitous grayness that seemed to permeate all the houses and buildings we passed like a stain.

I couldn't get Amka's middle-of-the-night call off my mind. The more I dissected it, the clearer it became that even Amka didn't know exactly what she was asking me for. The chief was right. She hadn't sounded like a victim of abduction. But her distress was palpable. And the one phrase—"Brianna understood"—lingered in my thoughts.

"I have a full slate of site visits and other real work stuff to get done today," Taylor said as she dropped me off outside of Evan's medical clinic. "I'll check in with you later this afternoon, OK?"

Inside, the same friendly receptionist led me down the hall to a small examining room at the end of the hallway. I'd held all my in-person appointments in the same room on previous visits to town. I rearranged the chairs, putting mine in front of the examining table and the other one by the door, in a feeble attempt to make the room seem more amenable to therapeutic intimacy than internal exams.

The receptionist brought in my first patient, Connie Ashevak, a middle-aged, fleshy Iñupiat woman who flushed in shyness at the sight of me.

I had been seeing Connie for almost four years. Her schizophrenia was relatively controlled on a combination of three medications, but she continued to have fixed delusions that certain Inuit deities spoke directly to her. Not only had I learned a lot about the local Indigenous spiritual customs from Connie, but she also reaffirmed for me that the religious delusions which were so common in Judeo-Christian cultures existed in hers, too.

"Connie, does Agloolik still speak to you?" I asked, referring to the evil sea god who was the central figure in her delusions. In Iñupiat lore, Agloolik was believed to flip boats and drown fishermen in his rage. Whenever her illness worsened, Connie obsessed over Agloolik. At the time of her original diagnosis, she had almost drowned after his demonic voice in her head commanded her to walk into the ocean.

"He tries," she said while chewing on her lower lip like it was gum. "But I don't listen to Agloolik now."

"Good, Connie. Very good."

She kept biting on the lip as she stared unblinkingly at me. I'd recognized her oral tic as a symptom of a movement disorder that was caused by the antipsychotic medications she'd been taking. But switching drugs had made no difference. The movement disorder was permanent. It reminded me again that despite the necessity of psychiatric medications, they often came with a significant cost.

I leaned forward in my chair. "Are you taking your pills every morning and night, Connie?"

"Always, Doctor. Otherwise Agloolik, he gets too loud in my head."

I nodded reassuringly. "Those pills are the best way to fight him."

"I hope Agloolik hasn't taken Amka."

I grimaced. "You heard about Amka?"

"She's my cousin's daughter. Tom told us someone took her."

"We think Amka is with a friend."

"I know that man. Rick." Connie folded her arms across her chest. "He is no friend."

I wholeheartedly agreed, but all I said was "There are lots of people looking for Amka."

"I hope Agloolik doesn't take her," she repeated.

"Why would he?"

"Agloolik took Uki."

I wondered how much Amka's older sister's death, her suicide in the freezing waters, had played into Connie's fixed delusion about the malevolent sea god.

"Amka has her sister's spirit," Connie continued wistfully. "The same sadness."

"Agloolik isn't going to take Amka," I said.

Eager to change topics, I asked Connie about other aspects of her daily routine. She excitedly explained how her sister had been teaching her to knit, which apparently helped to quiet her mind when it was most turbulent. She even promised to knit me a pair of socks. When our time was up, she shook my hand and reddened again at the contact.

After Connie left, I had successive appointments with eight more patients over the course of the day. Aside from Amka, and of course, Brianna, I was able to squeeze in every patient of mine who lived in the town.

After the final one left, I was sitting at my laptop, typing up the sessions' notes, when my phone rang. I lifted it up but froze as soon as I saw Beth's name on the screen. I wanted to answer and yet I couldn't bring myself to. I was still holding the phone like a mannequin when a text from her popped up on the screen. "We should talk, David."

"We definitely should," I said to no one.

I put the phone on the desk and returned to my charting, but I couldn't focus and kept retyping the same error-filled sentence. When the phone rang again, I answered without even glancing at the screen, expecting it to be Beth. "Hi."

"David? Hello. It's Yvette Berg calling. Do you have a sec?"

"Oh, hi, Yvette," I said, swallowing my disappointment that I had answered her call instead of Beth's. "Sure."

Yvette was a colleague of mine in Anchorage, but we hardly interacted beyond exchanging pleasantries at departmental functions. Friendly as she was, I found her to be overbearing and opinionated. And she didn't seem to enjoy my company any more than I did hers.

"I realize you're out of town," Yvette said. "But I'm on call for Psychiatry at the Regional today. And I just assessed a patient. A woman you admitted a few weeks ago. I wonder if you remember her."

I tensed. The calls from colleagues that began with "do you remember that patient?" inevitably ended with the revelation that some disastrous outcome, often death, had befallen the person. "Her name, Yvette?"

"Delores Nolan."

I had a mental image of the incredibly restless woman who'd paced the floors inside the psychiatric unit like a caged animal. "Of course," I said. "No history of bipolar disorder. Delores only had depression in the past, but I was convinced she was having an early manic break."

"She's in the ICU now," Yvette said with what sounded to me like a trace of satisfaction.

"What happened to her?"

"She overdosed. On massive amounts of aspirin, acetaminophen, and Ketopram. She's on life support now and requires urgent dialysis."

"Did you say Ketopram?"

"Yes," Yvette said. "That's what I wanted to ask you about. Why would you restart her on that after her last admission? Especially, as you said, when Delores was already exhibiting signs of mania."

"I was the one who took her off the Ketopram!"

"You didn't restart it?" Yvette sounded almost disappointed.

"No."

"The discharge summary from her last visit wasn't complete, and the prescription was called in by a resident. I just assumed you were the one who decided to put her back on the med."

"I wasn't."

"So who did?"

Theoretically, it could have been any psychiatrist who had covered the ward since I'd left. But my guts tightened. There was only one doctor in Alaska who would have restarted that medication.

CHAPTER 11

Two hours after Yvette's call—and her subsequent text confirming that Javier had indeed been the one to restart Delores on Ketopram—I was sitting in the same exam room where I'd spent most of my day. As tempted as I was to call and confront Javier over his decision to put a manic patient on Ketopram, I decided to first delve deeper. How could I ignore three attempted suicides? Anton Hayes, Brianna O'Brien, and now Delores Nolan. All of whom were taking Ketopram.

I logged onto my university library account and began to review the online data regarding the new antidepressant. As an early prescriber and user, I was intimately familiar with Ketopram's reported side effects in the scientific literature. Rereading the same studies now with a fresh eye, I noted they frequently commented on vivid dreams, but none documented an increased risk of suicidality. Statistically speaking, Javier had been correct when he told me that association was not evidence of causation. Coincidences did happen in medicine. But whoever said 'where there's smoke, there's fire' was also right. And in the case of Ketopram, the smoke was now billowing.

I looked up from the screen as Evan knocked on the open door. "Just heading out," he said from the doorway. "Can I give you a lift?"

"No. Thanks." I considered telling him about my suspicions regarding Ketopram but decided there was no point until I had something more concrete. "I still have to finish dictating my notes from today."

He nodded. "How much longer are you staying in town for?"

"A few more days, maybe. I want to see Amka found."

"Me, too." Evan sighed. "I've been calling everyone I can think of who might know her whereabouts. A bunch of her extended family are patients of mine."

"And?"

"Nothing."

His look of deflation was contagious. "That comment Amka made that Brianna 'understood,'" I said. "It felt as if she was telling me the two of them shared something."

Evan raised an eyebrow. "Like a secret?"

"Yeah, or maybe a trauma," I said. "Brianna once alluded to being abused as a teenager. Wonder if it all could be somehow connected?"

Evan shrugged. "They've both been my patients for years. You'd think one of them would've said something."

"Maybe," I said, my mind drifting back to Ketopram. "Don't worry about me. I won't be here much longer. And your office assistant gave me a spare key."

"OK." He waved half-heartedly. "I'll catch you later."

As soon as Evan left, I turned back to the laptop. I scanned through everything I could find online, even smaller studies, but none proved helpful. I found a number of case reports on adverse outcomes for specific patients, though I understood those kinds of anecdotal accounts were the weakest form of statistical evidence.

Only two of the reports involved patients who had attempted suicide while taking Ketopram. The first described a patient who had
blown the top of his head off with a shotgun only two days after beginning the medication. His suicide was deemed to have happened
too soon into treatment to have been caused by Ketopram. And the
second case—a woman who had slit both wrists but survived—had
low levels of the drug in her blood, indicating she had not been taking it properly.

I changed tacks. Since I knew that pharmaceutical companies sometimes buried the unfavorable studies they sponsored, I
searched for evidence of unpublished or aborted trials that might
suggest problems. I found precious few hits. A proposed trial of
Ketopram in Philadelphia never seemed to materialize. Another one
out of Miami had apparently completed the enrollment of patients,
but the results were never published. I was surprised to discover
that one of the most prominent early researchers on Ketopram, a
Dr. Avery Lincoln, seemed to have disappeared, at least in terms of
publications. He appeared to be a victim of the old academic adage:
publish or perish. Lincoln had been the lead investigator on the first
major study to show Ketopram to be effective in refractory depression. Pierson Pharmaceuticals had touted his research often in their
early promotional material. But those citations stopped abruptly
about three years ago, and I couldn't see a single mention of him
in any of the company's posts after that. When I went back and reviewed his groundbreaking paper more closely, I spotted a familiar
name. Javier was listed as one of the seven co-investigators on the
clinical trial.

Just as I called up Lincoln's profile on the University of Pennsylvania's faculty page, Taylor bounded into the room, almost startling
me. "How's it going?"

"Good," I said, rubbing my neck. "Any word on Amka?"

She frowned. "I just called Kai on my way over. Nothing so far."

"They didn't get anything out of Eddie?"

"Kai put the screws to him, apparently. But Eddie stuck to his story—that Rick owes him money and he's looking for him, too."

"Not sure I would take Eddie's word on that."

"Oh, God no! Not for anything. But he might actually be telling the truth about this one thing. Kai says Eddie's frantic to get his cash back."

"Must be a lot of money."

"Kai's convinced it's all related to the recent dump of coke in town."

"Great. So Amka's staying with the guy who ripped off the local drug lord?"

"At least Eddie doesn't know where to find them either." She nodded at my laptop. "What are you up to? You were so engrossed."

I considered telling her about my research into Ketopram and the reason behind it. But it was still such a nebulous theory, and I wasn't ready to put it into words for her, Evan, or anyone else. Instead, I closed the laptop and said, "Just finishing charting on my patients. How was your day?"

"Long. Not all that satisfactory, either."

"How so?"

"I just got back from the McDougals—Nevaeh's great-aunt and -uncle."

"I spoke to Kerry a few weeks ago," I said. "How are they doing? How's Nevaeh?"

"They're coping. Gus and Kerry are good people. But Nevaeh's a handful for them. Neither of them are in great health."

"Why is Nevaeh such a handful?"

"She's acting out. It's natural. The poor kid just lost her only parent. But she's throwing huge tantrums. Hitting them and sometimes even herself."

"That doesn't sound like the curious outgoing girl I remember from my videoconferences with her mom."

"Totally different. I used to drop by their place regularly. To help Brianna with her financial and housing applications. Nevaeh was such a happy, bubbly kid. Not today. I could barely get a word out of her. And not a single smile."

"Any luck tracking down her father?"

"Not yet. I got some calls in with our office in Anchorage. I almost don't want to find him. Doubt Dylan could manage Nevaeh on his own."

I thought of my earlier conversation with Evan. "Taylor, did Brianna ever mention anything about sexual assault or abuse?"

Her nose crinkled. "Of Nevaeh?"

"No, no. About herself."

Taylor shook her head. "But it wouldn't surprise me if she had been."

"Why do you say that?"

"It's common everywhere. But up here in the Arctic? It's rampant." She paused, and for a moment, her eyes clouded over. "And nine times out of ten, the abuser is someone in a position of trust."

I waited to give her a moment to expand on the comment. But instead, she motioned to the door and said, "Let's go."

I stood up and grabbed my laptop. "You don't mind dropping me off at the hotel?"

"Happy to." The carefree smile returned to her lips. "Are you hungry? We could grab a bite on the way."

"I'd love to. But after all the wine at Evan's last night and the really long day I've had in this office . . ."

"Yeah, yeah. I get it."

We headed out together to her truck. If Taylor was hurt by me turning down her dinner offer, she didn't show it on the ride back to the hotel. She chatted all the way. I wished I could absorb some of her positive energy.

After she dropped me off, I headed up to my room with the genuine intention of getting an early night. Once inside, I headed over to the mini-fridge and lifted the bottle of whiskey I'd brought from home off the shelf above it. I cracked open the bottle and poured myself a glass that was somewhere between a single and a double.

The scotch didn't help settle me. My mind wouldn't cooperate. As I lay on the bed, I ping-ponged between bouts of sorrow and anger. I felt betrayed by Beth and duped by Javier, even though I was aware the emotions weren't rational. I was also angry with Amka for calling me to ask for help without letting me provide it. And I was furious with Brianna for what she did to herself and tried to do to her daughter. But on further reflection, I realized I was angrier at myself for letting both young women down. And then there was my raging ambivalence over Ketopram. The drug I had credited for saving my life. The drug I had peddled to patients as if I worked for the company. Was it all just a fraud?

I had the sinking sense that if I stayed in the room, I would down the whole bottle and end up calling Beth or Javier. Probably both of them. Giving up on any hope of sleep, I rose out of bed, grabbed my coat, and headed downstairs.

It was after ten o'clock and still bright outside, but an icy breeze had whipped up. I tucked my hands in my pockets and bundled my coat tighter as I trod down the dirt road with my eyes fixed on the ground ahead of me and no specific destination in mind. At one point, I stopped to watch three skinny, collarless dogs, which looked to be at least part husky, amble past me. I'd seen similar animals wandering loose all over town like strays, but I'd been told that all of them had owners.

I soon found myself standing at the water's edge on the muddy bank of Barrow Beach. Beside me loomed the town's most iconic sculpture, a simple towering arch made from a bowhead whale's jawbone, with the skeletons of two canoes propped up on either side of it. The last time I'd stood on the same spot, in early April, so many ice drifts had filled the sea that it looked to me as if I could hop from one to another all the way to the North Pole. Now the ice was gone, and the blackish blue water rippled with desolate gray waves. And the beach was as empty as the sea, except for two ravens that glided low across the water in search of fish.

I thought of Amka's sister and imagined Uki steeling her nerves at the last moment as she threw herself out of her boat and into the unforgiving blackness. Did the freezing waters numb her angst? Had she found the relief she sought in Agloolik's embrace?

The chill cut through my jacket and I began to move just to warm myself. As I walked along the beach, I had a growing sense that I wasn't alone. I took a few more steps before I looked over my shoulder.

A stocky man walked about twenty yards behind me, far enough back that I almost mistook the balaclava over his face for bushy facial hair. I picked up my pace, but I didn't break into a run. At least, not until I heard the thuds of boots against the hard sand behind me.

Without glancing back, I took off in a sprint, my heart already pounding. Frigid air chilled my lungs, and my chest tightened with my usual exercise-induced asthma, but the loud footfalls at my back spurred me onward.

After running a few hundred yards, I stole a glance over my shoulder and saw that my pursuer had fallen back. I lowered my head and ran as fast I could toward the road in front of me, the same one I had come in on.

The moment I looked up again, I planted my feet so hard I almost tumbled forward. I was bewildered to see that my pursuer had somehow gotten ahead of me and was standing only yards away. Yet I could still hear the crescendo of boot stomps behind me. And I realized the guy in front of me was leaner than my pursuer.

A chill harsher than the Arctic wind hit me, as I recognized I was trapped between the two masked men.

I raised my hands in a gesture of surrender, but I'd barely got them halfway up when a heavy blow struck my shoulder blade and drove me forward. The shock blunted the pain as I slammed head-first into the hard sand.

Something thudded into my back again and blasted away the last of my breath. Gasping, I instinctively rolled into a crouch and covered my head with my arms. Two more hard blows landed on my back, and then something cracked across my arms so brutally that it felt as if both forearms had shattered.

I peered between the gap in my pulsating arms and saw two figures hovering over me. All I could make out were two sets of eyes peering out from behind the balaclavas.

"Take it," I croaked. "Wallet's in the back pocket."

They didn't move. Neither said a word. Time was filled only by the throb in my arms and chest. I wondered how many bones were broken.

"Get the fuck out of Barrow!" one of the men said as he heaved a club at me. They were the last words I heard before a searing pain tore across my forehead.

CHAPTER 12

The moment I opened my eyes, I regretted it. The glare of bright lights made my head throb, and I gagged from overwhelming nausea. As I raised a hand to my aching forehead, my arm felt as if it were weighed down by a bucket. My fingers rubbed the roughness of what I realized was tape. I pressed gingerly and felt thick padding around my scalp. I pulled my hand back and saw that my arm was wrapped in a plaster cast.

"Hi. How are you feeling?"

I looked to my left to see Taylor's smiling face. "I'm in hospital?"

"Yes, David. You still are."

"Still?"

"You've been here since last night, but you keep asking."

I shook my head in confusion, launching another wave of nausea through my body. "I don't understand."

"Evan says you suffered a severe concussion. And you've got anterograde amnesia. You keep asking us the same questions and forgetting the answers."

"How did I get here?"

"A young couple found you wandering on the beach, covered in blood from the gash on your forehead. They drove you to the ER."

The beach. The men in the balaclavas. "I was robbed."

Taylor shook her head. "You had your wallet on you. And your cash is still in it."

The warning. The one with the bat. "He called it Barrow," I muttered.

Taylor's face scrunched up. She laid her hand gently above my cast, on my upper arm. "Probably best for you to rest some more."

"Right before he clubbed me. He warned me to get out of town."

"Who did?"

"Their faces were covered. There were two of them."

"He's awake," Evan said as he suddenly appeared beside Taylor. "Hello, David. Enjoying your new digs? Do you remember any of our earlier chats?"

"No."

"That's normal. To have a gap in memory following a concussion like yours."

"What happened?"

Evan showed a lopsided grin. "In medical terms, you were the victim of a serious shit kicking."

Fan as I was of morbid humor, I wasn't feeling up for it now. "What specific injuries, Evan?"

He rubbed his chin. "Aside from the closed head injury, aka a severe concussion, you suffered a four-inch laceration to the forehead that I had to close in two layers of sutures just to the stop the hemorrhaging. You have three fractured ribs on your right posterior chest. One of the broken ribs punctured your right lung, and there's a partial pneumothorax. But the lung is only fifteen percent collapsed, so we didn't need to put a chest tube in. You've also got a fracture through the ulna of your right forearm, but the bones are well aligned and can be managed in a simple cast." He motioned to the plaster over my forearm. "Aside from that, you have multiple contusions to your chest and arms. And you lost a fair bit of blood from that gash. Your hemoglobin is down a little, but not low enough to require a transfusion."

Evan's description reminded me of a trauma service rotation I'd taken as a medical student, because the list of injuries sounded as if he were describing a victim of a major motor vehicle accident.

"The good news," Evan continued, "is that the pan CT scan from your head to your pelvis is otherwise OK. No bleeding around the brain. No neck fractures. No other lung collapses. And no internal bleeding. In other words, you won't need surgery. And you should make a full recovery."

I should have been more relieved to hear it, but my head ached, and my mood, which had already been low before my assault, only darkened. "Why?"

"We don't know," Taylor said.

"Who were they?" I asked.

"It's a small town. The cops will figure it out."

"She's not wrong, David." Evan took a step away from the bed. "I've got to run. I have another patient in the ER, but I'll drop in again this afternoon."

"I want to go home," I said, stopping him.

"To Anchorage?" He gave me a hard stare. "You can't fly. Not with that pneumothorax. It's small now but could easily increase inside a pressurized plane cabin. Won't be safe for you to fly for at least ten days. Probably two weeks."

"At least let me go back to my hotel."

"I'd prefer to keep you under observation for another day. I'll check in on you again this evening," Evan said as he headed for the door.

Minutes later, Kai entered and, glancing at Taylor, stepped into the space Evan had vacated. "Hey, Doc, how you doing?"

"Word is, I'm still alive." The conversation already felt repetitive to me, and this was only the first time I remembered having it. "Was Eddie behind it?"

"That's what we're trying to figure out," Kai said. "You didn't recognize the two guys?"

"They were masked."

"Did they talk to you?"

"Just once. The bigger one told me to get out of town. Specifically, Barrow."

"A lot of locals still call the town by the old name." Kai shrugged. "The one who warned you. Did he sound like Eddie?"

"No. Wasn't him. That guy was too big and burly."

"Makes sense." Kai scratched his cheek. "Eddie has an alibi for last night, which holds up. The girlfriend, Rita, and his sidekick, Gord Feenie, claim to have been with him until long after you showed up in the ER."

"Eddie would swear he wasn't present for his own birth," Taylor said. "Besides, he's more likely to have sent a couple of his boys, no?"

"We don't have much to go on. No witnesses at the scene." Kai turned back to me. "Did you tell anyone you were going down to the beach?"

"No."

"Did you go the first night you were in town?"

"No."

"So they must've been following you."

"Why would I matter to them?"

"That's a very good question, Doc."

My head pounded and I still had difficulty focusing, but the fog was clearing inside my skull. "They didn't want me asking about Amka."

"Maybe." Kai shrugged again. "Maybe not."

"Why else would anyone care?"

"Some locals—especially Eddie and his crew—don't trust outsiders of any kind," Taylor said.

"Especially right when they're gearing up for a big summer sale," Kai agreed.

Careful to keep my head still, I looked up at Kai. "Still no sign of Amka?"

"Not yet."

My heart sank, but I didn't comment.

"Better rest up, Doc," Kai said, backing away from the bed. "We'll find who did this to you. Meantime, I'm off to see Manny Irvine now."

"Who?" I asked.

"Eddie's main rival," Taylor explained.

"More of a wannabe than a rival, I'd say," Kai said. "Manny is lucky to still be alive. Was stabbed multiple times a year or two ago. Lost part of his liver."

"Eddie did that?" I asked.

"Manny couldn't say," Kai said. "Another masked assailant, like yours."

"As if Manny wouldn't know who was behind his attack." Taylor scoffed. "Mask or no mask."

Kai rolled his eyes. "These guys." And, without another word, he turned and left.

"So you're stuck in town for two more weeks, huh?" Taylor said, once he was gone.

"Can't be." I dug my elbows into the mattress and began to push myself up. Pain tore through the right side of me as if another brutal kick had just landed. I groaned.

"David." Taylor leaned forward as if to grab me. "Don't move."

"It's OK." I waved her back with my non-casted arm as I breathed heavily, aware of the movement of my ribs with each inhalation. "I have to be in Seattle next week. I promised my daughter."

"You heard Evan."

"I can't miss it, Taylor. I just can't."

Her face lit with a compassionate smile. "Next week is a ways off. Let's take it day by day. Things will work out, David. You'll see."

In my concussed state, the warmth of her expression almost brought me to tears. But I also had the uncanny sense that she was dead wrong. That nothing was going to work out.

CHAPTER 13

I checked myself out of hospital against medical advice just before lunch. I would have left sooner, but I had to wait for the second dose of hydromorphone—the opioid painkiller Evan had prescribed me—to kick in before I could stomach the pain enough just to rise out of bed.

Taylor dropped by as I was struggling to get my shoes on. She tried to talk me out of leaving, but once that failed, she insisted on driving me back to the hotel.

I had to lean on her shoulder while she boosted me into the truck, and the shame of my helplessness kept me quiet during the ride. But Taylor couldn't have been much more boisterous or chatty. I'd noticed that her gregariousness was, at least in part, a defense mechanism. The more anxious or unsettled she seemed to feel, the more sociable she tended to become.

Taylor pulled up in front of the hotel. I nodded to the TOP OF THE WORLD sign out front. "As long as I'm a guest here, they're guilty of very false advertising," I muttered.

"Yeah, well, it didn't book as well when they used to call it the 'Remote Frozen Wasteland.'"

Taylor shifted into park and reached for the door handle, making it clear she intended to get out and help me. I extended my non-broken arm, which still ached under the tensor bandage, and touched her elbow. "I can take it from here."

She eyed me patiently. "Everyone needs a hand now and again, David."

"I'm good, Taylor. Honestly."

She let go of the handle. "What if they come back?"

"Why would they?"

"Didn't they warn you to get out of town? I'm guessing they don't know a lot about the physics of punctured lungs and air travel."

"They're not coming back," I said with a certainty I didn't feel. "Thanks for everything, Taylor. Truly."

I gingerly reached for the door, holding my breath to minimize the pain, and eased myself awkwardly out of the truck. I planned out each step on the short walk through the lobby and over to the elevator. The shy young clerk behind the desk, who had never paid much attention to me before, watched me hobble past. "Need any help, sir?" he asked.

"I'm all right, thanks," I said, focusing on the five or six paces left to go.

I had no sooner gotten inside my room and lowered myself onto the bed when my phone rang. I'd been ignoring it all morning, and I had multiple "missed calls" and unopened texts waiting for me. But once I saw Ali's face on the screen, I had to answer.

Her jaw fell. "Oh my god, Dad! Are you OK?"

Through the fog of my concussion and painkillers, I'd forgotten I was answering with my camera on.

"I am, Bean. Honestly." I tapped the bandages across my forehead with my broken arm. "Just a few stitches and a cast." I forced a painful laugh. "Oh, and my pride has been fatally wounded, too."

"What happened?"

"I tumbled off a rental bike." I conjured a smile. "Maybe I'm not as graceful as you, after all?"

Her frown told me she wasn't buying it. "You don't look so good, Dad."

"Give me a couple days. I'll be back to normal."

"Will you still come down here?" she asked hopefully, and then added, "Can't wait to see you."

My heart fluttered, but the comment only made me sadder. "Next Monday," I said, determined that pneumothorax or not, I would somehow get there. "How's the driving? Has the terror of you behind the wheel cleared the streets of Seattle yet?"

"As if!" She showed her first grin. "Haven't even had time to practice once yet."

"And your recital?"

"I keep forgetting steps in rehearsal. I'm all nerves. Maybe they picked the wrong girl?"

"They absolutely picked the right one. Besides, anxiety is a protective emotion."

"Yeah, right."

"Trust me, Bean. Harness those nerves to perfect your routine. Every ballerina does. Maria Alexandrova probably still gets stage fright before she performs."

"Maria Alexandrova! You're so last decade, Dad," Ali groaned. "She retired from the Bolshoi in 2017. Hasn't danced since."

My chuckle made my ribs ache.

Distracted, Ali looked over her shoulder. "He says he's OK," she said away from the microphone.

Before I could stop Ali from the passing phone to her mother, the image on my phone shook and then Beth's concerned face filled the screen. "Since when do you bike, David?" she demanded.

"Got to do something to pass the time up here in Utqiagvik," I mumbled, conflicted at the sight of her.

"Your color is terrible. You don't look right at all."

"I have a mild concussion. I just need to rest."

"When are you going back to Anchorage?"

"A couple days," I said.

"Who's going to keep an eye on you up there?"

"I'll manage, Beth."

There was comfort in seeing her face. It reminded me of other crises she had seen me through over the years. From man-colds to the death of loved ones, Beth had been there for me. When I lost my parents, one after the other, she absorbed my grief and pain. But I kept pushing her away. The depression made me cruel to her at times. In the end, I didn't give her much choice but to leave.

"David . . ."

The unwelcome mental image of her with Graham popped into my head. "It's not your concern anymore," I snapped.

"I've never stopped being concerned about you. Never will."

"You've got a new partner now. One who's waited a lot of years to be with you. Why don't you focus on him?"

"It's not like that, David."

"You're not seeing Graham Blackburn?"

Her quick glance away confirmed the answer before she opened her mouth. "Graham and I have been dating, yes. It's early. And I don't know where—"

"Your business, Beth." My chest ached from more than just broken ribs. "I don't need to hear the specifics."

"Of course not." The kindness in her smile only made it worse. "Listen, David, I don't know how I can help you from here. But if there's anything I can do—anything at all—please let me know."

"Tell Ali that I'll call her back soon." I hung up without waiting for her to reply.

I dropped the phone on the bed and lay on top of the covers, pondering my sorry situation. I'd lost the love of my life to someone I thought had faded into obscurity years before. I was stuck—maimed and useless for reasons I didn't understand—in the northernmost town in civilization. I was at risk of missing the most important event in my daughter's life. And out of the eleven patients whose mental health I had been entrusted to manage in this hopeless town, one was dead and another missing.

My thoughts drifted again to Ketopram. I couldn't stop thinking of Yvette's call the day before regarding the overdose patient whom Javier had restarted on the medication. I slowly reached for my laptop on the nightstand. I carefully positioned it across my lap and opened it up. Typing with one finger, I had to repeat my previous search just to remind myself of the name of the prominent Ketopram researcher, Avery Lincoln. I found a contact phone number at the UPenn Department of Psychiatry. I dialed it and was surprised when the receptionist offered to patch me directly through to his phone.

"Hello," the man answered in a baritone voice.

"Dr. Lincoln? My name is David Spears. I'm a psychiatrist in Alaska."

"Alaska? Never been. My wife keeps threatening to drag me there on a cruise. But I keep telling her that we're too young to throw in the towel. A cruise!" He laughed deeply. "How can I help you, Dr. Spears?"

"I'm calling about your research on Ketopram."

He hesitated. When he spoke again, his tone was noticeably cooler. "It's no longer a research interest of mine."

"You authored the seminal paper on Ketopram."

"Maybe so, but I no longer study it."

"I was an early adopter of Ketopram, Dr. Lincoln. I've found it to be just as effective for my patients in refractory depression as your study suggested. If not more so. And my colleague, Dr. Gutiérrez, he is—"

"You work with Javier?"

"I do."

"I see," he said noncommittally.

"As I mentioned, I've been a proponent of Ketopram from early on, but lately there have been a few events that have given me . . . cause for concern."

"Events?"

"Adverse outcomes."

"What sort of outcomes are you referring to?"

"There have been a few suicide attempts in patients of mine who had been taking it."

"A few?"

"Three that I am aware of in the past month."

Avery paused again. "It's really not my area of expertise any longer, Dr. Spears. I have moved on."

I shifted uncomfortably. "Up until three years ago, you were arguably the world's leading clinical researcher on Ketopram. Your name was all over the scientific literature. And then it was as if you just . . . vanished."

"My funding ended."

"From Pierson Pharmaceuticals?"

"Among others, yes."

"Do you mind if I ask why?"

"Whether I mind or not is irrelevant. I cannot answer your question, Dr. Spears."

"Why not?"

"I signed a nondisclosure agreement."

"With Pierson?"

"Yes," he said. "Listen, Dr. Spears, I wish I could be more forthcoming, but my hands are tied. So if there's nothing else—"

"People—some of them my patients—have been trying to kill themselves, Dr Lincoln!" I snapped. "One of them succeeded. A twenty-two-year-old mother. I need to know if Ketopram was involved."

He went quiet for a long moment. "Ask Javier," he finally said.

"Ask him what?"

"About the study."

"Your landmark study?"

"No. The last one. The one that wasn't published."

I forced myself to focus. Feeling stoned on painkillers and concussed, it took me a moment to digest what Avery was telling me. There had been a subsequent study, one that had never been published. And then Avery had lost his funding and was silenced by a nondisclosure agreement. The only reason a drug company would want to bury a study and fire its preeminent researcher was if it had shown something alarming. And they would have done it early, before the results were considered more than just a "signal" and definitive proof of an issue, so they could prevent the study from ever seeing light of day.

"Why did Pierson Pharmaceuticals block its publication?" I asked. "What were they trying to hide?"

"Ask Javier, Dr. Spears."

CHAPTER 14

I was unsure whether it was due to the concussion or the hydromorphone, but I slept almost fifteen hours, until well after nine thirty a.m. If I'd woken up at any point during the night, I had no memory of it. I was relieved that the nausea had diminished, but I realized the painkillers had worn off as soon as I reached for my phone and relived the blows to my chest.

It took me a few minutes just to get to my feet and shuffle to the bathroom. I filled a glass with the acrid-tasting water that ran through the local pipes and gulped down two painkillers. I lifted the bottle of Ketopram off the narrow countertop and opened the cap. But instead of tapping out a tablet into my hand and popping it into my mouth as I had done for hundreds of mornings before, I stopped and studied the label. I reflected on my conversation with Avery Lincoln and his insinuation—or, at least, my inference—that Pierson Pharmaceuticals had covered up a negative outcome in a trial. I had no doubt how much Ketopram had helped me in the past, but I couldn't help thinking of the three patients who had attempted suicide in the past month while on the medication.

My hand wavered, alternating between the urge to dump the

bottle's contents down the toilet and to take my usual pill. I even fleetingly considered how easy it would be to swallow the whole bottle. In the end, I screwed the cap back on and lowered it without taking one.

I hobbled back to the bed, where I intended to hunker down until the hydromorphone kicked in. I'd just managed to position myself back on the mattress when my phone rang. When Taylor's name flashed across the screen, I decided to answer.

"I didn't wake you, did I?"

"It's almost ten, Taylor."

"How are you feeling? You OK?"

"I had a good sleep" was all I said.

"Do you need anything?"

"Just a bit more rest." I didn't mean the comment to sound as snitty as it might have, but I didn't have the energy to clarify.

"Totally get it. But I thought you'd want to hear the news."

"You found Amka?" I began to sit up and immediately regretted it.

"No. Only Rick."

"They're not together?"

"Not since yesterday apparently."

"Where's Amka?"

"Rick doesn't know. Or that's his story. I haven't spoken to him yet."

"Where is he?"

"Here at the police station."

"The police? Why?"

"He turned himself in."

"I'm on my way."

"You're in no shape to go anywhere, David!"

"I'll be there in fifteen." I hung up without giving her a chance to argue.

Gritting my teeth, I rose again from the bed and donned a pair of jeans and a button-up shirt. Socks were the biggest challenge.

Grunting, I managed to get them over my ankles. I had never felt more grateful for slip-on shoes.

I called the front desk and asked them to book a cab, and then I slowly made my way down to the lobby, relieved the painkillers were starting to kick in by the time I reached the front door. The skies were a volatile gray and summer snowflakes drifted down again, but maybe because of the hydromorphone, I didn't feel chilled.

The cab was idling out front. I waved off the driver's offer of assistance, which I almost regretted as I climbed painfully into the back of the SUV. Maybe the painkillers altered my perspective, but as we drove past the mishmash of houses lining the dirt roads, I found a degree of beauty in the chaotic townscape. It gave me renewed admiration for the defiance of the people and the town itself for existing at all in this isolated, inhospitable, and, in my opinion, uninhabitable clime.

The driver dropped me off in front of the police station. None of the staff stopped me as I hitched down the hallway to the chief's office, where he, Taylor, and Kai were sitting around his desk.

Taylor jumped to her feet. "David!"

"Shouldn't you be in hospital?" the chief asked in surprise.

"I'm all right," I said as I eased myself into a vacant chair.

"Could've fooled me," Kai said.

"Where's Rick?" I demanded.

The chief thumbed to the wall behind him. "We're holding him in the interview room."

"Can I speak to him?"

The chief shook his head.

"What did he tell you?" I asked.

"Rick claims Amka and he took a boat down the coast to Wainwright, four days ago."

"Where they hid out with one of his cousins who lives there," Kai added.

"When did he get back?" I asked.

"Last night," Kai said.

"With Amka?"

"So he says."

"Where did she go?"

"Rick claims not to know," Kai said. "Says Amka took off to find a bathroom while he was docking the fishing boat and never came back."

"He didn't go after her?"

"Says he kept expecting her to turn up on her own. Besides, Rick's a lot more concerned about protecting his own hide than hers."

"She's got to be somewhere in town," the chief said.

"Not at her parents'," Taylor chimed in. "I called her dad. He hasn't seen or heard from her."

I looked back over to Kai. "You said they were hiding out? From Eddie?"

"Yeah," Kai said. "Rick admits to owing him money. He's mighty vague about the details, though."

"Are you holding him?"

"Rick's not under arrest. Not yet anyway." The chief rolled his eyes. "He wants to be here. For his own protection."

"What if Eddie thinks Amka was involved in ripping him off?"

The chief glanced at Kai and then said, "She wasn't."

"What if he *thinks* she was?" I asked. "It could put her in more danger."

"We're going to find her," Kai said.

I raised my casted arm. "The same way you found the guys who did this?"

The smile left Kai's lips. "You aware of the stats on assaults in the US, Doc? Less than half of cases are ever cleared. Even when the assailants *aren't* wearing masks."

The chief shot Kai a cautionary glare and then turned to me. "You've been through a lot since you got here. Too much. But we are being more than transparent with you. And you need to let us do our job, David."

"I'm sorry," I said with genuine remorse. I touched the bandage around my head. "I'm not in the best frame of mind."

The chief accepted my apology with a small grin. "Who would be after that beating?"

"By the way, Manny Irvine wasn't much help with your attackers, Doc," Kai said. "Told me he has no idea who did it. For what it's worth, though, he did say Eddie wouldn't waste his time on a guy like you."

"That's reassuring," I muttered.

I took little solace from the fact that Amka had returned to town the night before. Where had she been staying since? And why hadn't she contacted her parents? I had to push myself up by both elbows to get out of the chair. "I'm going back to my hotel."

"I'm driving you," Taylor announced and followed me out.

As I was shuffling down the hallway, a door opened in front of me. A uniformed officer stepped out followed by a scrawny man in a black-and-red plaid jacket and a ball cap. Only when he glanced at me did I recognize him by his wispy beard and small eyes.

"Rick!" I called.

He looked up. "What?"

"Where is Amka?"

"How many times do I have to tell you all?"

"Do you know who I am?"

"Sure. The head-peeper. The one who planted all those shitty ideas in her brain." Rick waved a finger at my cast and bandage. "One of your patients finally get sick of your crap?"

"Matter of fact, I'm pretty sure it was the folks looking for you who did this." I took a slow breath. "You've put Amka in harm's way, you do understand that, right?"

"I was trying to protect her."

"By ripping off a local drug lord? That's how you protect your girlfriend?"

"You don't know shit." He sneered. "I got us to Wainwright. No one would've bothered us there. Amka made me bring her back!"

"Why?"

"Said she missed her family."

"Then why didn't she reach out to them once she got home?" Taylor asked.

Rick held up his palms and shrugged again.

"Why did you let her go?" I asked.

"I didn't!" he cried. "The crazy bitch took off on me as soon we hit the dock."

"And you have no idea where she might have gone?"

"Maybe Lana's or Kira's? She would've definitely gone to Bree's, if the chick hadn't offed herself."

The mention of Brianna made my chest ache again. And a thought occurred to me. "Was Amka taking her medicine while you were with her?"

"Those mental pills? Yeah."

"How do you know?"

"She made me get her a glass water to swallow them a couple times."

The confirmation she was taking her Ketopram didn't offer much reassurance after my conversation with Avery Lincoln. As I was turning away from him, Rick added, "Fat lot of good they did her."

I spun back toward him. Too quickly. A jolt of pain ripped through me and took my breath away. "What does that mean?" I panted.

"Nothing."

I wanted to shake him. "Tell me."

Rick only smirked in defiance.

The chief called out from somewhere behind me. "Tell the doctor, Rick!"

"I dunno," Rick said. "She was freaked out. We both were. But she was such a drowse the whole time. Going on about how Brianna figured it all out and all."

"Figured what out?" I snapped. "Her suicide?"

"Maybe. I guess."

I took a step closer to him. "Did Amka threaten to hurt herself?"

"Nah. Nothing like that."

"You weren't worried about her doing something rash?"

He squinted. "Rash?"

"Stupid. Impulsive. Like trying to kill herself."

"Nah. She was all right."

His nonchalance calmed me slightly. I knew from my training as well as my clinical experience that the risk of suicide was exponentially higher in people who had a specific plan for killing themselves, rather than those who just expressed passive suicidal thoughts.

"Except maybe that one time," Rick continued.

"Which time?"

"When she mentioned Uki."

I stiffened. "Her sister?"

"Yeah. On the way back on the boat. Amka was acting all quiet. Staring out at the water, like super-intense. And then she asked me if I thought Uki felt any pain at the end."

CHAPTER 15

The fatigue was more incapacitating than the physical discomfort. As soon I got back to my hotel room, I crawled into bed and napped for almost four hours despite the long sleep I'd had overnight. I only woke up at the sound of knocking.

I rose painfully from the bed and trudged to the door. As soon as I opened it, Taylor stepped past me carrying a cloth bag. The scent of curry wafted behind her as she headed toward the small table and chairs in the corner of the room.

"I hope you like Thai," she said, as she laid the bag on the table and began extracting Tupperware containers.

"There's Thai food in Utqiagvik?" I asked more out of disorientation than curiosity.

She laughed. "When I cook it, there is."

"Any word on Amka?" I asked.

"No." She glanced downward. "Nothing, so far."

"I'm worried, Taylor. Especially, after that comment she made to Rick about her sister . . ."

"Me, too. But the police are out looking. And there's nothing else to do. You, on the other hand, I can at least feed."

I didn't have the heart to tell Taylor that I had little appetite. "Thank you," I said, as I joined her by the table. "Thai is my daughter's favorite food."

"I like this kid of yours already," she said, as she began to dish the grub onto two paper plates, starting with the rice followed by heaps of red curry and pad Thai. "Tell me about her."

"Ali's a good kid." I couldn't help smiling at thought of her. "She just turned sixteen. She lives in Seattle with her mom, but I get to see her every month. Matter of fact, she was supposed to be in Anchorage with me right now—for the whole month of August—but her dance program got in the way."

"Ballet?"

"Yup."

"Cool. I used to dance as a kid, too. Ballet and hip-hop. Loved it!" Taylor bent her knuckles at right angles like a level and raised her hand in front of her face. "But I just kept shooting up into the giant you see before you. Not a lot of five-eleven ballerinas out there."

"Ali's petite like her mom."

"You must miss her, huh?"

I missed Ali terribly, and Beth almost as much. But all I said was "I do."

"Is that maybe why you're so protective of Amka?"

"Maybe." The thought had crossed my mind before. I wondered if I did exhibit more countertransference for the younger female patients in my practice because of my protectiveness over my own daughter. "You'd make a good psychiatrist, Taylor."

"Oh, probably. But I already have my hands full. Besides, counselling is almost all I do anyway."

"I bet." I took a first bite of the red curry. My mouth tingled from the spice, but I appreciated the taste of my first solid food in two days. "I have it easy. I only deal with one client at a time. You have to manage whole families."

"What can I say? Social workers are the unsung heroes of the system."

I chuckled. "Seems like."

"But I love the unpredictability of my job. On any given day, I might find new housing, do vocational counselling, advocate for child support, scrounge up food supplements, offer addiction counselling, or even help out with work and college applications. Some days, I'm doing all of them."

"I bet."

"I never get tired of advocating for my clients, David. It energizes me. It's just the other shit I hate so much."

"What other shit?"

"The interventions. Having to remove a kid from his or her home to place in foster care. Happens too often."

"You're advocating for your client then, too. The most vulnerable kind. A child."

"I suppose." She sighed. "Doesn't feel like it when I have to show up with a couple of cops in tow."

"I can't imagine, Taylor."

"No job is perfect, right? And on the plus side, while I work hard, my hours—as you might have noticed—are flexible. I define my own schedule, for the most part."

I finished another mouthful of the tasty curry. "How about your personal life? No family or partner?"

"Nope." She winked. "I'm just a lone wolf."

That surprised me. Not only because of her androgynous good looks or charismatic warmth. I had no doubt men and women—I still wasn't sure of her sexuality—would be drawn to Taylor. I'd already noticed her effect on Evan and Kai. But I was surprised someone so chipper and extroverted would choose to live in relative isolation, alone in such a remote locale.

As if reading my mind, she said, "Evan wasn't wrong when he

told you that most of us transplants to this town are running away from something."

"Including you?"

"Yup."

"Are you OK to talk about it?"

She put a forkful of curry and rice in her mouth and chewed slowly. "I was engaged," she said, once she finished. "Before I left San Diego."

I sensed it was best to let her explain at her own pace, so I said nothing.

"My mom, she was adopted," Taylor continued.

"Oh," I said, confused by the apparent digression.

"About four years ago, she started to forget things. And then she started to have these falls. So unlike her." Taylor twirled noodles on her fork without taking another bite. "It wasn't until she developed these jerking movements in her hands that the neurologist finally diagnosed her with the Huntington's disease."

"I've seen a few patients with it, Taylor," I said, thinking of the relentlessly progressive neurological disorder that robbed people of their minds and bodies. "I'm very sorry."

"Yeah, it was tough to watch such a strong, independent woman like Mom waste away like that. At least she went quickly. In under two years." Taylor nodded to herself. "I was equally shocked when I found out that my two brothers and I each had a fifty-fifty chance of inheriting the condition."

"That's so hard. I understand it's a huge dilemma for most offspring. Whether to get screened for the gene or not."

"Both of my brothers did the blood test. Sure enough, law of averages and all, the oldest carries the rotten gene while the youngest is scot-free." She looked away. "I couldn't do it, David. I just couldn't. If it came back positive and I had to live the rest of my life knowing for sure that I'm carrying some genetic time bomb inside me . . . I couldn't wrap my head around that. Still can't."

"I'm not sure I could either."

"My ex-fiancé, Gabe. He's a great guy," she said. "It didn't faze him. Huntington's gene or not. He didn't even care if I got tested. Said it was up to me. That he'd love me no matter what. He saw my mom near the end, so he knew what to expect." She cleared her throat. "But Gabe wanted kids even more than I did."

I suddenly understood, but I let her keep talking.

"How could I bring kids into the world if I knew there was a good chance I'd be passing on a death sentence to them? How selfish is that?"

"What about adoption?"

"We talked about that. Or even getting a donor egg. But I couldn't raise children just to have them watch me decay in front of their eyes the way my mom did . . ." She swallowed as if she still had a mouthful of food. "In the end . . . I don't know. The more accommodating Gabe was, the harder everything got for me. I could see everything I was doing wrong, but . . ."

I could relate, but I only said, "It must've been hell, Taylor."

"For Gabe, anyway." She forced a chuckle. "Of course, we broke up. My doing. Because he never would have. And then I needed to escape the memories. Not only of Gabe. Of Mom . . . my brothers . . . California in general. And Utqiagvik was the farthest place away I could find without having to renew my passport." She waved the subject away with a sweep of her fork and smiled again. "Anyway, that's all behind me now."

Despite her breezy dismissal and familiar grin, the hurt still burned in her eyes. My personal troubles suddenly seemed small compared to her flip-of-a-coin deadly dilemma.

"Speaking of families," she said, clearly wanting to change the subject. "I tracked down Nevaeh's dad."

"Dylan, right?"

"Yeah, he's living in Fairbanks. He hadn't heard what happened to Brianna. He was devastated."

"Is he planning to come back for Nevaeh?"

"No. Not right away, anyway. He recognizes that he doesn't have the means or circumstances to support a four-year-old."

"Probably for the best."

"It was weird, though. As hard as Dylan took the news about Brianna, he didn't seem all that surprised."

I lowered my fork before it reached my mouth. "He expected her to kill herself?"

"Not exactly. He just said that when Nevaeh was about six months old, Brianna changed completely. As if overnight. 'The light went off,' as he put it."

"Did Dylan mention any specific instigating events?"

"Nope."

The incompleteness of it niggled. "Do you mind sending me his number?" I asked. "I'd love to speak to him."

"Sure. Will do."

I ate as much food as I could through my lingering nausea. And Taylor didn't push when I put my fork down beside my half-finished plate, but she did insist that I keep the leftovers in the room's bar fridge.

After she left, I headed over to the shelf where the bottle of whiskey stood. Although I knew better than to mix alcohol with my painkillers and my concussion, I craved a drink. But I poured carefully, allowing myself only a single shot.

The familiar warmth of the whiskey tickled my throat, but it didn't compensate for my disconcerting thoughts. I felt for Taylor and her terrible conundrum. And I couldn't stop ruminating over Brianna. All accounts of her initial mood disorder suggested that something more than just an imbalance of neurochemicals had tipped her into a depression as suddenly as a tree crashing in a windstorm. And if a specific event had precipitated the first episode, when Nevaeh was only a baby, maybe something had happened again right before her suicide to send her spiraling down that deadly path.

True to her word, Taylor texted me the contact number for Dylan. I was about to lift up the phone to call him when it rang with an incoming video call from Javier. I probably wouldn't have answered were I not so determined to get some clarity on what Avery had shared with me about Ketopram.

Javier's face creased into a grimace as soon as he saw me. "You look like you were runover by a snowplow, David. And then it backed over you a couple times for good measure."

"Something like that," I said.

"What the hell happened?"

"It's a long story."

"Beth told me you fell off a bike?"

I gritted my teeth. "You're talking to Beth now?"

"She called me out of the blue. She's very worried, David. She doesn't believe your story."

"It's not her business," I said. "Not really yours, either, Javier."

"I beg to differ." And I could tell by the contemplative look in his eyes that he was wondering why I was being so short with him. "What's going on in that town, David?"

"A lot more questions than answers. But that's not unique to Utqiagvik, is it?"

"How so?"

"Delores Nolan, for starters."

"Ah. You heard about her suicide attempt?"

"Which happened after you restarted her on Ketopram. The same medication I had discontinued."

He hesitated. "Delores had severe depressive symptoms."

"She was bipolar, Javier."

"I am not arguing that. But when I evaluated her, she was depressed. And I started her on the appropriate treatment."

"Another patient on Ketopram, another suicide attempt."

"It's not rocket science, David," Javier said evenly. "Mood disorder patients attempt suicide. With or without medication, sometimes."

"But lately, seems like a lot of them have been attempting it while on one very specific medication."

"If I didn't know you better, I might think you were sounding a little paranoid, David."

"Except I'm not the only one."

"What does that mean?"

"I spoke to Avery Lincoln."

Javier's face went still on the screen for a few seconds. "And what did he have to say?"

"Not very much. He couldn't. Because of his NDA with Pierson Pharmaceuticals." I let that sink in for a moment. "But he did tell me there was another drug company–sponsored trial. One that was never published. And he suggested I talk to you about it."

"That trial only ran for a couple of months before it was aborted."

"Come on, Javier! Drug companies don't abort their own studies without damn good reason. What did it show?"

"It didn't show anything. It was never completed."

"You know what I think? That a signal was developing in the early data. Something the drug company never wanted to come to light. And neither did you. So you pulled the plug on the study."

He sighed heavily. "They panicked, David."

"Who did? Pierson Pharmaceuticals?"

"We were only about a month or so into enrollment when a thirty-year-old man jumped off a bridge in Portland. Turns out he had a troubled past. Multiple suicide attempts before. He should've never been released from hospital so soon. Or enrolled in the study in the first place."

"But you thought Ketopram might be blamed?"

"The powers that be at Pierson did. They insisted we stop the study. Avery refused."

"Yet you still went along with it?"

"What could I do? Pierson was funding our research. It was their call." He rubbed his eye. "Avery couldn't be convinced, though. It became a matter of pride for him. He fought them tooth and nail. He didn't leave Pierson any choice but to fire him."

"And you were OK with all of that?"

"Did I have concerns about stopping the trial? Yes. About Ketopram? No. This was a phase four post-marketing study, the year after the drug had been released. By then, I had already found it to be safe in my practice."

"The bridge jumper was just a coincidence then?"

"I didn't believe one suicide among hundreds of study patients could be directly attributable to Ketopram."

I could feel my indignation stirring. "The same way the three attempted suicides that I've been directly involved with this summer weren't related to them all being on Ketopram, either?"

"It's freakish, David. I'll give you that. But everything has changed since COVID. The rate of suicides has been climbing steadily. Besides, go scan the literature. Show me the case reports of other links to Ketopram."

"I already did. I found two case reports."

"Two cases! Among tens of thousands of patients taking the drug? And in both, there were seriously extenuating circumstances."

I found it curious that he was already aware of both cases, but I didn't comment.

"Listen, David," he continued. "I can't explain your recent cluster of suicide attempts. But I'm convinced Ketopram is safe. I wouldn't prescribe it if I had any doubt."

"Convinced enough to risk your patients' lives?"

His eyebrow cocked. "You haven't stopped taking your medication, have you, David?"

"I'm on a shitload of painkillers since I got out of hospital."

"What does that have to do with it?"

"I don't how they'll interact with Ketopram."

"They won't," Javier said.

"You're convinced of that, too, obviously."

"Do you remember what you were like before you began taking Ketopram?"

I did. Vividly. But I no longer trusted the medication. Or, for that matter, Javier. "I can take care of myself."

"I'm not the enemy, David."

I wished I could believe that. My chest ached, and I felt bone-weary. "I have to lie down, Javier."

"I am coming up to that godforsaken town."

"Don't bother."

"Believe me, it's not like I want to," he said. "But you're not yourself. And, whether you realize it or not, you could use a friend right about now."

CHAPTER 16

I was dozing off at around nine thirty p.m. when a heavy rap at my door jolted me awake. My breath caught, but from fear, not pain. *Did the thugs from the beach track me to my room?*

"Doc, are you in there?" a familiar voice on the other side asked.

Relaxing, I gingerly rose and opened the door for Kai, whose smile was wide as ever. Somehow, though, it struck me as a little less friendly each time I saw it.

"Amka?" I asked, hopefully as he joined me inside the room.

"Not yet. But a lot of folks are out looking for her."

"It's not that big a town."

"Big enough if you don't want to be found." The detective shrugged. "Shouldn't be too much longer."

"Let's hope," I mumbled.

Kai motioned to my cast. "How's the convalescence?"

"Great. I should be kickboxing by tomorrow."

"Wouldn't recommend it." He chuckled. "At least, based on how you performed in your last altercation."

While I might have misinterpreted the lack of warmth in his smile, there was no accident in Kai's choice of terms for my ambush, or the resentment that underlay it, despite his attempt to disguise it as a joke. Was it because I was a nosy outsider? Or was he jealous of all the time I was spending with Taylor? Either way, I was too tired to confront him beyond saying, "Speaking of my altercation, any new leads on the assailants?"

"Possibly," he said as he pulled his phone out of his pocket. He flicked his finger across the screen a few times before turning it outward to show me an image. "Recognize this guy?"

I studied the photo of the bearded, brown-eyed man who glared back at me, but he didn't look familiar. "They both wore balaclavas, Kai," I said.

"Hmm." Kai turned the phone back toward himself and repeatedly flicked at the screen again before he eventually spun it around. This time, I saw the man in motion, folding his arms across his chest, the veins popping on his thick neck. Kai's voice came over the phone's speaker though he must have been standing off camera.

"George, who was with you when you beat the crap out of the doc?" Kai asked.

"Who's that?" the man grunted.

"The guy you and your buddy jumped at the beach."

George shook his head. "Nope."

"You had nothing to do with it, huh?"

"Nah."

Listening intently, I tried to match his voice to the man who clubbed me, but his monosyllabic answers made it impossible to tell.

"Georgie, Georgie, Georgie," Kai said in a singsong. "With what we found in your truck, your future's not looking so promising."

George only snorted his contempt.

"You're from Barrow, aren't you?" Kai asked.

"Barrow?" George scoffed. "Who the fuck calls this place Barrow anymore?"

"It's not him," I said. More than his indignation over the detective's use of the old colonial name for Utqiagvik, the cadence and pitch were all wrong. My attacker's voice—low and gravelly—was etched in my memory. And it wasn't George's.

Kai stopped the video and put his phone away. "Could George have been the other guy? The silent one?"

"No. The second guy was a lot slighter than him."

"Too bad." Kai sighed.

"Who is George, anyway?"

"No one, really. Low-level muscle. But we found a half a kilo of coke, two bottles of liquid ecstasy, a couple hundred tabs of molly, and forty bottles of vodka hidden in his truck. Someone was planning a good old-fashioned fire sale on check day."

"Eddie?"

"Probably. George couldn't have pulled something this big off on his own. He was just the driver." Kai tucked his phone back into his pocket. "When will you be cleared to go home?"

I wasn't sure whether it was a question or a hint. "Soon, I hope."

He turned for the door. "Meanwhile, the search goes on for your two boys."

"I'd rather you found Amka." Realizing how ungrateful I must have sounded, I added, "Thanks for the effort you're putting into this."

"We'll find them all," he said with a confidence I didn't share. "I'll catch you later, Doc."

After Kai left, I stared at my empty whiskey glass, fighting the urge to pour another. To distract myself, I picked up the phone, found Taylor's text, and dialed the number she had forwarded me.

A man answered on the third ring. "Hey."

"Dylan?"

"Who's this?"

"Dr. Spears," I said. "I was Brianna's psychiatrist."

He went quiet for a few seconds. "Why'd she do it?"

"I'm still trying to figure that one out."

"Yeah," he said distantly.

"Dylan, I was hoping you could fill in a few blanks for me."

"Doubt it."

"What happened with you and Brianna?"

"Fuck if I know," he grumbled. "I thought we had a good thing."

"Brianna didn't?"

"Yeah, she did! Or she used to. Money was tight and all, but we were happy. Those first few months with Nevaeh everything was cool. A real family."

"And then?"

"It came back."

"What did?"

"Her darkness. Just like in senior year. Except worse."

"What happened in senior year?"

"Teenage girl drama. She feuded with some friends and shit. Then her favorite teacher left."

"Brianna was that close with her teacher?"

"All the girls used to crush on him. And the asshole was so full of himself. I just think him leaving in the middle of that year was like the final straw or whatever. Anyway, that first time, in senior year, Bree snapped out of it pretty quick."

"Not so the second time? After Nevaeh was born?"

"She went even darker. And it just didn't lift."

"Can you tell me about the darkness, Dylan?"

"She cried. Got pissed off. Had nightmares. All of it."

"Nightmares?" I immediately thought of Ketopram but realized Brianna wouldn't have been on the medication back then.

"She'd call out in her sleep sometimes," Dylan said. "Wake up in a sweat."

"Did she tell you about the nightmares?"

"Bree wouldn't tell me shit! When she wasn't in tears, she was mad at me twenty-four-seven. I couldn't do anything right."

"And that's why you left?

"Bree told me to go!" he groaned. "Said she hated me. Told

me I wasn't good for her or the baby. Said I wasn't a real man. I thought . . ."

"What did you think, Dylan?"

"That it'd pass. I thought if I went away for a bit, she would miss me. So I went to Prudhoe Bay to work the rigs. But I didn't hear nothing from her. She didn't even respond to my texts. I just gave up after a while. Moved to Fairbanks."

"And this darkness of hers, it came on suddenly?"

"Like boom. One day to the next."

"Without any reason?"

"Nothing I heard of."

There it was again—a depression that fell as suddenly as a curtain. "Dylan, did she ever mention anything about being abused?"

"What the fuck are you saying?"

"No, no. Not you! I mean, earlier. Was there ever a suggestion she might've been sexually abused or assaulted as a kid?"

"Nah, nothing like that," he said, his voice calmer. "But . . ."

"Yes?"

"I saw this show on Netflix a while back. About these women who'd been sexually abused when they were young. How they got that post-traumatic whatever. The shame and self-hating and shit. The way they described it made me think of Bree. Especially her nightmares."

"I thought she wouldn't talk about those."

"She wouldn't," he said. "But sometimes in her sleep she'd get all restless and she'd mumble shit like 'I can't' or 'Not again' or 'Don't.'"

"I see." I didn't want to put too much stock in his amateur analysis, but it was hard not associate it with what Brianna had insinuated herself. "Victims of sexual abuse typically know their abusers."

"That's what the show said."

"And there's no one in Brianna's life you could think of who might have . . ."

"Her dad skipped on them when she was super-young. Never met the guy. But the uncle . . ."

"Gus? What about him?"

"Super-quiet dude. Hardly says two words. Opposite of his wife in every way. But I thought Gus was kinda creepy. The way he looked at Bree sometimes."

"The uncle, huh?"

"What's it matter? She's gone."

But it mattered to me. Especially when I considered how Gus was now Nevaeh's guardian.

The thought must've occurred to Dylan, too. "Kerry and Gus have Nevaeh now, huh?"

"Taylor will check it out. She'll make sure Nevaeh is safe."

"I'd love to take her in, but there's no way I can look after her on my own." His tone softened. "Maybe one day."

"I understand," I said, but my thoughts were already moving elsewhere. "Dylan, do you know Amka Obed?"

"Yeah. We were all in the same class. Amka was super-tight with Bree. And she was always cool with me. How's she doing?"

"She took off last night on her boyfriend."

"Rick?"

"Yeah."

"Amka finally left him, huh? Good! He's an asshole."

"She's AWOL, though. Do you have any idea where she might have holed up?"

"Nah. Wouldn't know. I haven't been in touch with anyone up there since I left."

Disappointed, I thanked Dylan for his time and hung up. I checked my watch and realized I was due my ten o'clock dose of painkiller. Since the throb in my head and chest had lessened, I decided to wait a bit longer. The nausea had also diminished. I was even feeling a little hungry, so I went over to the bar fridge and pulled out the leftover Thai food.

I had just begun to pick at some rice and curry when there was a light knock at the door. I opened it to find Evan standing there.

"What brings you over?" I asked.

"Just checking up on my most challenging patient," he said as he joined me inside the room. "How are you?"

Evan looked tired to me. His eyes were more sunken and his hair even more tousled than usual. I sensed how much responsibility he was carrying as one of the few doctors who covered the whole town. "A bit better, I think," I said. "Thanks for checking in."

"Don't mention it. I get to bill extra for house calls." He chuckled. "How's the headache?"

"Improving. The nausea is almost gone."

"Good. Very good. And the breathing? No cough or shortness of breath?"

"Nope. And if I'm careful how I move, the chest pain is manageable. I haven't needed to take as much hydromorphone lately."

"Don't be too stoic, OK? That's why I gave you plenty of pills. It's not uncommon to develop pneumonia after rib fractures if you're not breathing properly." He nodded at me. "But you know all this."

"No one would ever mistake me for stoic."

"Still, you should have another chest X-ray tomorrow to ensure the lung is re-expanding." Evan reached for the bottle of the Macallan on the shelf above the fridge. "The good stuff," he said, whistling appreciatively.

"You a scotch aficionado?"

"Not really. But I do appreciate a good single malt now and again."

"Would you like a glass?"

"That's OK." He replaced the bottle back on the shelf. "And it's probably best if you don't indulge either until you're off the painkillers and the concussion has settled."

"Wouldn't dream of it," I said.

"Which is doctor-speak for no more than two glasses per night, am I right?"

We shared a quick grin, before his expression turned somber. "I kind of expected Amka to turn up at the same time as Rick," Evan said.

"Me, too."

"Her friends and extended family must be sick of hearing from me by now, but I can't stop checking in with them." He rubbed his eye. "Don't know how else to help her poor parents."

"Must be agony for them."

"They're beside themselves, David. Can't blame them, after what the family went through with her sister."

"Uki was your patient, too, right?"

"The whole family." He sighed. "Uki was such a sweetheart. Strong, too. When her mom's rheumatoid arthritis got worse, Uki stepped up to take care of her as well as her little sister. She was so protective of Amka."

Amka had mentioned her mother's arthritis, but I didn't realize how extensive it was. It explained why I hadn't heard from or seen her mother since I came to town.

"Uki's death came as such a bombshell," Evan continued. "I had no idea she was depressed. She never complained about any kind of mental health issues. Only reason I ever saw her was because she brought her mother in for appointments."

"Such a waste, huh?"

"Tell me about it." Evan exhaled a slow breath. "Suicide runs through this damn town like the flu."

"For what it's worth, I spoke to Brianna's ex."

Evan frowned. "Nevaeh's dad?"

I nodded. "Dylan."

"How did you track him down?"

"Taylor did. In Fairbanks."

"What did he have to say?"

I relayed Dylan's description of Brianna's sudden darkness. And then I mentioned our discussion about potential sexual abuse and Dylan's suspicion regarding her uncle.

Evan folded his arms, appearing uncomfortable with the whole subject. "Gus?" He frowned. "I can't see it. The man's a gentle giant."

"You might be right," I said. "But I'd like to find out for myself."

"How? By accusing him?"

"By talking to him."

"To what end, David?"

Evan had a point. Dylan's association of Brianna's behavior to a Netflix documentary was hardly proof of anything. Earlier, I was blaming Ketopram for her suicide, and now I was searching for a theoretical sexual predator. Perhaps I was tilting at windmills, eager to blame anyone but myself for what happened to her. But I knew in my heart I couldn't let it go.

"If she was abused as a teenager then maybe it continued after Nevaeh was born," I said. "Maybe even right before she died."

"Sounds like a fishing expedition," Evan said. "That family has already been through so much. Imagine the unnecessary grief you might cause them by turning over those rocks."

"I have to, Evan," I said. "If it did happen, then we're talking about more than just sexual abuse."

"More?"

"If I'm right, it was the flashpoint in her life for everything that followed. Including her death."

"You're saying her abuser—if he even exists—killed Brianna?"

"Basically, yes."

CHAPTER 17

"Can't be helped" was all Taylor said the following morning, when I shared Evan's concerns about further traumatizing Brianna's family by raising the specter of potential sexual abuse.

"No one looks forward to these conversations," she said, as we walked up to the front door of the McDougals' modest bungalow. "But there's a right way to have them."

When the door opened, Kerry and Gus McDougal stood side by side, but they were almost cartoonishly disproportionate in stature. Gus had to be at least six five and pushing three hundred pounds, while Kerry stood barely five feet. Her stooped posture only made her appear that much smaller.

"Good morning," Kerry rasped, while Gus only nodded.

"Hello, Kerry, Gus." Taylor motioned to me. "Meet Dr. Spears."

"Nice to meet you in person, Mrs. McDougal." I had to look up to meet Gus's eyes. "Mr. McDougal."

"What happened to you, Doctor?" Kerry asked, motioning to my cast.

"An accident." I was relieved the bandages wrapped around my scalp had been replaced by a simple Band-Aid covering the sutures on my forehead. "I'm already on the mend."

Before she could ask anything else, Nevaeh squeezed out through the gap between their legs. She put her thumb in her mouth and looked down shyly.

"Hiya, Tiger." Taylor knelt and extended her arms. "No hugs, today?"

Nevaeh hesitated and then took a couple of tentative steps into Taylor's arms, allowing herself to be embraced by the social worker without hugging back.

After Taylor released her, I bent down and said, "Hi, Nevaeh. Do you remember me?"

She nodded without making eye contact. "From Mommy's TV."

"That's right."

In person, Nevaeh's resemblance to her mother was even stronger, particularly in her heart-shaped face. I fought off a shudder at the thought of how close Brianna had come to taking her daughter to the grave with her.

"Go watch your show now, Nev," Kerry said.

As Nevaeh pivoted and walked past Gus, he tousled her hair, his hand cupping her scalp like a mitt over a softball.

"Come in," Kerry said to us, and we followed them inside. The stench of burnt cigarette grew even stronger with each step closer to the living room, but there was no smoking paraphernalia in sight.

Taylor and I sat down on a worn leather couch across from the two green upholstered chairs where Kerry and Gus sat.

"How's Nevaeh coping?" Taylor asked.

"Good days and bad," Kerry replied, and Gus nodded.

"Can't be easy," Taylor said. "For any of you."

"She's hitting less," Gus said in an unexpectedly soft voice.

"It's true." Kerry hacked out a smoker's cough. "Those first weeks after Brianna . . . Nevaeh was punching and kicking at us. At everyone. Her best friend got a gash across her cheek after Nevaeh struck her with a doll stroller. Had to be glued shut."

Taylor nodded sympathetically. "It's natural to lash out after such a trauma and loss."

"She's too young to make heads or tails of it," Kerry agreed.

Taylor leaned forward in her seat. "We wanted to let you know that we spoke to Dylan."

Kerry's eyes went wide. "You found him?"

"In Fairbanks. He's working construction down there."

Kerry turned to her husband with a helpless look. Gus reached out and laid his hand across his wife's entire bony shoulder. "Does Dylan plan to take Nevaeh there?" she asked. "To Fairbanks?"

"No," Taylor said. "Obviously, he was crushed to hear about Brianna. But he's not ready or able to be a single father. He was relieved to hear Nevaeh was in a stable home."

Kerry relaxed visibly, and Gus withdrew his hand. "He's welcome to visit anytime," she said. "Would be good for the girl to know her father."

"Thank you. I'll tell him." Taylor glanced over to me and then back to the McDougals. "We also wanted to ask you about Brianna."

"Bree?" Kerry viewed her with a frown. "What more is there to say?"

Taylor inhaled. "I think Dr. Spears mentioned already that Brianna once alluded to a potential incident of abuse."

Gus's face remained impassive, but Kerry looked down, clearly embarrassed by the subject. "Never heard such a thing before he brought it up," she mumbled. "Still don't believe it could've happened."

"I imagine." Taylor leaned in even closer. "Dylan didn't exactly corroborate the story, but he did have a few concerns of his own."

"What kinds of concerns?" Kerry asked coolly.

"That Brianna exhibited some . . . behaviors that could have been consistent with her having been abused," I spoke up.

Kerry's prominent crow's-feet deepened. "Behaviors?"

"Signs of post-traumatic stress disorder," I said. "Mood swings, anxiety, and sleep terrors. Sometimes, apparently, she would call out in her sleep."

"What does any of that prove?" Kerry scowled.

I shifted on the couch, and Taylor shot me a glance that silenced me. "Nothing," she said. "It's all just hypothetical, but I have to follow up on even the least suggestion of this kind of thing."

"We never heard about any of this from Bree," Kerry said with another harsh cough.

Taylor turned to the husband. "How about you, Gus?"

He jutted out his lower lip and shrugged.

"Statistically speaking, children and teens are most likely to be molested by someone they trust," Taylor said. "Can either of you think of anyone who might have been involved?"

"No, no one like that," Kerry said without hesitation, while Gus shook his head.

An awkward silence descended on the room, which I broke. "Do you remember when Brianna fell into her first episode of depression? During her senior year?"

A pained look crossed Gus's face.

"Of course, we do!" Kerry said. "We were there. It was hell for her. For all of us."

"By all accounts, it came on suddenly," I said.

"I'd say," Gus said.

"Dylan mentioned a conflict with some of her friends. He also said something about one of her favorite teachers leaving?"

"Usual teen stuff." Kerry waved it away impatiently. "You're the expert, aren't you? Isn't depression caused by some kind of chemical imbalance in the brain?"

"That's true," I said. "But often, especially with a precipitous or sudden depression like in Brianna's case, it can be set off by a specific emotional event. Like grief or stress or . . . trauma."

"Trauma?" Kerry eyed me warily. "Like someone molesting her or something? That what you're suggesting?"

"Maybe."

"Bree's in the ground," Kerry said, rising from her chair but gaining little height. "This isn't about her, is it? You're here about Nevaeh. You're worried she might be at risk. Which means you think we were somehow involved in this nonsense with Bree."

Taylor held up a hand. "We are only—"

"You're accusing us of having abused our own niece?" Kerry's voice rose with each word. "Barely a couple weeks after we buried her! The goddamn nerve of you two!"

Still seated, Gus lifted his arm and easily reached Kerry's shoulder with his hand. "They're only doing their job, hon." His voice was as unmodulated as ever.

"Can't imagine how difficult this is to talk about, Kerry," Taylor said. "We're just trying to be as thorough as we—"

Kerry waved a hand in front of Taylor's face. "Leave me. Get out. Go!"

I gripped Taylor's elbow as I stood up, and she rose, too. Kerry fumbled in the pocket of her cardigan and extracted a pack of cigarettes and a lighter. Her hand was trembling as she lit one. She ignored our goodbyes, but Gus walked us silently to the door.

After we got back into Taylor's truck and pulled away from the house, I said, "Either Gus wasn't involved or he's one hell of an actor."

"Yeah, well, people will surprise you," Taylor said.

"What's your take?"

She sighed. "My gut tells me that if Brianna was abused, those two were in the dark."

"Mine, too."

Taylor glanced at me sidelong. "You all right?"

"Yeah. Why?"

"You're a bit . . . flatter today."

"Guess my natural sunniness was beaten out of me."

She grinned. "They still haven't found the attackers, huh?"

"Kai came by last night to show me images of a suspect, but it wasn't him."

"He'll track them down."

"Hope so." I looked over to her. "I don't think he likes me much."

"I think you might be misreading him."

"Not convinced I am. Regardless, I'm quite sure he'd rather you and I didn't spend so much time together."

Keeping her eyes forward, she shook her head. "Nah. That's just Kai. He's slow to warm up to outsiders. And to be honest, I think he's a bit intimidated by you. And maybe a bit territorial about the investigation into Amka."

Kai didn't strike me as being intimidated, but I didn't care enough to argue. I wasn't sure if it was just in my head or related to the relentless cold and dreariness, but I did feel different after skipping my dose of antidepressant for a second day in a row. I'd been detached throughout the emotionally charged exchange with the McDougals. Even Amka's disappearance weighed less on my mind. It reminded me a little of the time, the winter before last, when I'd stopped caring about anything.

But as Taylor pulled up to the front of the hotel, the sight of a familiar figure in a camel-colored wool overcoat carrying a compact suitcase jolted me out of my numbness. "He didn't," I muttered to myself.

"Huh?" Taylor asked. "Who didn't what?"

Ignoring her question, I hopped out of the truck so quickly that another jolt of pain ripped through my rib cage, but that didn't stop me. I didn't even realize Taylor had followed me inside until I caught up with Javier at the registration desk.

"Hello, David," Javier said as he ran a finger in a circle above his scalp. "Glad to see you've lost the mummy wrap."

"You actually came?"

"I thought I was quite clear," he said, and then turned to Taylor. "For David, the art of politeness is still a work in progress." He laid a hand on his chest and bowed his head slightly. "Javier Gutiérrez. Pleasure to meet you."

"I'm Taylor Holmes," she said with a smile. "One of the social workers in town."

"Of course, Taylor. David here has told me good things. Such good things."

With Javier's innate flirtatiousness, it was hard to tell whether he was actively trying to chat her up. I doubted the thirty-year difference between Taylor and him would deter Javier, but I had no patience for his playfulness this morning. "I think you might have wasted a flight."

"Only time will tell, David," Javier said. "Besides, whether you're happy to see me or not, the Arctic has been on my bucket list for quite some time."

"You live in Anchorage and you've never come to the Arctic before?" Taylor asked.

"It's a crime, isn't it?" Javier emitted one of his stuttering laughs. "But whenever I have time on my hands, I immediately head south. I'm genetically programmed to seek warmer climes."

Taylor grinned. "I know the feeling."

"I get tired easily after this concussion," I said, as I turned away from them. "I'll catch up with you later, Javier."

"You might not be excited about my visit, David," Javier said. "But I think you need me here."

"Is that why you've come?"

"Why else?"

Maybe to protect your precious wonder drug? But the fatigue was incapacitating. And I couldn't even see the point in confronting Javier anymore.

CHAPTER 18

I spent the rest of the afternoon in bed. I tried to nap but couldn't. And my mind was too unfocused to read or even pay attention to the program I tried to watch on my laptop. I ignored two calls and three texts from Javier. Only when Ali video-called me did I answer my phone.

"Dad!"

The sight of my daughter's smiling face perked me up for the first time in days. "Hi, Bean."

"You look better without all the bandages."

"Feel better without them."

She bit her lower lip. "Is everything OK?"

"Yeah. Why?"

"I don't know. Your voice. You sound kind of . . . down."

"Just tired. Concussion and all." I summoned a smile. "I'm eager to get back home. Can't wait to see you. Not to mention your performance!"

Her eyes lit. "Next week, Dad!"

"And? How's rehearsal going?"

"I'm harnessing my nerves like you told me to. At least, I hope I am. I got enough of them." She giggled. "But Miss Warner says my timing is better."

"Can't wait for the recital, Bean."

"Me, neither," she said. "But I'm sorry we're going to miss the Rockies and Banff. I was jazzed to see them."

"Next summer."

"Promise?"

"Promise." I could see from the shifting background on the screen that she was on the move. "Where are we heading?"

"Kitchen," she said. "I'm thirsty."

The screen stilled and I could see a fridge behind her.

"No snacking, Ali." Beth's voice came from somewhere off-screen. "We're eating in fifteen."

"Chill, Mom! I'm just getting a drink."

The camera panned over Ali's shoulder, and I saw Beth standing in the family room. She wasn't alone. Even though I hadn't seen the man beside her in almost twenty years, I recognized Graham immediately.

The image on the screen flicked back to a close-up on my daughter's face. Ali looked embarrassed, as though she realized she had revealed more than she should have. "Hey, Dad, can I call you to-morrow? I got to go . . . um . . . have dinner."

"Of course," I murmured. "I love you, Bean."

"Love you, too, Dad." And then she was gone.

The visual of Beth standing with Graham told me nothing I didn't already know, but it hurt more than my attacker's club. I headed straight for the shelf and pulled down the bottle of the Macallan. I didn't even try to measure the glass as I filled it well above the halfway mark.

I had just finished my third sip when a knock came at the door, and I heard Javier's voice from the other side. "Are there any Michelin-rated French restaurants in this town? I have a hankering for boeuf bourguignon."

When I didn't answer, he rapped again. "Come on, David. We need to talk."

Too numb to resist, I trudged over and opened the door. Javier was wearing a button-down shirt with a sweater carefully tied over it, as if dressed for a modeling shoot for some European driving magazine.

He nodded to the drink in my hand. "Isn't this a dry town?"

"Not that dry."

"Maybe, in your case—with the concussion and all—it ought to be a little more arid?" He walked over to the shelf and pulled down the bottle and another glass. "You mind?"

"Go ahead."

He poured himself a single shot, sat in the chair, and crossed one leg over the other. "What gives, David?"

"No idea what you're getting at."

"All of it. This wild goose chase you've come up here on. The beating you took. You stopping your medications. Your paranoia over Ketopram and, frankly, me."

I stared at him, unwilling to engage. I almost surprised myself when I blurted, "Beth has a new boyfriend. An ex-classmate of ours."

"Oh." He clicked his tongue. "I'm sorry, David. I've been there."

"With wife two or four?"

"Four hasn't been determined yet." He chuckled in his distinct way. "Your point is valid, though. Beth was the love of your life. I hear you. But two years later and living thousands of miles apart, there was a certain inevitability to this."

"It wasn't inevitable that I'd see her together with an ex-classmate on my daughter's phone."

"Maybe not, no," he said, lowering his glass. "It's just hurt piling on hurt now, isn't it?"

I only shrugged.

"Do you know what worries me, David?"

"No."

"Your flatness."

"My flatness?"

"Yes. And your detachment, too."

I took another long sip of my whiskey. "It's not your concern, Javier."

"At this point, I'd feel reassured seeing some more of that outrage and anguish you showed over Brianna's death."

"I'm about tapped out of both, I'm afraid."

"I see that," he said. "But can you put on your professional lens for a moment?"

"Why? To analyze myself?"

"Exactly. If you were your own patient. Someone with a history of a major mood disorder. Who has stressors mounting right, left, and center. Who is noncompliant with his antidepressant. Who—"

"I'm not noncompliant," I said. "I chose not to stay on Ketopram."

"Because you think it's somehow dangerous?"

"As might you, if you weren't in the back pocket of the parent drug company."

"You really believe that, David?" He snorted. "That I would stake my reputation—my whole career—on some shares and a few paid speaking gigs?"

"How else do you explain it?"

Javier rose slowly to his feet. "My grandparents left the tropics for the subarctic to find food and work. I'm the first person in my family to get a college degree, let alone a professional one. For Christ's sake, you know *Mama*! Nothing would crush her more than if I tarnished all of that."

It was true. I'd had several delicious dinners at his mom's house. Even though his doting, eightyish mother had grown up in Alaska, she always cooked traditional Honduran fare and, more often than not, addressed Javier in Spanish. Her pride in her only son was her oxygen.

"Then why, Javier?" I asked. "Why did you allow Pierson Pharmaceuticals to bury your study?"

"There was nothing else I could do."

"You could've walked away. Like Avery did."

"I believed in Ketopram. Wholeheartedly. I still do."

"And you still think it's safe? Despite all the bad outcomes of late?"

"I do." He stared hard at me. "Particularly for you."

"I wish I shared your conviction." But the doubt was back again, intensifying like a migraine. Javier was a world expert on the medication. What did I really know?

"You want to blame it all on Ketopram, David. I understand that. But if our roles were reversed, you would see it as clearly as I do. The depression is taking a grip on you like someone wrapping their fingers around your neck."

"Is it depression, though, Javier?"

"What else could it be?"

"Maybe just the realization of how badly I'm failing in my personal and professional lives."

"No. The depression—no doubt aided and abetted by your concussion, the painkillers, and the stress—is obscuring your judgment. And the last time you fell into this kind of mental quicksand, Ketopram was the only thing that pulled you out of it. You need to get back on your medication, David. Before . . ."

"Before I do something stupid?" I emptied the last of my glass in one gulp. "Problem is, Javier, I no longer trust Ketopram. Or you."

CHAPTER 19

I slept in again the next morning, but I couldn't blame it on the hydromorphone. I was learning how to manage the chest discomfort with only Tylenol. I hadn't popped a tablet of hydromorphone in almost twenty-four hours. The haze from the concussion had lifted, too. But I still could barely drag myself out of bed. More than fatigue, I was immobilized by an overwhelming sense of futility.

At about nine o'clock, I finally got up and went to the bathroom. I eyed the bottles on the counter, focusing on the nearly full container of Ketopram. I considered what Javier had told me. Maybe my growing apathy was an indicator the major depression was coming back? Maybe the warning lights were flashing again? But I couldn't bring myself to even touch the bottle. Despite Javier's impassioned argument, Ketopram was sullied in my mind. I associated it with death.

I dressed carefully so as not to aggravate my injuries, but I was indifferent to the end result. Evan had texted me earlier to prompt me to get my follow-up chest X-ray taken at the hospital, and if only to escape the monotony of my room, I headed downstairs to meet the taxi I had called.

The sun was out, and the bright daylight only reminded me how much I missed the dark of night. The streets were quiet as ever as the cab rumbled down the dirt road. The discrepancies in design between neighboring houses that we passed made them seem unrelated to one another and struck me as a metaphor for the isolation of the community.

As the driver pulled up in front of the hospital, I noticed an ambulance and two NSB police SUVs lined up in front of the ER's entrance. I would have ignored them, except I spotted Chief Bedard standing beside the ambulance and talking to one of the paramedics, so I veered away from the main entrance and toward him.

"Thanks, Lorna," the chief said to the young, uniformed Iñupiat paramedic. "I will take it from here."

She nodded solemnly and then headed for the open driver's door of her rig.

When the chief turned to me, his face was impassive, but his eyes were deeply troubled. "We found Amka."

Emotion stirred in me for the first time today. "In the ER? Is she hurt?"

"She's not there."

"Not there? Then where is she?"

He hesitated. "The morgue."

His words hit me like a rockfall. "How?" I croaked.

"She drowned."

Just like her sister. I couldn't believe it. "I want to see her."

"What for?"

"Please, Chief. Let me just see her."

He wavered a moment. "I'm heading in there now."

I followed him inside, and we trudged down the hallway to the morgue. Neither of us spoke a word. *How could this be happening again?*

We entered the cold gray room where two gurneys stood, only one of them occupied. It was Amka. She lay on top, fully dressed down to her boots. Her coat looked waterlogged, and a few strands of wet hair stuck to her forehead, but otherwise, she appeared as if she were already embalmed and prepped for an open-casket funeral. Her eyes were closed, but her expression was mercifully peaceful.

"It's the water temperature here," the chief said. "It preserves the bodies."

"Who found her?"

"A fisherman, earlier this morning. She was floating just off-shore." He cleared his throat. "Not far from where we originally found her sister."

I couldn't help but think of Amka's schizophrenic cousin, Connie. How empty my reassurance to her had been. Agloolik had taken Amka, after all. "Definitely suicide?" I asked, resisting the temptation to sweep back the stray hairs from her forehead.

"Looks to be. But we'll need to investigate. No one has corroborated Rick's story about her ditching him as soon as they got ashore. In fact, no one has seen her in days. It's possible he pushed her out of the boat."

Intuition told me otherwise, but I said nothing.

I heard a sound behind me. I looked over my shoulder and saw someone in scrubs opening the door for Taylor.

"No," she cried, as she barged into the room. "For fuck's sake! No, no, no . . ."

Elbowing her way between the chief and me, she stepped up to the gurney, leaned over, and stroked Amka's cheek. "You're so cold," she murmured.

None of us said anything for a while as Taylor hovered over the body. Finally, she straightened up and turned for the door without a word to the chief or me.

I followed her down the hallway and out to her truck. I climbed into the passenger seat without waiting for an invitation.

"Have they notified the family?" Taylor asked, as we sped away from the hospital. Her tone was businesslike, but her eyes glistened.

"Not sure," I said. "They just recovered the body."

"I'll confirm with the chief. If her parents haven't heard already, they will soon. I should go see them."

I couldn't imagine how crushed the Obeds would be to find out they had lost their second daughter, the same way as they had their first. And I couldn't stomach the idea of being there when they did. "Do you mind dropping me off at the hotel?"

"All right."

We drove another mile in silence, before Taylor glanced over to me. "Are you going to be OK?"

I shrugged. "Amka was one of my first patients from this town."

"I'm sorry, David."

"The second patient of mine to take her own life in the past month."

"It's not your fault."

I turned my gaze to the window. "That remains to be seen."

"How do you mean?"

"I drank the Kool-Aid, Taylor."

"What are you talking about?"

"I put them both on the same antidepressant. Ketopram. Turns out it's a very dangerous drug."

"Come on, David."

"When something seems too good to be true, it usually is. But I was an unquestioning convert. Jumped right in blind. Wasn't willing to wait for wider clinical experience to accumulate. I turned my patients—Brianna and Amka, included—into guinea pigs."

Taylor pulled up in front of my hotel. "You're hurting, David. I get it. But don't mistake grief for guilt."

"I know exactly what it is," I muttered.

Taylor put her hand over my forearm and squeezed it lightly. "You're going to be all right, David. Aren't you?"

"I need to go home."

"You still have to wait for your lung to fully re-expand before you fly. No?"

As I reached for the door handle, a sense of gratitude edged through the numbness. I turned to her with a smile. "Thank you, Taylor. For everything. You've been the one bright spot here."

"Why don't I come back? After I've spoken to the Obeds?"

"No." I gently eased my arm free of her grip. "I just need to a little time to myself. I'll catch up with you later."

As I entered the hotel, I kept my head down and walked toward the elevator.

"David!"

I looked over to see Javier sitting by the lobby's fireplace. He shut his laptop, rose to his feet, and joined me where I stood. "Where have you been?" he asked.

"The hospital."

"What did the chest X-ray show?"

"Didn't get it."

He cocked his head. "Why not?"

"Amka showed up."

"Oh, that's encouraging."

"Would've been. If she were still alive."

He winced. "Oh, God."

"Can't be helped, right? She was on the best medication possible."

"David . . ."

"What? You're going to give me another lecture on the safety of Ketopram? How your buried study was irrelevant? How all the corpses piling up on top of those expensive pill bottles are just some kind of coincidence?"

"I can't explain this, David. I can't. But I do know that now is not the time to jump to conclusions."

"You've gaslit me enough for a lifetime."

"There's that paranoia again."

"Maybe I'll take my paranoia public. What do you think, Javier? Perhaps it's time to let the world know just how dangerous Ketopram is." I turned away quick enough to send a stab of pain through my ribs.

"David, listen . . ."

The moment I felt his hand on my shoulder, I spun and, without thinking, swung my casted arm. My fist smashed into his jaw. His head snapped to the side, and he moaned as he stumbled and fell to the floor, his laptop clattering loudly against the tile.

"Hey!" the clerk behind the desk called.

Javier gaped up at me, his eyes clouded with a look of betrayal.

I couldn't believe what I had done, but I also didn't care.

"Turns out I did have a little outrage and anguish left in me after all," I said as I turned from him.

My chest throbbing, I strode right past the clerk as he rushed over to Javier. I headed straight up to my room and collapsed on the bed. I eyed the whiskey bottle on the shelf but didn't have the energy to pour myself a glass.

The memory of my middle-of-the-night call with Amka tormented me. Her comment that "Brianna understood" echoed in my head. It was the second of the last-chance calls, after the one I had with Brianna, that I had bungled. *Surely, I could've talked sense into at least one of them?*

I was still on the bed an hour later, overcome by hopelessness and inertia, when I heard a knock at my door. Assuming it was Javier, I ignored it.

Another knock.

"David?" Evan called from the other side.

Reluctantly, I got out of bed and opened the door.

"I can't stay long, but I had to see you." Evan's eyes were bloodshot and his expression crestfallen as he trod back into the room with me. "Amka's cousin was in my office for a checkup. I was grilling her about where she thought Amka could be when the chief called with the news."

The best I could conjure was a sympathetic sigh.

"I still can't believe it, David," Evan continued. "That poor, poor family. Jesus! It's like one endless tragedy for them."

"Endless," I echoed.

He pinched the bridge of his nose. "Why does everyone in this fucking town seem to think suicide is the answer?"

I didn't have the energy to share my theory about Ketopram, so I just looked at him. *Besides, maybe for some it is the right answer?*

"Not a month after Brianna," he murmured.

I couldn't think of anything reassuring to say. We fell into a despondent quiet.

Evan finally broke it by saying, "Did you ever talk to the Mc-Dougals?"

"Yeah."

"How did that go?"

"I don't think Gus abused Brianna. In fact, I'm sure neither of them even knew about it."

"Maybe she was never abused then? Maybe it was just a desperate cry for help?"

"Trust me, Evan. It happened. I think she'd kept it to herself for years. I don't even think she meant to tell me when she blurted it out."

"I guess," he said, skeptically.

"You know what else I think?"

"What's that?"

"Bringing her abuser to light might be the only way left to get any semblance of closure for that family." But even as I said it, I realized the closure I really sought was for myself. "He needs to be exposed."

Evan viewed me for a long moment, as if he might argue. Instead, he reached over, picked up the two-thirds-full bottle of scotch up off the shelf, and weighed it in his hand. "Fuck it." He pulled down two glasses. "Clinic or not this afternoon, I need a drink. How about you?"

I wasn't sure what I needed. It felt to me as if my whole life had capsized. And I couldn't see the point in struggling to right it anymore. "Yes."

PART II

TAYLOR

CHAPTER 20

This fucking town.

I had had such high hopes for Amka. But Utqiagvik had brutalized them. The town had a knack for doing that.

Why do I stay?

Normally, my morning mindfulness routine grounded me and chased away this kind of negativity. As clichéd as it was for the woke Californian I considered myself to be—or at least aspired to be—meditation had helped see me through some of the worst periods in my life. Since Mom's diagnosis. Since I fled San Diego. Since, well, Gabe. But even an extended meditation session combined with a tall glass of my homemade kombucha didn't soothe me this morning.

I couldn't shake the look in Amka's father's eyes. Terms such as "grief" or "despair" didn't do it justice. It was more of an existential fury—outrage at fate for claiming not one but both of his daughters in the same cruel manner.

I'd spoken to Tom Obed yesterday afternoon outside his house, since he hadn't invited me in. The depth of his emotions, quiet though they were, was so overpowering that the only way I could process it was to default to basic social work practicalities. "Will you need any help with the funeral arrangements, Mr. Obed?" I asked.

"No."

"Is there anything you and Mrs. Obed need right now? Food? Transport? Help with filling in the forms? Anything at all?"

"No."

"Is Mrs. Obed home?"

"Yes."

"Do you think I could I say hello? To offer my condolences?"

"She don't need them."

"Is she all right?"

Tom looked past me. "Where's Rick?"

"With the police, still."

He turned, entered his house, and shut the door behind him, leaving me on the doorstep, fighting back tears.

I pushed aside the memory, frustrated I'd let it own me as much as it had. Besides, I had no time to dwell on the past this morning. Check time had hit Utqiagvik. And if the previous year was anything to go by, I would be swamped.

Before I'd experienced last year's distribution of the Arctic Slope Regional Corp.'s dividend checks, I'd assumed the mood in town would be upbeat, celebratory even. But I soon discovered the monetary windfall had unexpected consequences. Alcohol and drug use soared, and with it so did the incidence of domestic abuse and other violence. I wasn't surprised when the chief told me that arrests peaked every summer during the two weeks after the checks had been distributed.

I'd already received a call this morning from the ER regarding a woman who had been so viciously assaulted and raped by her estranged husband that she had to be admitted to hospital for care. With their mom hospitalized and their dad jailed, their children, a six-year-old daughter and nine-year-old son, needed temporary guardianship. They had no other family, so finding foster parents for those kids was my priority this morning. Everything else on my schedule would have to wait.

I was just pouring myself a second glass of kombucha when my phone rang with a caller who was identified as only "private" on my screen. I answered anyway.

"Hello, Taylor? Javier Gutiérrez here."

"Oh, hi, Javier," I chirped, reflexively burying my despondence.

"I hope you don't mind me calling you. The hospital gave me your number."

"No worries, Javier." I'd warmed to David's colleague the moment I met him. But I wasn't oblivious to his potential for mischief, either. He reminded me of one of my old profs—the sort of cultured, older gentleman whose seemingly innocent flirtatiousness carried far more intention than the harmless act suggested. "What's up?"

"Have you spoken to David recently?"

"Not since I dropped him at the hotel yesterday afternoon. To be honest, I sensed he needed a bit of space."

"Me, too," Javier said. "But I haven't been able to reach him this morning."

"Maybe he slept in?"

"Possibly. Or maybe he's screening my calls. Lord knows, he wouldn't be the first. But he didn't answer when I knocked at his door just now."

"Let me see if I can reach him."

"Please."

"How do I get back to you, Javier? Your number only comes up as 'private' on my phone."

"Let's rectify that criminal oversight, this instant," he said with a laugh that sounded like a motor turning over, and then he recited his number.

As soon as I said goodbye, I phoned David, but it rang through to voicemail. Instead of leaving a message, I texted him. "Thinking of you. Call me."

I slurped down the rest of my drink and headed to the hospital to meet my battered client, Miranda Davidson. She had raccoon-patterned bruising encircling both eyes, and one of her front teeth was broken off at the base. Miranda spoke with a timid fatalism that was so typical of the chronically abused. Her two kids were even quieter. It was hard to imagine what they had seen their dad do to their mom, but neither said more than a word or two to me the whole time I was with them. Even after I took them for burgers and milkshakes. By the time I dropped the children off with the older foster couple who'd agreed to take them in temporarily, I was already nearly two hours behind schedule.

The rest of my day flew by in a whir of on-site visits, follow-up calls, and electronic documentation. On my drive home, I realized David still hadn't gotten back to me. Rather than try calling again, I decided to just drop in at the hotel. I parked out front, headed straight up to his room, and knocked at his door. There was no answer.

I pounded on the door with the side of my fist and called, "David! Open up, please."

"He won't answer, Taylor," Javier said from somewhere behind me. "I've tried multiple times. My room's just down the hall."

I sensed Javier's worry as if it were a weight on my neck and shoulders. It only ratcheted up my own. As soon as I turned to him, I spotted the bruise that extended all the way along the right side of his jaw. But I was too preoccupied to ask what had happened. Instead, I hurried past him and down the stairs to the front desk. I flashed my government identification to the bored-looking teenager behind the desk and demanded a key to David's room. The kid didn't blink an eye or bother to ask why a social worker was insisting on access to a guest's room. He ran a plastic room key through the magnetizer and handed it to me. I raced back upstairs and along the hall to where Javier paced in front of the door.

I suddenly froze. Entering homes and residences where I wasn't invited was a routine part of my job. This felt different, though.

Javier gently plucked the key card from my fingers and ran it over the sensor. When the electronic lock buzzed and clicked, he pushed opened the door and stepped inside. I followed him in, my heart in my throat.

The stale stench of alcohol and vomit drifted to me, but Javier blocked most of my view into the room. All I could see was a pair of legs jutting out along the end of the bed.

I almost ran into Javier when he suddenly stopped.

"Jesus Christ, David," he muttered.

Javier's words broke my spell, and I nudged past him. David was lying fully dressed on the bed, eyes closed, and neck craned to the left. A bluish streak ran down from his mouth, across his chin, and down to his neck where the rest of the multicolored vomit puddled over his shirt collar. An empty whiskey bottle lay beside his head.

"Call 9-1-1!" Javier barked at me, before lunging for the bed. His hand shot up to David's neck.

As I fumbled to get my phone out of my pocket, Javier looked back over his shoulder at me, his color almost as pale as David's. He shook his head once.

"Do something, Javier!" I cried. "CPR!"

Javier didn't budge. "He's as cold as this room."

I stumbled back a step. "Can't be."

"He's dead, Taylor."

"No . . ."

"He's gone."

A devastating stillness fell over the room.

Javier dropped his head and muttered, "I never thought he would try it again."

CHAPTER 21

No one said a word, as Natan, Evan, and I watched the paramedics seal the black bag over David's head and hoist his body onto the gurney. I kept thinking of the time David mentioned his daughter and her ballet and how, at that moment, all the tension had drained from his features, replaced by only love and pride.

The sadness would come. I could feel it building like water rising against a buckling dam. But right now, outrage consumed me. What a waste. All these pointless suicides. But David, of all people, should have known better. I'd given him every opportunity to talk about what was troubling him. I'd even opened up to him about my most guarded secret. Why hadn't he shared his with me?

Natan nodded at the open door to the bathroom, inside which the empty pill bottles still lay on the countertop in the same jumble Javier and I had found them in. "What do you think killed him?" he asked Evan as the paramedics wheeled the body past us and out the door of the room.

"We won't know for certain without the tox screen, Chief," Evan said, still looking as stunned as he had the moment he arrived. "Obviously, the bottle of whiskey contributed, but my best guess is he died mainly from an opioid overdose."

Natan grimaced. "Like fentanyl?"

"Hydromorphone. I'd prescribed David two weeks' worth, what with his multiple rib fractures and broken wrist and all. Last time I saw him, he told me he wasn't using them much for the pain. But he must have gone and swallowed the whole goddamn bottle." Evan's cheeks colored. "Never once crossed my mind he might . . ."

"Why would it have, Evan?" My heart went out to him. I resisted the urge to reach over and stroke his shoulder.

Natan's eyes narrowed. "There were a lot of different colors in what he vomited up. I assume he took other pills, too?"

"True." Evan motioned to the bathroom. "There are empty bottles of ibuprofen and Dramamine in there, as well. And the dark blue came from an antidepressant he was taking called Ketopram."

"Could any of those have killed him?"

"Maybe the ibuprofen and Dramamine contributed. Probably not the Ketopram."

"Why not?"

"Like most newer antidepressants, Ketopram is usually relatively harmless to overdose on."

Harmless? One of the last things David ever told me was how dangerous he believed the medication to be. I had no idea he had been taking it himself. "Weren't Brianna and Amka also on Ketopram?" I asked.

"Yes," Evan said.

Natan clicked his tongue. "Doesn't sound like much of an antidepressant to me."

Evan sighed again. "No, I suppose not."

"And David didn't leave a note, huh?" Natan mused. "Neither did Brianna or Amka."

"Suicide notes aren't as common as people assume," I said. "Only about one in four people who kill themselves actually leave a note." I knew the statistics well since I'd presented on the subject in my final year of college.

"What now?" Evan asked, his voice hollow.

Natan rubbed his eye. "We'll keep his body in the morgue, and I'll report it to the Medical Examiner's Office in Anchorage. Once we have the toxicology back—as long as there aren't any surprises—I'm sure they'll agree to sign off on it as a suicide and release the body to the next of kin. Meantime, we'll poke around a bit more."

Evan frowned. "Poke around?"

"The usual," the chief said. "Ask a few questions. Make sure there was nothing suspicious about his death."

"I suppose," Evan said.

"He was jumped this week by unknown assailants," Natan pointed out. "And then he takes his own life a couple days later? It's kind of a coincidence."

"It is," I agreed. "And even by this town's standards, three suicides in under a month is way above the norm."

"Yeah. Let's dot all our *i*'s and cross our *t*'s on this one," Natan said. "We owe the doc that much."

"We do," Evan said. "David did a lot for his patients in this community."

Natan looked over to me. "Will you track down his family in Anchorage?"

"Of course. I think his colleague, Javier, is trying to contact David's ex-wife in Seattle." I stopped to swallow. "Where his teenage daughter lives, too. But I'll reach out as well."

"A daughter, huh? Jesus." Natan grunted, as he turned for the door. "I have to head back to the station. I'll catch you both later."

Once the chief had left, Evan angled his head and viewed me with concern. "How are you holding up, Taylor?"

"Who knows?" I sighed. "This is insanity. Like a domino effect of suicides."

"All of them connected by underlying depression." He exhaled so heavily that his breath whistled. "David took Amka's death so hard. Especially after Brianna . . . He blamed himself."

"Did you know David was on antidepressants?"

"Only when he showed up in the ER after his assault. But he told me he'd recently stopped taking them."

"Why would he do that?"

"He never explained it. To be honest, I didn't push. I was more focused on his injuries."

"Yeah, of course."

Evan's dejected face broke into a slight smile. "I don't know about you, but I could really use a glass of wine right now."

The offer was tempting. Aware of my current vulnerability, though, I suspected I would just wind up back in Evan's bed if I joined him. And I was determined not to repeat that mistake. We'd drunk so much wine that night, back in early June, that I couldn't remember how I ended up naked with him. Evan had been nothing but understanding ever since, despite my evasiveness. I still found him sort of attractive in a rumpled kind of way, but it hadn't felt right the first, and only, time I slept with him. And I knew I would only end up hurting him worse, if he were serious about a relationship with me.

"I could use a drink, too, Evan," I said. "But I've got to go see Javier. To find out what's going on with the family."

"Of course." He turned for the door. "I'll talk to you tomorrow?"

"Sure."

I followed Evan out of the room, but instead of accompanying him to the stairs, I headed in the other direction, toward Javier's room.

Even without the bruising across his lower cheek and jaw, which was even more noticeable now, Javier would've stood out since he was wearing a paisley robe over his pajamas. "I am afraid I don't have anything to offer you but water," he said apologetically as I stepped inside the room.

"I'm fine, thanks. Did you reach David's ex-wife?"

"No answer. But Beth will get back to me soon."

"Can you tell her that I need to speak to her, too? Regarding the funeral arrangements and, um, David's remains."

"Of course."

"Thank you." I motioned to his face. "What happened?"

He grimaced. "David."

"He *hit* you?"

"With his casted arm. It carried quite the punch."

"Why?"

"He blamed me."

"For what?"

"Everything," Javier said distantly. "I wasn't just his friend, Taylor. I was also his psychiatrist."

"That's why you came up here?" I drew my head back in surprise. "You were that worried about your patient?"

"My friend, my patient. Both. David wasn't himself. It began with Brianna's suicide and kind of spiraled from there. When his other patient went missing . . ."

"Did you know he'd stopped taking his antidepressant?"

"I just found out a few days ago. That was one of the reasons I decided to come up to see him myself." He paused. "A lot of good that did."

I didn't have words to reassure Javier any more than I'd had for David after Amka's death. The guilt and recrimination from these suicides spread worse than smoke off a campfire. Instead, I said, "Back in David's room, you made it sound as if he'd attempted suicide before."

"He had."

"When was this?"

"A year and a half ago. Maybe a little more. Right before we admitted him to hospital."

"He tried to overdose then, too?"

Javier closed his eyes and shook his head. "He almost jumped off his balcony."

"What stopped him?"

"One of his neighbors spotted him sitting on the balcony for hours. It was winter and he wasn't wearing a jacket. She called 9-1-1. When the cops broke into his condo, David climbed over the railing. One of the cops was able to distract him while the other grabbed him and pulled him in."

"Oh my god. A psychiatrist . . ."

"We're not immune, Taylor."

"I guess not." Early on in my training, I'd realized that social work often attracted people to it who'd survived early life traumas. I didn't doubt the same held true for psychiatry. But none of it helped me make any more sense of David's death. And it certainly didn't excuse it. "The last time I saw David, he was very upset over Amka's suicide—"

"Believe me, I'm aware," Javier said.

"No, I mean he believed that antidepressant, Ketopram, was involved. That it contributed to Brianna's and Amka's deaths. And he blamed himself for prescribing it to them."

Javier touched his bruised cheek. "He also blamed me."

"Why?"

"I was the one who first convinced David of Ketopram's effectiveness."

"Effective? You still believe that? After all these suicides?"

"I do."

"Why?"

"Well, for one reason: David."

"David?" I held up my palms. "I'm not following."

"When he sank deep into his depression that winter, only Ketopram pulled him out of it. He used to credit it with saving his life." Javier motioned in the direction of David's room. "And look what happened once he stopped taking it."

CHAPTER 22

I put the kettle on and sat in my favorite chair, spine straight, hands on each thigh, shoulders drawn slightly back, chin tucked in, jaw open, and eyes lightly shut. I stilled myself, focusing on my breathing, on the rise and fall of my chest. My foolproof pose. But try as I might, I couldn't clear my head or shake the lingering sense of loss.

It reminded me of the darkest period in my life, after I'd first learned of my mom's diagnosis and how the defective gene that was rapidly eroding her body, mind, and soul had a fifty-fifty chance of doing the same to mine. I'd struggled with bouts of outrage over the unfairness of my fate that were invariably followed by tidal waves of guilt over my selfishness, aware that Mom was the one who was suffering. And through it all, poor Gabe just wanted to support me, to understand my anguish. And the harder he tried, the more detached I felt from him.

For months during my mom's decline, I'd been unable to meditate. Not properly, anyway. God knows, I tried. I worked harder at it than ever before, but I could never center myself or focus. It wasn't until I moved up to Utqiagvik that I could stay in the moment long enough to experience mindfulness again.

But the deaths of Amka and David had reheated the familiar toxic stew of anger, sorrow, and guilt, blocking any hope for meaningful meditation. Giving up, I checked my watch and saw that it was after eight a.m. I lifted the phone and called the number Javier had forwarded me.

"Dr. Raymer?"

"Yes," David's ex-wife said. "Who am I speaking to?"

"My name is Taylor Holmes. I'm a social worker here in Utqiagvik."

Beth went quiet for a long moment. "Javier told me."

"I'm so sorry for your and your daughter's loss."

"Thank you."

"Do you have a couple minutes?"

Beth hesitated. "Yes, of course."

"Shouldn't take long. I'm trying to work out a few logistics."

"Such as?"

"To begin with, we need to establish Dr. Spears's next of kin."

"His parents are dead. And David was an only child. I suppose that would make our daughter, Ali, his next of kin. But she's only sixteen."

"Legally speaking, that would give you power of attorney to make the decisions on her behalf. Do you know if Dr. Spears had a will, Dr. Raymer?"

"He did. He gave me a copy of it. I can email it to you." Her voice softened. "And please, Taylor, call me Beth."

"All right, Beth. Thank you."

"Javier told me you and my ex-husband were close."

I considered my words carefully. "I only met David in person last week, but we shared a few clients, remotely, over the past two years."

"Oh."

"I liked him, Beth. A lot. He was always kind to me and dedicated to his patients. But I think what I appreciated most was the respect he showed me. He treated me as an equal. Not all doctors do."

"Sounds like David."

I didn't know what else to say, so I changed the subject. "Do you know what his final wishes were for his resting place?"

"He wanted to be buried. Matter of fact, we were supposed to get side-by-side plots, but we never got around to it. Not that it's relevant anymore." She cleared her throat. "David would've wanted to be buried in Anchorage. Near his parents. I can say that with certainty."

"That's really helpful, Beth. I can arrange to get his remains to Anchorage, but from there . . ."

"I'll take it from there, Taylor. Thank you. I'll contact one of the funeral homes." Her tone was businesslike. "How long do you imagine it will take to organize the transport?"

"The flight isn't the issue. They go daily. The problem is that we don't know when the Medical Examiner's Office will release his . . . um . . . body."

"Why would they hold it up?"

"The circumstance of his death. The mixed overdose. Apparently, they're waiting for final toxicology results."

"What difference could those make?" she asked. "Everyone knows how he died."

"There's been a lot going on in this little town. And after David's assault, the police chief wanted to—"

"What assault?"

"You didn't hear? Shortly after he got to town, he was jumped on the beach. He got a concussion, some fractured ribs, and a broken arm."

"The biking accident," Beth muttered.

I frowned at my phone. "Biking accident?"

"Never mind," she murmured. "That goddamn bastard."

Confused, I said, "There were two of them who jumped him."

Beth breathed rapidly, sounding as if she were fighting back tears. "I meant David."

"Oh."

"I can't believe it. And what this is doing to Ali! I can't get her out of her room. She's a mess." Beth paused to get her voice to cooperate. "I'm so sorry, Taylor, but David didn't bother to say goodbye. He didn't even leave a note." She faltered again. "I just can't believe he would do that to his own daughter. To be so selfish."

"I . . . don't know what to say, Beth."

"It makes no sense, Taylor."

I felt compelled to defend him, to somehow rationalize it to Beth. "One of David's patients was found the day before he died. She drowned herself in the—"

"Javier told me about her. And the other girl who killed herself in the garage. David told me about her himself."

"He took their deaths so hard, Beth. So personally. One right after the other."

"He was a psychiatrist." She paused. "I'm one, too. It's the job hazard we all dread. But we don't deal with suicides in our practice by taking our own lives."

"No, of course not," I said. "What about the previous time? Did David leave a note then?"

"Previous time?" Her voice rose. "What are you talking about?"

"In Anchorage. Right before he was hospitalized. Javier told me he tried to jump off his balcony."

"Javier told you that?"

"Yes," I said, worried I'd overstepped.

Beth went quiet again "I didn't know he had tried before. David never told me. We were already separated by then."

"I'm sorry, Beth. I shouldn't have said any—"

"I knew about his mood disorder, of course. He was diagnosed before we even met. But through most of our marriage, he was so good. So . . . even. Then he lost his dad and mom, one right after the other. And the grief swallowed him whole. It tipped him into a major depression that lasted years."

"That's a lot," I said weakly.

"I would've never left," she went on, as if talking to herself. "But the whole thing became impossible. I tried, I really did. But he resented me so much."

"I'm sure it wasn't you, Beth. We both know how depression—"

"He sure took it out on me. I never stopped loving him, though. But it was so hard on Ali. She was too young to understand. And I couldn't let her watch how he treated me. What kind of message would that have sent our daughter?"

"Must've been so difficult."

"I'm sorry, Taylor," she said again, her tone more even. "I didn't mean to lay all that on you. I think I'm still in shock."

"Beth, I get it. I do. I can't imagine what you're going through."

"Not that suicides ever make sense, but this one . . ." Beth exhaled. "Even at his worst—and trust me, I'd seen David at his very worst—I still can't believe he'd do this to Ali."

We both went silent for a few moments. I thought again about my last conversation with David. Finally, I asked her, "Do you know much about Ketopram?"

"I don't prescribe it much myself, but yes. David told me how much it helped him."

"Right before he died, David told me he had concerns about the drug. The two women—both his patients—were taking it when they killed themselves."

"They were?"

"Yeah, but then again Javier says Ketopram saved David's life. And the reason he killed himself was because he'd stopped taking it."

"He'd stopped?"

"Apparently."

"For how long?"

"Not sure."

"Could you find out?"

"I could try. But why does it matter, Beth?"

"Antidepressants take time to start working." She sniffled. "And they also take a while to wear off."

I considered it. "If David had stopped taking Ketopram within a few days of his death, say, then it shouldn't have affected his state of mind that much?"

"Probably not."

I bit my lower lip. "It really doesn't make any sense, does it?"

"I just can't help thinking there has to be more to it." She sighed. "Or maybe, I just need to believe that."

It saddened me to consider all the unanswered questions that would continue to haunt his family, potentially forever.

"It's kind of ironic, though," Beth went on. "David died on the twenty-second of August. The same day of the month we got married."

"Your anniversary?"

"No. We were married on the twenty-second of May."

I didn't see any real significance in that small coincidence, but I didn't comment.

"On the twenty-second of every month, no matter what, David used to acknowledge it with some kind of gift. From a single flower to a new car, once." She laughed softly. "And then, after he got sick, the presents stopped. Not at first, but eventually. When the third month in a row passed without the usual gift on the twenty-second, I just knew . . . I'd already lost him."

CHAPTER 23

The next morning, when I stepped into the chief's office, I found Natan leaning back in his chair with his hands folded on his belly as he stared out the window. "G'morning, Taylor," he said without taking his eyes off the street.

"Hiya, Chief."

"Did you know Utqiagvik is one of the oldest settlements in North America?" he asked, apropos of nothing.

"I heard that. The remains of those sod houses—buried down there in the mounds off Barrow Beach—date back over a thousand years, right?"

"Older. The Birnirk—the prehistoric forefathers of my people—first settled here fifteen hundred years ago. We Iñupiat have been here ever since."

"That's a long stay," I said, as I dropped into the chair across from him.

"Wonder if this place had the same effect on my ancestors back then, too."

"What effect?" I asked, intrigued.

"To make 'em desperate enough to want to end it all, too."

"Could you blame them, if it did?" I said, trying to lighten the mood.

His laugh sounded more like a grunt. "In our culture—at least our traditional one, before the missionaries forced us into Christianity—all beings have their own *inua*."

"*Inua*?"

"A person's—or animal's—spirit. What you would call a soul."

"That's cool," I said, unsure where he was heading.

"And where your *inua* goes after death depends on where you die. Amka would have gone to the sea, David and Brianna to the sky."

"So no heaven or hell?"

He shook his head. "To me, it's never been clear which is preferable. They say the sea is more fun for an *inua*. But I'm going with the sky, because I'd hate to be wet all the time."

"You're OK, right, Chief?"

"All good." Chuckling, he pulled his gaze from the window, sat up, and spun his chair to face me. "What brings you by?"

"Just following up on my client, Miranda Davidson. You're holding her husband in cells."

"Oh, yeah, that piece of work."

"That's the one. Will the charges stick this time?"

"They should. No bail. This is his third charge."

"Good. I'm trying to determine if it's safe to let the family back in the house."

"Should be all right. We got zero plans to release him, but if the judge lets him out on bail—and even if he can somehow pay it—I'll give you plenty of notice before we do."

"Thanks, Chief," I said. "What about Rick?"

"Yeah, he's still here, too. We haven't found any proof that Amka made it back to town with him. But there's nothing to suggest he pushed her in the water, either. My gut tells me he wasn't involved."

I shifted in my seat. "Do you think I could talk to him?"

Natan raised an eyebrow. "About . . . ?"

"Three suicides in less than a month, Chief. All interrelated."

"In what sense?"

"Brianna's suicide tormented Amka, and both of their deaths devastated David."

"Maybe, but what's that got to do with Rick?"

"He's got to know more about Amka's mindset around the time of her death. The Obeds have lost both of their daughters. I figure they deserve some closure." I tapped my chest. "So do I."

"We're just about to take him to the hospital to visit his grand-mother. Sonya fell and broke her hip. She's going to have to be airlifted to Fairbanks for surgery."

I clicked my tongue. "That poor woman has been through too much already."

"Tell me about it."

"I only need about ten minutes with him, max. Please, Chief."

He closed his eyes, as if considering it for a moment, then opened them again. "All right. I guess you and the Obeds deserve that much."

Natan called out to one of his officers, and five minutes later, I was sitting in the interview room, across from Rick. His beard was even more scraggly, and his hair was ponytail-free and fell past his shoulders. Even though his expression was set in the same defiant scowl as before, I could sense a sadness in his eyes.

"I'm sorry about Amka," I said.

He shrugged. "The cops think maybe I shoved her out of the boat."

"I don't, Rick."

He stared down at his hand. "Doesn't matter. I know what I know."

"Speaking of the boat, you mentioned that on your trip home she was talking about her sister."

"It was just talk."

"Given what happened, it was probably more than just that, Rick," I said gently. "Were there other signs, do you think? Maybe things she said or did?"

He glanced up at me. "She wasn't right after Bree killed herself. She couldn't stop talking about it."

"Amka told Dr. Spears that 'Brianna understood.' Any idea what she would've meant by that?"

"Those two . . ." He scoffed.

"What about them?"

"Bree and Amka were always so . . . so serious . . . when they got together. All hushed, too. Like they were sharing the biggest secret or something."

"What kind of secret?"

"No fucking idea. That's the whole point of a secret, isn't it?"

I offered a sympathetic smile, trying to defuse his defensiveness. "Dr. Spears wondered if maybe Brianna had been abused—sexually—at some point."

He only shrugged. "Wouldn't be surprised."

"Why not?"

"Bree and me, we used to get along OK. But she changed after she had her kid. After Dylan hit the road. She had no time for me, that's for damn sure. But not just me. Any dude."

"How so, Rick?"

"Brianna was smoking hot, OK? Guys were always hitting her up. But she'd have nothing to do with any of them."

From my perspective, lacking interest in Rick's friends might have been just a sign of good judgment or, at least, a reflection of her mood disorder. But I wondered if there could have been more to it. "So Brianna never dated after Dylan?"

"Nope. Never."

"What about Amka?" I asked. "Any chance she might also have been abused?"

The corner of his lip curled. "Amka was cool that way. She liked me just fine."

I held up my palms. "No judgment, Rick. Just asking."

He sighed, slumping back in his chair. "They say it could happen to anybody, right? Especially in this shithole town."

I leaned in closer. "I don't get it, Rick. Why did you run? And why did Amka go along with you?"

"None of your fucking business."

"I'm not a cop, all right? I don't give a crap whether it was legal or not. I'm just trying to make a bit more sense of Amka's death. For the sake of her family." I paused. "Mine, too."

He rubbed his chin roughly. "She had a soft spot for the powder, OK?"

"Coke?"

"Yeah, more blow than we could afford. Especially after Bree's death. She went nuts for it. She went through it like it was dishwasher detergent."

"So you cut a little off the top of Eddie's supply? Kept some for yourself?"

"For Amka!"

"But Eddie wasn't so understanding?"

"I would've paid him back."

"Yeah, but gang leaders don't take kindly to being ripped off by one of their own dealers."

"Fuck you!" he snorted. "And you can get off your high horse, too. You should see the blue bloods in this town. Who do you think is buying up most of this shit?" He affected a haughty voice. "Professionals like you. Pillars-of-the-community types. They all like their product plenty."

"I don't doubt it, Rick."

"Blow, shrooms, E, you name it. They like it all. Even got one high roller who's got a sweet tooth for the liquid ecstasy. Or maybe he just like to roofie his dates," he muttered, and laughed.

"Who's that?" I asked in surprise.

He blew out his lips with contempt. "Whatever."

One of the younger cops opened the door and poked his head inside the room. "If you want to see your grandma before she's flown out, we got to leave now."

Rick hopped up from his chair and darted past me without so much as a glance.

I was still digesting what I'd learned as I pulled on my coat and walked out of the station.

"Afternoon, Taylor," Kai called out from the other side of the street.

"Hi." I stopped and waited for him to cross.

Kai had never expressed that he was interested in anything more than friendship, but I suspected he might be by the way he sometimes looked at me. And my internal radar was rarely wrong.

He motioned to the POLICE sign above us. "What brings you by?"

"Came to see about a client's husband," I said. "I ended up talking to Rick, too. Did you know Amka had a coke habit?"

He nodded. "Rick was skimming from Eddie to support it."

I frowned. "Why didn't you tell me?"

"Didn't think it would matter to you anymore since Amka and Doc are both gone."

"Fair. It's just that with all that's happened lately, guess I'm trying to find a bit of meaning in it all."

"Good luck with that." He snorted. "I'm still trying to get someone to cop to the doc's beating."

"Who could David have spooked enough for them to go the trouble of trying to scare him off like that?"

"Not sure." Kai scuffed at the ground with his boot. "Got to assume it was one of the usual suspects, probably Eddie. Just can't figure out why he'd care enough."

I heard the door to the station opening, and I turned to see

Rick step out with the uniformed cop behind him. Our eyes met, and I couldn't decipher if there was understanding or blame in the look.

Just as he broke off eye contact, two loud, firecracker-like pops sounded somewhere behind me, making me flinch.

Rick's upper torso twitched. His jaw fell open. I could swear his shocked eyes found mine again.

Before I could move, Kai shoved me to the ground and threw himself on top of me. I peered out from beneath his arm, desperate to understand what was happening.

Rick staggered a step or two, teetering for a moment before his legs gave way and he crumpled to the ground in a motionless heap.

CHAPTER 24

Kai kept me pinned me to the ground for what seemed like forever before one of the other officers called out an all clear.

By the time I got to my feet, the chief was straddling Rick's chest and compressing it frantically. Blood sprayed from Rick's mouth with each thrust. I heard a woman scream. A siren whined in the distance. Despite his strength, I sensed Kai's anxiety as he hovered beside me.

The next twenty minutes passed in a blur of noise and activity. I couldn't wrap my head around the happenings. I felt disembodied. Not only was it the first shooting I'd ever witnessed, but I'd been speaking to the victim only minutes before.

Three or four uniformed officers scrambled, with guns drawn, to search the neighborhood for the shooter. Two paramedics took over the CPR from Natan. But within minutes, the female paramedic stopped the compressions and shook her head as she rose to her feet.

Rick was dead.

Uninvited, I followed Kai back into the station and down to the chief's office, where Natan sat behind his desk, his white shirt splattered with Rick's blood.

"Shooter's gone," Kai told him.

"Witnesses?" Natan asked.

"Nope," Kai said. "But we found the spot across the street that looks to have been his perch. Under a truck lifted on blocks. Direct frontal view of the station. Can kind of see an imprint in the dirt. But no one in either house saw anything."

Natan sighed. "Eddie."

"Yeah, probably."

I looked from Natan to Kai. "Why would Eddie shoot Rick if he still owed him money?"

"Maybe he knew Rick was going to flip on him?" Natan said.

"Was he?" I asked.

"Yup," Kai said.

"Question is, how would Eddie have known?" Natan asked. "Or that we even had Rick in protective custody?"

"Probably from Rick himself," Kai reasoned. "He was on the phone just this morning. He might've inadvertently tipped someone off about heading to the hospital today, too."

"Maybe."

Kai scratched the side of his head. "We need to check out Amka's dad, too. Tom was no fan of Rick's."

I had a vision of Tom with his hunting rifle slung over his shoulder and that faraway stare in his eyes. I hoped Tom wasn't involved in the shooting, but based on what he'd said about Rick, I wouldn't have ruled him out as a suspect.

"We already have a suicide crisis in this town," Natan muttered. "Now a targeted hit on someone in our custody outside our own station? What the hell is going on?"

"Check time," Kai said.

"It's more than that." The chief groaned. "You better go track down Eddie and Tom."

"My next two stops," Kai said, as he turned for the door.

I walked alongside Kai out to his SUV. As I opened the passenger door, he asked, "What're you doing?"

"Coming with you," I said as I climbed into the passenger seat.

"This is a homicide investigation."

"I know them both, Kai. Probably better than you. I can help."

He eyed me for a few seconds, and then started the car.

We drove away from downtown in silence. The first time I had heard the sparse few blocks constituting Utqiagvik's commercial center referred to as "downtown," I'd almost laughed in the person's face. But now I threw the term around without a second thought like any of the locals.

I tried to focus on anything other than the murder I'd just witnessed as we made our way. There wasn't a cloud in sky and the temperature hovered in the mid-fifties, balmy by regional standards. The sunshine had the effect of a fresh coat of paint on the town. The houses appeared less dilapidated, and even the abandoned cars were less noticeable as we drove through the residential streets and pulled up in front of the Obeds' home.

Tom was sitting in a chair on the dirt in front of his front door with a knife in one hand, whittling away at a piece of wood in the other. He didn't look up as we approached.

"Rick's dead," Kai said and waited for a response.

Tom said nothing. He didn't even take his eyes off his carving, which took no identifiable form that I could make out.

"Two rifle shots," Kai continued. "Fired across from the police station."

"Can't say I'll miss him," Tom muttered.

"We didn't think you'd miss him," Kai said. "I'm more interested in whether or not you shot him."

"Someone tell you I did?"

"No."

"There you go."

"You won't mind if I check your rifle then?" Kai asked.

"Nope."

"Do you want to show me where it is?"

"As soon as you show me your warrant."

"Where have you been in the last hour, Tom?"

"Here."

"Are there any witnesses to that?"

"Don't know. Wife's asleep."

I knelt in front of his chair. "I get it, Tom. If I were in your shoes, I might want Rick dead, too."

Tom whittled aggressively at the piece of wood for a few moments. "Hope you're never in my shoes."

"If you were involved, I can help."

He stopped carving and locked eyes with me. "Don't want your help. Never did."

"I'm going to go get that warrant, Tom," Kai said, turning for the street.

"You do that."

"I'm so sorry about Amka, Tom," I said. "Please call me if there's anything I can do, OK?"

But Tom didn't acknowledge the offer as I straightened up and followed Kai back to his car.

"You hanging in there, Taylor?" he asked as he put the car into gear.

"Hasn't been the happiest few days."

"I'd say. Amka, Doc, and now Rick." He glanced over at me. "That must be a load to carry."

The kindness in his eyes almost made me tear up. Rick's murder was jarring enough, but it was the deaths of Amka and David that clung to me. It was hard enough to lose a client I cared about, but with David's passing, I lost a meaningful friend despite how little time we'd spent together. I hadn't told anyone in Alaska about my mom's death and the potential implications it had for me, and yet it had felt so natural to share with David. I kept thinking about Beth and his daughter, and the hole his suicide would leave in their world. Not that any suicide made sense from the family's point of view, but David's even less so. I wanted to find out more about his antidepressant and the role it might've played. And after what Rick had told me, I wasn't done digging into Brianna's abuse. David had been fixated on getting to the bottom of that, and I felt obligated to continue his quest.

But I didn't share of any of that with Kai. Instead, I laid my hand on the back of his hand and gave it a squeeze. "Thanks for checking, Kai. But I'm a social worker. Tragedy and loss are our stock and trade. Besides, I'm tougher than I look."

He chuckled. "You've always looked plenty tough to me."

I grinned. "Yeah, well, multiply that by two, at least."

Kai slowed the car as we pulled up to Eddie's place.

"Looks like he's home," Kai motioned to the truck parked in front of us, a shiny black Ford F150, decked out with aftermarket alloy wheels and extra racks.

Eddie's latest girlfriend, Rita, opened the door for us. She was a thirtyish woman with dirty blonde hair and a bruise over one of her tired eyes. Without a word to us, she looked over her shoulder and yelled, "Ed! Cops are here." She wandered back into the house, leaving the door wide open behind her.

From the doorway, I could only see part of the living room. A huge TV screen covered much of the far wall, with a hockey game playing on it. A flashing pinball machine stood in the corner.

A minute or two later, Eddie limped up to the door, listing to his left with each step. "For fuck's sake, you haven't been here enough lately?" he asked Kai, ignoring me altogether. He stretched a hand toward the living room. "You want to search it again? Be my guest."

"Actually, Eddie, I want to ask you about Rick's shooting," Kai said.

"Just heard 'bout that. Too bad. Good kid."

"He's a good kid now?" Kai chuckled. "You already forgive him for stealing from you?"

Eddie only smirked. "He wasn't perfect, that's for sure."

"Is that why you shot him?"

"Riddle me this, Detective. How do I get my money back by shooting the little prick?"

"Maybe you get something even better?"

"Like?"

"Freedom."

"I don't look free to you?"

Kai shot out a hand and grabbed Eddie's collar, yanking him forward. "I bet you needed his silence a lot more than the few ounces of coke he skimmed off of you."

"A few ounces? He tell you that?" Eddie scoffed, and shook free of Kai's grip. "What he stole from me was valuable. Very valuable. And how do I get it back now that he's been iced?"

"Just how valuable?"

Ignoring the question, Eddie cleared his throat aggressively. "I'm not the only one he ripped off, neither."

"Manny?"

Eddie only shrugged and backed into the house. "If there's nothing else, *Detective*, I got a g-note riding on this game."

"Eddie!" I snapped, stopping him. "The doctor I came here with me the last time. Who jumped him?"

Eddie nodded to Kai. "Like I already told this one. Don't have a clue."

"It wasn't you?"

"Why the fuck would I care enough to beat up some random outsider like him?"

"Because he was asking questions about Amka and Rick."

"Yeah, well, so were you. And I don't see no bruises on you." He spun and slammed the door on us again.

CHAPTER 25

I stared at the computer screen, trying to focus on one of my client's half-completed and mistake-riddled applications for temporary housing. But my concentration was as hopeless as his incomplete form.

I'd never been so immersed in death. A man I'd known had been murdered yards away from me this morning. His demise coming only days after I'd stroked the lifeless cheek of one of my clients and seen my friend zipped up in a body bag. It was times like these that I missed Gabe's calming presence. He was the best listener I'd ever known. If he were here now, he would've helped me muddle through my shock and grief, probably without uttering more than a few words.

I'd wanted to stay in touch after I broke off our engagement, but Gabe said it would hurt him too much. Regardless, I continued to follow him on social media, even after I'd moved to Alaska. I was genuinely pleased for him when another woman—a Spanish beauty named Teresa—began to appear in his posts. Her stunning looks were only the tip of the iceberg. Teresa was also an assistant prof who taught environmental sciences. Moreover, she came with an instant family, in the form of an adorable two-year-old son who had huge brown eyes and curly locks. I could handle being replaced, but it wasn't as easy for me to swallow the fact that Gabe might have actually found an upgrade on me. But after all I'd put him through, I was happy for him. Even when I read that he and Teresa were engaged. Even after Gabe announced online that they were expecting a child, although that revelation took a bit more time to absorb.

I wasn't normally prone to loneliness, not even during the long, lightless Arctic winters. I'd come to this remote tip of the continent to escape my previous life and the uncertainty of my future. Work fulfilled me. Usually. But today I felt particularly isolated and trapped beneath my avalanche of loss.

Desperate for a distraction, I was relieved when Javier texted to ask if I'd heard the results of the toxicology screen on David. I responded, telling him that I would drop by to discuss it in person and asking him to meet me in the lobby.

Javier was waiting just inside the main door of the hotel. Despite his welcoming smile, I sensed his subdued mood before he opened his mouth to say hello.

"I thought you'd have gone home to Anchorage by now," I said, as we sat down in front of the fireplace.

"Tomorrow, probably," he said. "I promised Beth I would oversee the arrangements."

"I can handle things on this end, Javier."

"Thank you," he said. "But I was hoping they would release David's remains soon. Have the toxicology results come back?"

"Not that I've heard."

He frowned. "Do you know how much longer they might take?"

"Honestly, no," I said. "It's not exactly a common occurrence up here."

"Is there anyone I can call to expedite it?"

"Do you happen to know the ME in Anchorage?"

"Matter of fact, I do."

I wasn't surprised. "Guess it wouldn't hurt to ask him. But I doubt even he can speed up a lab test."

Javier sighed. "Poor Beth."

"I spoke to her, too."

"So I heard."

I shivered. *Why didn't they have the fire on?* "Beth is very angry with David."

"Can you blame her? I am, too. Furious with him. David was one of my best friends."

"Such a waste."

"Such a selfish thing to do," Javier said as he ran his fingers over the bruise along his jawline. "The number of times we discussed it, too. His guilt. After the first episode, and what he almost did to his daughter. He promised me, Taylor. He swore he would never do that to Ali."

"Then why did he?"

"Listen, as hurt as I am by what he did, you can't rationalize someone's behavior during a major depressive episode. It changes a person. Sometimes beyond recognition. And more often than not, it shatters their judgment." He paused. "I blame myself as much as him. More, maybe."

"About the Ketopram?"

He grimaced. "No. Not for that." His expression softened. "I was his psychiatrist. I saw the changes in him. The downward spiral."

"And you came up here to keep an eye on him."

"Look what that accomplished."

We were quiet for a short while. "About the Ketopram, Javier . . ."

I thought I saw his jaw clench momentarily, but his tone was friendly as ever when he asked, "What about it?"

"Obviously, I don't know much about pharmacology, but it's hard to ignore the coincidence of three people in one tiny town all committing suicide while on the same medication."

"David wasn't taking his anymore."

"Beth told me that even if someone had stopped taking it a few days before, he would still basically be under its influence."

Javier eyed me for a few seconds. I couldn't discern what lingered behind the blank stare—defensiveness, defiance, apology, or something else altogether—but he finally said, "I agree, Taylor. It's freakish. But *coincidence* is the right word."

"How can you be so sure?"

"Because I've lived and breathed this medication for the past three years," he said. "I've participated in or reviewed every single study on it. There is no wide-scale association between Ketopram and suicide."

"Until now, maybe?"

"Medicine doesn't work that way. Neither does science."

I saw no point in arguing. Not only was Javier the expert, but he wore his devotion to the drug more prominently than his brand-name clothing. It was more than just science for him. It was clearly his religion, too. "There now have been four potentially related deaths," I said.

"Four?"

"Amka's boyfriend, Rick, was gunned down this morning."

Javier's eyebrows furrowed. "But how is that related to the other deaths?"

"It's possible Amka's father was involved. If so, it would mean Brianna's suicide led to three more deaths. Including Rick's."

He nodded. "I see."

"Did David talk to you much about Brianna's suicide?"

"Not so much her suicide, as his reaction to it."

"Did he ever mention that he believed she'd been sexually abused?"

"No." Javier frowned. "You mean as a child?"

"More recently, too. After her baby was born. And maybe again right before her death."

He shook his head. "Did David know who might've been abusing her?"

"No."

Javier considered it for a moment. "In such recurrent cases, the abuser is usually closer to home."

"I've seen it depressingly often in my work." I sighed. "David and I went to see Brianna's aunt and uncle. They said they were in the dark. And we believed them."

"But you intend to keep looking into it?"

"I feel like I owe it to David, if no one else, to try," I said. "There are a few cousins I'm going to track down. Also, I'm going to see if I can reach any of Brianna's old teachers or coaches. Nevaeh's dad told David about a teacher who left during Brianna's senior year. Apparently, she was upset to see him go. Maybe he knows something?"

"Maybe," Javier said half-heartedly.

"I'm not convinced it'll go anywhere," I said. "But this whole tragic mess really does start with Brianna's death."

"Let's just hope it ends with Rick's."

My phone vibrated, and I glanced at it to see a text from Kai that read: "Call me."

"Sorry, Javier, I've got to run," I said as I rose to my feet.

He smiled and waved me off with a backward flick of his hand. "Go, go."

As soon as I was back inside my truck, I called Kai over the Bluetooth speaker. "Hey. What's up?"

"Do you know Cupun Meelak or Jim Harris?" he asked.

I considered it a moment. "The first one sounds kind of familiar, but I can't place him."

"We've had the two of 'em under surveillance for the past week. Suspicion of bootlegging. We just pulled their truck over today and busted them with several crates of vodka and gin. Street value north of twenty grand."

"That's a flush street," I said, not seeing the relevance.

"When we searched their truck, we didn't just find booze," Kai said and, clearly enjoying the reveal, waited for me to comment.

I played along. "What else did you find, Kai?"

"Two balaclavas."

I gripped the steering wheel tighter. "They're the guys who jumped David?"

• "They certainly fit the description. Jim's a big boy and Cupun is a wiry kid."

"Did they admit it?"

"Nah. They've lawyered up already."

"Do they work for Eddie?" I asked.

"Nope." He paused again to draw the news out. "Manny."

CHAPTER 26

"Thanks again for letting me tag along," I said to Kai from the passenger seat of his SUV.

"Against my better judgment." But his gruffness wasn't too convincing.

I punched him lightly on his thick shoulder. "Come on, you could use the company."

He chuckled. "Maybe I could."

I'd definitely played on whatever feelings Kai might have for me to weasel my way along for the interview, and I felt a bit guilty for it. As much as I liked him, there wasn't enough of a spark there for me to consider anything more than a friendship. But I couldn't wait to hear what Manny had to say.

Between Eddie's bitter divorce—which involved assault allegations and a restraining order—as well as his penchant for enlisting troubled youths in his criminal trade, I'd had several professional run-ins with him since I moved to Utqiagvik. Not so with Manny. I'd only met him once. In many ways, he was the opposite of Eddie. He was short and lean, with dark curly hair to match the rest of his

Semitic features. He was educated, too. Apparently, he had come to Alaska, specifically Prudhoe Bay, to work as an oil and gas engineer. How he ended up in this town as a second-tier drug and alcohol trafficker was a lingering mystery.

Manny's freshly painted blue house stood at the end of the block, and the grounds were immaculate. He met us at the door after two knocks. Rather than a rifle, he carried a water bottle in his hand. His face was flushed, and his shirt sweat-stained.

"Hello, Detective. The wife insisted on one of those spin bikes with the live classes from New York or wherever. Now I'm hooked." Manny laughed as he motioned to me with his bottle. "Tyler? No . . . Taylor, right?"

"Yes."

Manny waved a beckoning hand. "Come in."

We followed him into the front room, where his spin bike stood in front of yet another huge wall-mounted TV screen. There were a couple of tasteful paintings on the wall and even a colorful throw rug that tied the room's colors together.

"Did you hear about Rick Neakok?" Kai asked.

Manny jutted out his lower lip. "Brazen, I'd call it. Gunned down in broad daylight."

"Is that like self-congratulations or something?"

"Never fired a gun in my life, Detective." Manny laughed. "But if I had, your only crime scene victims would've probably been windows and tires."

"What do you know about the shooting, then?"

"Nothing except that somebody must've really wanted the kid dead."

"Not you?"

"Kill him? He wasn't even on my radar."

"Basically, the same way you were in the dark about the shrink who got jumped on the beach?"

"This town is getting violent." Manny rubbed the side of his abdomen where, I assumed, he'd been stabbed. "And I'm missing a third of my liver to prove it."

"You think Cupun Meelak or Jim Harris might know something more about the aggravated assault at the beach?"

Manny shrugged, not the least fazed. "Why don't you ask them? I hear you have them in custody."

"Yeah, along with thousands of dollars' worth of your booze."

Manny licked his thumb and used it to wipe away a tiny smudge on the handlebar of his spin bike. "My booze? Was it labeled?"

"No, but Cupun and Jim practically are. Everyone knows they work for you."

"They've done work for me in the past," Manny said. "I'm not Walmart or something, Detective. I don't have employees."

"Come on, Manny. Those two halfwits aren't beating or threatening anyone without your say-so."

Manny held up his hands. "Don't know what else to tell you, Detective."

"Rick owed you money."

Manny's face creased. "He did?"

"We've been told."

"Even if that were true—and it's not—killing him would make no sense. Execution probably isn't the most effective way to collect on a debt."

Kai took a step closer to him. "This all points to you, Manny."

"So you're saying I had Rick killed because he owed me money, and I had the doctor jumped for . . . what? The hell of it? Anything else you want to add to my tab? Maybe throw in the Kennedy assassination?"

I couldn't hold my tongue any longer. "How did you get mixed up in all this, Manny? How does an engineer end up as a bootlegger in a remote Alaskan town?"

"That's the best question I've been asked today."

"So enlighten us," I said with a smile.

"What I do is my business, but how I ended up here?" For the first time, bitterness crept into his tone. "You can blame that on the Arctic Slope Regional Corp. A clusterfuck happens on the line. A pipe bursts. And the mothership needs a fall guy. Who better than the little Jew from Vermont? They stripped me of my license and my livelihood."

"And after all you went through, you still chose to stay in the Arctic?" I asked.

"Chose?" Manny cried out. "Where else is a disgraced engineer supposed to go? So, yeah. I chose to join all the other escapees and misfits who are hiding out here at the end of the earth."

Kai's glance to me suggested there was no point to this. "All right, Manny, I'm off to have another chinwag with Cupun and Jim," he said. "Make them realize how much better their lives will be by opening up about you. Anything you want say before we leave?"

He only grinned. "Tell them I say hello."

We headed back to the car.

I'd never seen Kai as frustrated. "That little prick," he grumbled as he jammed the gearshift into drive and pulled out onto the street. "Too smart for his own good."

I'd noticed that Kai seemed most defensive whenever he sensed that his own intellect was being challenged. I'd picked up on the same insecurity around David. It made him uncharacteristically irritable. "Manny does come across as pretty sharp, Kai," I said gently.

"No one in the drug trade is that smart. Manny is going to fall soon. Very soon if Cupun or Jim rolls on him."

Kai drove us in sullen silence back to the police station, where my truck was parked. As we were pulling up front, we ran into the chief, who was just about to climb into his vehicle.

If Natan was surprised to see me getting out of Kai's car, he didn't show it. "Toxicology screen just came back on David," he announced as he stepped up to Kai's open window. "It was positive for alcohol, hydromorphone, Ketopram, ibuprofen, and . . . what was it. Oh, yeah, Dramamine. No other drugs or illicit substances."

"We can sign it off as suicide then?" Kai asked.

"Guess so," Natan sighed.

I hadn't expected anything different, but the finality hit me with a flush of sadness. "Does that mean you can release the body now?" I asked.

"We already did. Got the word from the ME's Office earlier."

I suspected Javier had a hand in that. He really was as connected as advertised. The thought of him reminded me of our earlier conversation about Brianna. "Chief, David was convinced that Brianna had been sexually abused," I said.

"Hmmm," Natan said. "And he thought that was somehow related to her suicide?"

"Yeah. I'm still looking into the possibility. Neither of you remember any incidents involving Brianna, do you?"

"Nothing," Natan said. Kai only shrugged.

"I was planning to talk to her cousins," I said. "This would've started long before I got here. Can you think of anyone in her orbit who would be worth talking to? Dylan told David something about a favorite teacher who left during her last year of school."

Kai glanced at Natan and then said, "Could be that English teacher?"

"Brianna's teacher?" I asked.

"Probably," Kai said. "The school's not that big."

"But that incident had nothing to do with her," Natan cautioned.

I frowned. "Incident?"

"It didn't involve Brianna."

"Please, Chief, just tell me."

Natan hesitated a moment, and then said, "About four or five years back, a mom came forward. Accused the English teacher of seducing her daughter. The girl was only sixteen at the time. We investigated. There were some rumors, but nothing concrete we could dig up. A lot of the girls had crushes on this one teacher. But the girl in question refused to corroborate her mom's story, and we had to close the file."

"Is he still teaching here?" I asked.

"No. He left soon after and headed back to the Lower Forty-Eight."

"Must be the same teacher, then," I said. "What about the girl and her mom?"

Natan eyed me skeptically. "Yeah, they're still in town."

"Can you give me a name?"

"It was a confidential investigation, Taylor," Natan said. "You know that."

"I'm a social worker, Chief. I look into these kinds of things all the time. Discreetly. Please . . ."

Natan looked over to Kai, who nodded encouragingly. He turned back to me. "Mary Taslak. Her daughter is Amy."

"Thanks," I said. "And the teacher involved?"

"Keefer Willesdon," Kai answered for him.

"That's a mouthful," I said, but I was relieved he had such a distinctive name, since it would make him easier to track down.

Eager to speak to the Taslaks, I turned for my car, but the chief's voice stopped me. "Oh, hey, Taylor, do you know an Avery Lincoln in Philadelphia?"

"I don't think I know anyone in Philadelphia," I said. "Why?"

"We just got ahold of David's phone records. Lincoln's was the last call he ever received. At least, the last one he picked up."

CHAPTER 27

Once home, I sat down at my laptop and began researching the names I'd just learned from the chief, starting with Avery Lincoln. I was burning to find out what he and David might have discussed right before the psychiatrist died. Googling his name gave me a strong clue. The first twelve entries all referenced studies on Ketopram that Lincoln had either led or participated in. I noticed that Javier's name was also included on a few of the hits.

It was dead simple to track down a phone number for Lincoln's office at UPenn. Though it was late in the evening out east, I dialed and, predictably, it went straight through to voicemail. I left a message identifying myself and explaining that I wanted to speak to Dr. Lincoln. And, for good measure, I described David as "the late Dr. Spears."

Next, I turned to the other names Natan had given me. Through my office's database, I quickly found numbers for both Mary Taslak and her daughter, Amy. I decided to try the mother first.

Mary answered on the second ring. "Hi, Mrs. Taslak," I said cheerfully. "My name is Taylor Holmes. I'm one of the social workers in town."

"A social worker, huh? What's this about?"

"I'm looking into the allegation regarding inappropriate sexual behavior of one of the high school teachers, Mr. Willesdon."

"Five years after the fact?"

"I realize the police already investigated—"

"That was more of a cover-up than an investigation."

I resisted the urge to defend my friends. "Regardless, new information has come to light."

"About my Amy?"

"No, Mrs. Taslak. Concerning another student."

"I knew it!" she said.

"That there would be others?"

"With men like that—*predators*—there are always others!" she said, almost triumphantly. "He's a sociopath, that one. There were rumors of more girls at the time, but the police didn't do anything about them."

"I'm pursuing it now."

"About time."

"I don't have access to the original police complaint, Mrs. Taslak. I was hoping you could fill me in on some of the details regarding your daughter."

Mary didn't need further encouragement. "Yes. Well. Amy was thrilled to get Mr. Willesdon in her sophomore year. She loved poetry. And he introduced her to all different kinds, especially Inuit poetry. She was just a child. Fifteen. And an innocent fifteen-year-old, at that." She exhaled heavily. "By the time Amy was in his junior class the next year, she'd changed so much. Too much. She'd go to school with her faced caked in makeup, fake eyelashes, and half-tops exposing her midriff. I knew something was up. I just knew it."

"Why did you think Mr. Willesdon was involved?"

"I didn't. Not at first. But one day when she was in the shower, I checked her phone. I'd started to do it regularly after she began to act that way," she said unapologetically. "Back then she only had a password-protected phone. And one of the conditions of her getting it was that her father and I would always have the password."

"Clever," I said, although it seemed a bit invasive to me.

"I scanned through her texts while she was showering. The last chat was with a 'KW.' It had only two entries. A text from Amy that read "Dying to see you again tonight." And a photo of—" Mary swallowed. "A selfie of my sixteen-year-old lying naked on the bed except for the tiniest thong."

"That couldn't have been easy for you to see, Mrs. Taslak," I said. "And you're sure 'KW' was Mr. Willesdon?"

"I tried the number, of course! It went straight to voicemail. But it was his voice. No question."

"There were no texts back from him?"

"That's exactly how the police defended him!" she cried. "There must have been other texts, for sure, but my daughter had been careful enough to delete those. She knew we had her password. And I saw from the time stamp that she'd only sent the text and the photo right before she stepped into the shower. If I'd waited another ten minutes, she probably would've deleted the two texts I saw, too."

It made sense. "Amy wasn't willing to identify him, though?" I asked.

"She did to me! As soon as I confronted her. She said they were in love. In love!" Mary cried. "A sixteen-year-old child and her teacher!"

"She wouldn't admit anything to the police, though?"

"No. As soon as I went to them, she changed her story. Denied everything. And she had already deleted those incriminating texts and even his contact by then."

"That must have been crushing for you."

"Worse than crushing." Mary's voice cracked. "That man molested my daughter. He ruined her childhood. And the worst thing was . . ." She swallowed again. "Amy blamed me. Me! For wrecking her life."

"I can't imagine." If I'd been in the room with Mary, I would have offered her a hug.

"It's never been the same between Amy and me," she said wistfully. "What that man did to her. To us. My only child. She hasn't looked at me the same since."

"Does Amy still live with you?"

"Hardly. She left the minute she could. She shares an apartment with a roommate in Browerville and works down at the general store. Matter of fact, she's there right now, I think."

"Thank you, Mary," I said. "I won't let this go. I promise."

"I hope not. Not again."

As soon as the call ended, I searched "Keefer Willesdon" on all major social media pages. I only found two matches on Facebook, but one was a kid and the other an elderly man living in Wales. When I Googled the name, I got a few more hits. I found a Keefer Willesdon who was a roofer in Orlando, and another who was listed on the faculty web page of a private English-language school in Seoul. I couldn't find photos of either of them, but I had no doubt which one I sought. There was a phone number and an email listed for the Korean school, but I decided to speak to Amy before tracking Keefer down.

I headed on foot to the general store, which was less than fifteen minutes from my home. Late August was my favorite time of year in Northern Alaska, especially on a sunny evening like this one, when the light dusk rolled into town in what seemed like slow motion. The walk also helped to calm me and dissipate the negative thoughts about all the lives lost or destroyed in recent days.

I reached the shiny new Alaska Commercial Co. building, one of the largest in town, and walked through the sliding doors of the general store. At the information desk, I asked a gangly teenaged boy, who pointed me to a young, thickset set woman working one of the nearby tills.

I waited a few moments, pretending to shop, until her line

cleared, and then approached. It was impossible not to notice Amy's mesmerizing brown eyes and perfectly arched eyebrows, which matched her lustrous dark hair.

"Hi, Amy. I'm Taylor. A social worker in town. I was hoping to chat with you."

Her face creased. "Me? Why?"

"I had a few questions about a teacher of yours, Amy."

Her eyes darted around as if the whole store might be suddenly listening. "No, no, no," she said in a hush without asking which teacher I was referring to. "I got nothing to say to you."

"I'm not going anywhere until we talk about this," I said, deliberately raising my voice slightly.

Her eyes went wider. "OK, OK, my break's in fifteen," she muttered. "I'll meet you outside by the shopping carts?"

"I'll see you there," I said, as I walked away from the till.

I waited outside beside the penned-in area for returning the shopping carts. A few yards away from me, a mangy dog stood on his hind legs with his front paws resting on the edge of an overflowing garbage can as he nosed through it in search of scraps. About ten minutes later, Amy skulked over to where I was. "Why are you doing this?" she demanded as soon as she reached me.

"I need to ask you a few questions about Mr. Willesdon."

She shook her head. "Haven't seen him in years. Besides, I already told the police everything I know about him."

"I don't think you did, Amy," I said gently. "I spoke to your mom."

"My mom! She's crazy, batshit crazy."

"I believed her, Amy."

Amy bobbed from one foot to another. "Yeah, well, maybe you're crazy, too, then."

"Do you know where Mr. Willesdon is now?"

"I don't care."

"South Korea."

Her face scrunched again. "Korea?"

"He's teaching English there now."

"He is?"

"I think he went because he knows how difficult it would be to extradite him from over there."

"You're just guessing, aren't you?"

"Can you think of another reason he'd move that far away?"

"Why can't you people leave it alone?"

"Because you probably weren't his only victim, Amy."

Her head jerked back, but she said nothing.

"Amy, did you know Brianna O'Brien?"

She looked down. "Bree was a year ahead of me at school."

"You heard what happened to her?"

She nodded.

I extended my hand toward her shoulder, but Amy recoiled from my touch. "I think Mr. Willesdon might have taken advantage of Brianna, too."

Amy just gaped at me for several seconds. Then her eyes misted over and tears began streaming down her cheeks. "I fucking knew it," she sobbed. "Bree was so gorgeous."

"What did you know, Amy?"

"One day after school, I saw Bree getting into his car," she choked out. "Keef told me he was just giving her a ride because her aunt couldn't pick her up. He promised me there was nothing more to it."

"Men like him, they do that, Amy. They make you feel so special. Like you're the only person in the world. And then they take such advantage of you."

"He told me I was the only one . . ." she whimpered.

CHAPTER 28

I assumed the ringing came from my phone's alarm clock. I wasn't even sure why I set it anymore, since I almost always woke up before it went off, especially in the summer. But as it continued to ring, I realized it was my phone, not my alarm. As I lifted it to my ear, I glanced at the clock, which read 5:23 a.m. "Hi," I said, stifling a yawn.

"Is this Ms. Holmes?" a low male voice asked.

"Yes. Taylor, please."

"This is Dr. Lincoln, from the University of Pennsylvania, returning your call."

I sat up, shaking off the mental cobwebs. It occurred to me that Philadelphia was three hours ahead of us, which must have explained why he was calling so early. "Thanks for getting back to me, Dr. Lincoln."

"It sounded on your voicemail as if you had said something about the *late* Dr. Spears."

"David is dead, Dr. Lincoln."

"Dead?" his voice rose. "What happened?"

"He committed suicide."

Dr. Lincoln went quiet for several seconds. "I just . . . I spoke with him only a few days ago."

"According to his phone records, you were the last person to ever speak to him."

He exhaled slowly. "That must be why the police are looking for me, too. I was going to call them right after you. What happened?"

"He took an overdose."

"Of what?"

"A mixture of substances, including alcohol, opioids, ibuprofen, and Ketopram."

"Ketopram?"

"Yes."

"Dr. Spears was taking Ketopram? For himself?"

The shock in his tone was almost palpable.

"Yes," I said. "Or he had been. He'd stopped a few days prior to his death."

"I don't understand."

"David was on Ketopram for depression. He'd had a . . . umm . . . previous suicide attempt, apparently. But after he began to suspect Ketopram was somehow linked to his patients' deaths, he stopped taking it." It still felt foreign to talk about David in the past tense. "I don't know if you heard, Dr. Lincoln, but he had a bad concussion a few days before his overdose. Maybe it affected his judgment, too. We'll probably never know."

"He never mentioned any of this."

"Do you mind telling me what you did speak about?"

"I supposed there's no one's confidentiality left to protect now," he sighed. "Dr. Spears called me last week to voice his suspicions over Ketopram. More specifically, he wanted to understand why we had aborted our study—the one I was lead investigator on—into the drug's adverse effects."

"Why did you?" I blurted.

"I wish I could answer that. However, as I told Dr. Spears, I am bound by a nondisclosure agreement with the sponsor company—"

"The company that makes Ketopram, right?"

"Precisely. Pierson Pharmaceuticals. Legally, ethically, I couldn't go into the details with him. No more than I can go into them with you now. All I told Dr. Spears—all I could suggest—was for him to speak to Dr. Gutiérrez."

"Javier?" I frowned. "Why him?"

"You know Javier, too, then?"

"Yes," I said without elaborating.

"Javier was one of the other investigators on the aborted study. I thought he might answer Dr. Spears's questions more fully than I could."

"Sorry, but I don't quite understand, Dr. Lincoln. If you already told David all of this on your first call, then why did you call him back the day he died?"

"To let him know his friend had threatened me."

"Javier threatened you?" I gasped.

"Yes. Threatened."

"With what?"

"He accused me of violating the terms of our NDA. He said he would let Pierson's legal team know that I was spreading malicious rumors about their product. Me? Violate the NDA? I've done everything within my power—often against my conscience and my better judgment—to abide by the terms of that miserable NDA."

Javier? I was struggling to align the amicable, sophisticated man I knew with the bully Dr. Lincoln was describing.

"More than just threats, he had the gall to blackmail me," he continued. "Or at least try to."

I was flabbergasted. "How? What could Javier blackmail you over?"

"He said that if I called Dr. Spears and downplayed the significance of our aborted study, he would—and I quote—'stop the
corporate lawyers from descending on me like a pack of starving
wolves.'"

"And that's why you called David? To downplay the study?"

"Absolutely not!" He snorted. "I told Javier exactly where he
could take his two-bit street thug act."

I couldn't believe what I was hearing. "So why did you call
David?"

"To warn him about his so-called friend. Even before the study
all fell apart, I never trusted Javier. My instinct told me he was only
ever in it for himself."

"How did David take it, Dr. Lincoln? When you did reach him."

"I must admit, I was hot under the collar. I didn't hold back.
I told him everything Javier had said. And I shared my general
low opinion of the man." He paused. "I suppose I would describe
Dr. Spears's reaction as subdued."

"Subdued? You mean he wasn't outraged?"

"More as if he wasn't surprised."

"Oh."

"And I even thought . . . No, never mind."

"Please, Dr. Lincoln, tell me."

"It's pure speculation on my part, but I had the sense that
Dr. Spears might have been drinking."

"Why is that?"

"He was slurring some of his words. And it wasn't even six p.m."

Which meant David would've had to have been drinking in the
mid-afternoon or earlier here, but I didn't point that out. Instead, I
asked, "Did anything else stand out about that last conversation?"

"Not really. It's just Dr. Spears was so indignant the first time
we spoke. And the last time—despite his colleague's outrageous
conduct—he seemed, well, almost disinterested . . ."

"That doesn't make sense, does it?" Then again, putting the events of the past month together was beginning to feel like trying to assemble one jigsaw puzzle out of random pieces from ten sets. "But thank you so much for the information and your time, Dr. Lincoln."

"You're welcome." And just when I thought he was about to hang up, he added, "Dr. Spears said Javier was in town with him. Is he still there?"

"Yeah."

"Don't make the same mistake I did, Ms. Holmes. Do not trust that man."

As I said goodbye and laid the phone back on the nightstand, I almost felt dizzy absorbing what I had just learned.

While I wouldn't have described myself as antimedicine, I did my best to avoid drugs of any kind—over-the-counter, prescribed, or illicit. I didn't even believe in health supplements. For me, mindfulness, exercise, and a balanced diet were the keys to good health. Unless, of course, I did carry a time bomb in my DNA that I'd inherited from my mom. In which case, nothing would help anyway.

I could think of only one person who might be able to explain the science behind Ketopram, so I texted Evan and invited him out for breakfast. Despite the early hour, he responded immediately, saying he would love to meet me.

The diner was three-quarters empty when I walked in just after seven a.m. Evan was already sitting in a corner booth with a black coffee in hand. His hair was as unruly as ever, and the collar of his sweatshirt askew. But his grin was as bright and welcoming. "What a lovely out-of-the-blue invitation," he said.

"I need to kind of pick your brain, Evan," I said with an apologetic smile. "But I'm definitely buying."

He shrugged, unperturbed, as I sat across from him.

"What do you know about Ketopram?" I asked.

"Just that it's been the talk of the town ever since David got here."

"Come on," I encouraged.

"OK. It's in a new class of antidepressants. Similar to the serotonin and norepinephrine reuptake inhibitors, but also chemically distinct." He paused to see if I was following, and I nodded. "It's only been on the market for two or three years. And I probably would've never prescribed it if it weren't for David. He was a big advocate."

"Not by the end, he wasn't." I went on to tell Evan about my conversation with Dr. Lincoln.

Evan was gaping by the time I finished. "Holy shit! That is one tangled web."

"Could David have been right? Do you think those suicides might've been linked to Ketopram?"

"It's possible. Other antidepressants have been associated with suicides before."

"Say that Ketopram did contribute to those deaths. Why would a guy like Javier want to cover that up?"

Evan sipped his coffee as he considered my question. "No one would be so stupid as to go to those lengths for professional pride alone. Just to be right about a medication."

"Then what else?"

Evan took another long sip. "Maybe Javier has a financial interest in it?"

"How would that work? Like he owns part of the rights to the drug?"

"No. Pierson Pharmaceuticals would own those. But drug companies often pay doctors—generously at that—to act as their spokespeople. To lecture to other doctors or to influence our prescribing practices. Javier must have done a helluva good job, too, because David once told me that Alaska had the highest use per capita of Ketopram anywhere in the world."

"Yeah, but would that be incentive enough to want to cover up suicide?"

"Probably not." He squinted, deep in thought. "Maybe Javier owns a bunch of stock in the company, too? Ketopram is Pierson's premier product. News of something this potentially disastrous would crash their share prices. Maybe Javier stands to lose a bundle?"

"Couldn't he just sell them?"

"I think that would be illegal, wouldn't it? Insider trading or something?"

"Yeah," I said. "Maybe. I don't know beans about the stock market."

Meg—the sweet maternal server who was a staple of the diner—interrupted us. "What can I get you for, dolls?" she asked in her usual rasp.

I ordered the oatmeal while Evan chose the farmer's breakfast with sausages. Once Meg left, Evan said, "I realize I'm here only as your pharmaceutical expert, Taylor . . ." He looked almost bashful. "But I've got to say, I'm still happy you reached out."

"Listen, Evan." I cleared my throat. "We never really spoke after that time I . . . um . . . slept over."

"No, we haven't."

"Truth is I drank way too much that night. To be honest, the whole thing is very fuzzy."

He brought a hand to his chest. "I drank just as much or more, Taylor. I wasn't forcing the wine on you."

"No, not at all." I reached over and touched his other hand. "I didn't mean it like that. No regrets. I like you. And I like your company. It's just that I left a very messy situation back in California. It's . . ."

"You've been here a couple years now, haven't you?"

"It's complicated, Evan. I haven't felt emotionally available since

I got here." I pulled my hand away from his. "Not sure when . . . or even if . . . I ever will be again."

"OK," he said, breaking off eye contact.

We lapsed into an awkward silence. After several seconds, I said, "I also wanted to ask you about Brianna?"

"Brianna? What about her?"

"David was convinced she'd been sexually abused as a teen. Not only that, but that it contributed directly to her death."

He looked skyward. "First David blamed Ketopram? Now sexual abuse? Which was it exactly?"

"Both, maybe?"

"I didn't think David found anything to substantiate the abuse theory."

"He didn't," I said. "But I might have."

He leaned forward. "What did you find?"

"Do you remember a high school teacher named Keefer Willesdon? Lived here a few years back."

"Keefer? Yeah, sure. He was a patient of mine." He sat up straighter. "You're not suggesting . . ."

"The mother of one of his students alleged he'd seduced her daughter." I went on to summarize my conversations with the Taslaks, and how I'd tracked Keefer down to Korea. "And I think Brianna was another of his victims."

"Huh." Evan grunted, his expression faraway. "I always found Keefer to be kind of slippery. One of those guys who was too nice and too happy all the time for it to be genuine."

"Typical predator."

"So, what's next?"

"I'm going to track Keefer down."

"In Seoul?"

"Yeah."

"Good luck with that," he sighed. "And what about Javier?"

"No idea what to do about him." It was all too much to think about. I felt like the girl from that popular streaming series who was playing speed chess on multiple boards at the same time. "I might have to leave Javier to the cops."

CHAPTER 29

I had just reached my office when I received an urgent call from the older foster parents who had taken in the two Davidson children while their mother was still recuperating in hospital from her assault. They were struggling with the nine-year-old boy's aggression. He'd knocked over the foster mom and put out her back, leaving her essentially bedridden. It took me most of the morning to find a suitable home to relocate the kids.

Shortly after three p.m., I double-checked the time in Seoul and confirmed it was just after eight in the morning there. I dialed the number for the English language school, and a receptionist answered in Korean.

"Is there anyone who speaks English?" I asked.

"Yes. Me, I do," said the woman in a high-pitched voice.

"I would like to speak to Mr. Willesdon, please."

She paused. "He has class. I pleased to take message for him."

"It's kind of urgent."

"I get him message right away."

I didn't trust him to call me back. "Please, this concerns an urgent matter in the United States involving Mr. Willesdon." And then

I added, "I work for the government. I must speak to him right away."

"Oh, yes. The government. I will put through to his line."

The line buzzed five or six time before a man picked up. "Hello," he said in a singsong voice.

"Keefer Willesdon?"

"Yes."

"My name is Taylor Holmes."

"I'm sorry, do I know you?"

"No, you wouldn't. I'm calling from Utqiagvik. I work in government services here."

"Oh, I haven't lived there in years." Keefer's tone remained pleasant, but I thought I picked up on a note of suspicion.

"Of course," I said. "But you were a standout of a teacher. Very popular with the kids. You're still remembered here."

"They were great kids. Very motivated. I'll always treasure my time teaching there."

"I didn't live here at the time, but apparently everyone was sorry to see you go," I said, hoping to disarm him further with false praise.

"Thank you, Taylor. That's most kind." He paused. "I still don't understand how I can possibly be of help to you from the other side of the planet."

"Oh, it's an administrative matter. We're looking into the files of a couple of students you taught up here."

"Which students?"

"Amy Taslak and Brianna O'Brien."

"I taught a lot of kids up there," he said without missing beat. "I vaguely remember Amy. I can't even place Brianna."

"I thought your memory would be more vivid." I paused. "Especially after the police investigation."

"Who are you again?" The friendliness in his tone evaporated.

"Taylor Holmes. I work in social services here."

"What the fuck is this about? Really?"

"Allegations that you were sexually involved with your students."

"No way. Uh-uh. The cops checked into all of that. I was fully cleared."

"The difference is, the victim is now corroborating the story."

"Which victim?" he blurted. "I mean accuser, obviously! There are no victims. I didn't do anything."

"Amy Taslak."

"Amy! Her mom must've gotten to her then," Keefer huffed. "The woman was on a crusade!"

"What about Brianna?"

"Who the fuck knows? Come on. Kids talk. They scheme all kinds of stuff. They probably worked out this whole plot together."

"Sex with a minor is a serious criminal charge, Keefer."

"They were sixteen at the time! In Alaska, that's the age of consent!"

"And how do you know they were claiming to have been sixteen when the abuse began?"

"I don't. How could I? But most of my contact with my students was during their junior or senior years. So I just assume that if they were going to accuse me—and I'm not admitting a goddamn thing—that's when they would've probably claimed it started."

"It is a serious criminal offense in Alaska for a high school teacher to have sex with his student. Regardless if they were sixteen or the sex was consensual. Two huge ifs, by the way, Keefer."

"This is insanity. Slanderous, actually. What proof do you have? Only the word of two fucked-up kids who had crushes on me?"

I didn't want to let him off the hook, so I bluffed. "How hard do you think it was to recover photos and texts from their phones?"

The line went dead quiet. "I'm not saying another word without legal representation."

"Brianna is dead," I spat before he could hang up.

I wasn't sure he was still on the line until he finally croaked, "Dead?"

"She killed herself."

"I . . . I didn't know," he stuttered, sounding genuinely flustered. "It's been years since I've seen her. But dead? This . . . it's got nothing to do with me."

"Nothing, huh? Brianna killed herself with carbon monoxide in her own garage, Keefer. And she tried to take her four-year-old daughter with her."

"Oh, God." His voice trembled. "Is the kid . . ."

"She's alive." I hadn't considered the timing before, but the realization jolted me as if I'd touched a live wire. *Keefer could well be Nevaeah's biological father!* "Did you know about her daughter?"

I heard his stilted breathing. "I heard she was pregnant," he finally said.

"By you?"

"I'm not admitting to anything." His denial was less forceful than before.

"Brianna's suicide is directly linked to how you abused her."

"Abused?" he said in a panicky voice. "It wasn't like that."

"She was a child!"

When he spoke again, his voice fluctuated between panicky and pleading. "Look, Brianna was sixteen, and . . . and I was only twenty-four. Practically a kid myself. Could you really blame me if something did happen? You have any idea what it's like to be young and alone in Utqiagvik."

I wasn't about to tell him that I did. "Did you know about her daughter?"

"Bree told me she was pregnant. Before I left. I thought she was going to . . . to take care of it. Anyway, with Amy's mom stirring up so much shit, I couldn't stick around that town."

"And you never heard from Brianna after you left?"

"Right after, she used to text me. A lot. But I didn't . . . engage. And then nothing for a year or so."

"What happened after a year?"

"I'd already moved to Seoul. I changed phone numbers and dropped off social media. But I still had my old email address. Bree wrote me." He took a breath. "This crazy rambling email."

"Why crazy?"

"It made no sense. She was threatening to expose me."

"That makes perfect sense to me."

"No. Not like that! Bree was totally paranoid. She thought I was trying have her baby taken away. For being an unfit mother or something. She was threatening to expose me if I tried to claim custody."

"Why would she have thought you wanted to have her daughter taken away?"

"How should I know? It was irrational is what it was. I had no idea she'd even kept the kid." Keefer paused to take a halting breath. "After I left, I worked so hard to put Utqiagvik behind me. I hardly even thought about it. As if I would want to get involved with anything to do with that horrible place ever again."

"Must've been nice to put it all behind you. To not even think about all the carnage you left behind."

"I didn't mean it like that—"

"Brianna wasn't crazy. She was depressed and suffered from PTSD. No wonder, after the way you took advantage of her. But she was a good mom."

"I . . . I'm sure she was. Even if I'd known about the kid . . . and I was the father . . . I never would've dreamed of trying to take her from Bree."

CHAPTER 30

"**S**on of a bitch," Natan said from behind his desk, where he had sat utterly motionless while I recounted the phone call with Keefer. "When I interviewed him five years back, I had my doubts. I thought he was a little too smooth. Too tolerant of the accusation against him. He played the concerned teacher to a tee."

"What could you do, Chief? Amy wouldn't talk. All you had was the mom's word against his."

"It should've been enough," he sighed. "We'll get statements from the Taslaks and then forward the complaint to the regional US Attorney's Office. Not sure how extradition works with South Korea, but maybe those girls will see some justice yet."

"Amy, maybe. It's too late for Brianna."

"Son of a bitch," Natan muttered again. "What do you think of the email he claimed Brianna sent? Do you believe him?"

"What would be the point of making up a story like that up? It only incriminates him more."

"I suppose." Natan leaned back in his chair. "So either Brianna was imagining things or someone else convinced her that Keefer was threatening to have her daughter taken away?"

"Or maybe she was getting anonymous threats?" I speculated. "Online or whatever. And she just assumed Keefer was the one behind it?"

"For what purpose?"

"That's the twenty-million-dollar question. If we knew the why then we could figure out the who."

"It's probably worth talking to her aunt and uncle again. They might be able to add something more."

"Maybe Dylan, also?"

"Probably him, too," he said glumly.

I sensed the chief was blaming himself for not having done more to stop Keefer five years earlier. It made me hesitate a moment before sharing my next thought. "I wished I'd thought to also ask Keefer about Amka while I had him on the line."

"You don't think . . ."

I'd been thinking about it almost nonstop since I hung up. "Remember how on that final call to David, Amka told him that Brianna 'understood'? And when I was interviewing Rick, he suggested the two girls shared some kind of deep, dark secret?"

"You think Keefer Willesdon was that secret?"

"It would make a ton of sense, Chief."

"Son of a bitch," Natan repeated for a third time.

"I tried phoning Keefer back, but he wouldn't take my call."

"Doubt he'll take anyone's calls from now on." Natan shook his head. "He was always too damn smooth . . ."

"The damage he's done . . ." I could feel my neck and cheeks heating. "Could you imagine how vulnerable some impressionable fifteen- or sixteen-year-old would be to a charismatic teacher like that? Amy's mom was right. The guy's a total predator."

Natan didn't comment, but his eyes were pained as he turned his head to look out the window.

Wanting to change the subject for his sake as much as mine, I asked, "Any leads on Rick's murder?"

"Nothing concrete. We've seized rifles from both Eddie Snyder and Tom Obed. It might take a while to get a ballistics match back from Anchorage."

"What about Jim and Cupun?"

"They're not saying squat."

"Manny doesn't seem like a guy who'd intimidate a lot of people."

"Don't fall for his harmless city-boy-trapped-in-the-wild act," Natan said, turning back. "Manny is still a suspect in a shooting of one of Eddie's crew, a couple years back. We could never pin it on him, but we think it's the reason he got knifed."

"This town," I said, wondering for the umpteenth time what I was still doing here.

"It's not all bad, Taylor. Look how the community is rallying around the Obeds. Tom told me they ran out of freezer space for all the food folks brought over."

"Generous folk."

Natan shrugged. "By the way, Dr. Lincoln in Philadelphia called me back."

"Yeah? What did you make of him?"

"He's no fan of Dr. Gutiérrez."

"I'm not much of one myself, anymore, either," I said. "Javier hasn't leveled with us since the second he landed here. And I don't buy that he flew all the way up because he was worried about his patient."

"You think he came to protect his interest in that medication?"

"Yeah. Basically, to bury the bodies." The second I mentioned "bodies," something occurred to me. "You know, Javier might've been the very last person to have seen David alive."

Natan folded his arms. "And?"

"Javier tried—and failed—to blackmail Dr. Lincoln. What if he pulled something similar on David?"

"What if he did?"

"Javier's sporting a huge bruise on his jaw. He admitted David cuffed him with his casted arm. What if . . . what if the fight didn't end there?"

"You were in David's room with me, Taylor. It was an overdose."

"But aren't there ways to stage those?"

"Staging suicides, maybe. But an overdose on the victim's own medications?"

"I'm just brainstorming here, Chief." The idea chilled me, but once I'd lifted the manhole cover into this sewer, I couldn't stop from climbing down into it. "What if Javier spiked David's drink with that date rape drug—"

"GHB?"

"Yeah. Liquid ecstasy, right? Rick told me there was a demand for it in town."

"We already got the toxicology screen. They didn't find any GHB."

"I guess not, huh?" I said, feeling a bit deflated.

"It's a good theory. But at some point you just have to—"

"Hey, Chief." Kai appeared in the open doorway. "Got a minute?"

I saw that he wasn't alone. Beside him stood a skinny boy with short spiky hair who barely reached the level of the detective's chest. I recognized the shy ten-year-old immediately. Jesse was the youngest of the five Adjuk boys. His parents were kind and hard-working but struggled at times to feed their large clan. I'd had to help secure food and housing supplementation on a few occasions since I'd come to town.

"Hello, Jesse," I said with a big smile, as he and Kai joined us inside in the office. "How are you doing?"

"Hi," he said softly without making eye contact.

Kai placed a hand on Jesse's head and mussed his hair affectionately. "Jesse has some vital information for us."

"Do you, Jesse?" Natan asked.

"I guess," Jesse mumbled.

"Jesse was playing soccer yesterday across from the station, when the . . . incident happened," Kai said. "He's a bit of a soccer star. His mom tells him he might go pro one day soon."

"As if!" Jesse said with a pleased snort.

Kai looked down at him. "Why don't you tell Taylor and the chief what you saw yesterday?"

Jesses scratched his head. "Can you say it?"

"Would be better if it came from you," Kai said.

I winked at Jesse. "And we'd way rather hear you talk than Detective Kai."

Jesse shrugged. "There's a good patch between the houses over there." He thumbed toward the window. "Mr. Qayaq, my coach, he lives in one of them. He told me it's OK to practice there. I set up a goal against his wall. And I was taking penalty kicks. That's when I heard them."

"The bangs?" Kai encouraged.

Jesse nodded. "Rifle shots. I know rifle shots. I've hunted with Dad and my brothers. The shots, they sounded close, but I couldn't tell where."

"What did you do?"

"Everyone was running around out front of the police station." He looked down and his voice went quieter. "It freaked me out. I . . . I hid."

"Very smart, Jesse," Natan said. "Where did you hide?"

"Mr. Qayaq is working on his old fishing boat out back of his house. I kind of squeezed in behind the hull."

"Good thinking. And then what?"

"I waited awhile. To make sure it was like . . . safe. I was just about to go home when I saw him. He crawled out from under the truck in the Katoos' yard."

"Who crawled out?"

Jesse hesitated a minute and Kai gave him an encouraging pat on the shoulder. "Mr. Obed," he said.

My heart sank. "You sure, Jesse?" I asked.

"Yeah, he hunts with my dad sometimes."

"And Mr. Obed had his rifle?" Natan asked.

"Yeah, he kind of stopped and strapped it over his shoulder. Then he ran off in the other direction."

CHAPTER 31

I stopped by Evan's clinic just after 6:30 p.m. He was so focused on the computer screen that it took him a moment to notice me standing in the doorway to his office. Once he did, he yanked his glasses off and grinned.

"Twice in one day, Taylor? Didn't think I had that kind of luck."

I appreciated how, with one quick greeting, Evan wiped away the lingering awkwardness from our breakfast discussion. "I'm almost embarrassed to tell you that I need to pick your brain a bit more. Is now an OK time?"

"Perfect. Just finishing my charting." He motioned to the chair across from him. "What now? You need me to explain the second law of thermodynamics?"

"No." I laughed, as I sat down across from him. "Mr. Fischer tried that a couple times in junior year chemistry. A total lost cause."

His smile disappeared. "You heard they arrested Tom Obed, huh?"

"I did."

"To lose both daughters to suicide?" Evan blew out his lips. "Terrible. Would probably drive anyone mad. Besides, Tom blamed Rick for everything that happened to Amka."

"The drug use?"

"That. Her suicide. All of it. Tom's as stoic as they come, but the happiest I've ever seen him was right after Amka broke up with Rick last year. He thought she was finally 'on the path,' as he put it."

"The collateral damage just doesn't end. Ever since Brianna . . . it's like one tragedy fuels the next."

Evan rubbed his eye. "Sure seems that way, doesn't it?"

"I actually came to ask you another medical question. Well, more of a pharmaceutical one."

"Fire away." He chuckled. "Ask old Alexa here."

"Yeah, that's you. For all things medical, at least." I cleared my throat. "Do you think a suicide could be staged? Specifically, an overdose like David's?"

"What . . . what are you talking about?"

"Humor me," I said. "It's a wild hypothesis but hear me out. We know Javier has been less than honest about what he's been up to. Let's say he did come here because David was asking too many questions about Ketopram and its connection to the recent suicides."

Evan nodded, but his expression remained deeply skeptical. "All right."

"Javier was trying to talk David out of digging any deeper into Ketopram. Both of them told me as much. And judging from the bruise on Javier's cheek, I think we can assume the discussion didn't go so well."

"Taylor . . ."

"Javier was staying just down the hall from David. And he might be the last person to have seen him alive."

"How would Javier force David to swallow four different bottles of pills?"

That was the sticking point in my scenario. "What if he drugged him first?" I speculated. "And then, when David was totally out of it, Javier somehow coaxed him into swallowing the pills?"

"Pretty weak, Taylor," Evan said. He picked up a pen and waved it in the air. "First of all, what would he have drugged him with?"

"Something like GHB? I know it didn't show up in his toxicology screen—"

"Exactly." He tapped the pen on the desk.

"OK, what about one of the other drugs they found in his system like the hydra . . . what's it again?"

"Hydromorphone." Evan shook his head. "You can't roofie someone with it. You'd have to dissolve a huge number of pills in their drink. He would've tasted it in one sip. Besides, the drug just doesn't work that way. The onset would be way too slow." The pen clicked on the desk, as if keeping time.

"You don't see any way that Javier could've staged David's overdose?"

"No. Honestly, I really don't."

"Ugh," I groaned. "Something's off about the whole situation."

After a moment, Evan tossed the pen aside and reached a hand across the table toward my arm but stopped a few inches short. "I get it, Taylor. You've lost people you care about. You want to make some sense of their deaths. I would love to, too. But it doesn't always work that way."

He was right. But I couldn't let it go that easily. I needed to speak to Javier again. I needed to hear it from his lips.

"Thanks, Evan," I said, as I stood up from the chair.

Still seated, he looked up at me with a sad smile. "You definitely look as if you could use a drink. And I'd invite you for one, but after our chat this morning . . ."

"Soon, maybe. Right now, an early night is what I need more than anything."

I headed out to my truck, intending to go straight home, eat dinner, and crawl into bed. My phone rang before I'd barely pulled away from the clinic. I answered as soon as I saw Kai's name on the call display.

"Whereabouts are you?" he asked.

"Just heading home."

"You think you could stop by the station?"

"What's up?"

"Tom Obed. He wants to talk to you."

"To me?"

"Yes, you."

The idea made me uneasy. In the past week, Tom had lost his second daughter and killed her boyfriend in retribution. I wasn't sure how I felt about seeing him. But I had no real choice. It was my job.

Kai met me inside the station and guided me to the interview room, where Tom was waiting, dressed in a brown jumpsuit and handcuffed to the table.

"Hi, Mr. Obed." Not knowing what else to say, I added, "How are you doing?"

He shrugged indifferently.

"The detective said you wanted to speak to me," I said.

"You offered to help."

"I did. And I meant it."

He nodded. "It's my wife."

"How can I help with Mrs. Obed?"

"The arthritis. It's bad. Some days she can't even get out of bed."

"That must be so hard. I'm sorry." Tom hadn't let me visit his wife in months, but the last time I had seen her, it was obvious how badly the rheumatoid arthritis had ravaged her. Her fingers were knobby and angled to the point of disfigurement. And her back was so stooped that she resembled a hunchback.

"Amka and me, we did the cooking. And the cleaning." Tom looked away in embarrassment. "Sometimes—on the bad days—we needed to even help her with her washing and . . . the bathroom. She can't be alone."

"I can help, Mr. Obed."

"How?"

"I'll ensure she has a home-care worker visiting her twice a day."

"They can help her with those things?"

"Sure," I said with an encouraging smile. "We call them ADLs—activities of daily living. Our home-care workers do it all the time for folks with conditions like your wife's."

"Amka and I were with her most of the day. What if she still can't manage?"

"Hopefully, with help, she will. But if not, we can move her to the assisted living facility in Browerville. It's nice there. People have their own apartments, but there are nurses and caregivers on-site around the clock." Anticipating his next question, I added, "The government covers the costs."

"Good." He nodded, satisfied. "That's good."

I leaned forward. "There's something I wanted to ask you, Mr. Obed."

"I already told the cops everything."

"No, it's not related to the shooting. It's about Amka."

"Amka?" he asked warily.

"Do you remember a teacher of hers from high school by the name of Mr. Willesdon? Keefer Willesdon?"

"Yeah, I remember him."

"What do you remember about him?"

"She liked him. A lot." He frowned. "Why does that matter now?"

I had to bite my tongue before I said too much. After all Tom had been through and might still be facing, it seemed cruel to suggest to him that his daughter might have been molested before her death by one of her teachers. "His name has come up in relation to another student at school. I'm just trying to gather some background info."

Tom accepted the explanation with a disinterested shrug. "Because of him, Amka got interested in poetry. She even brought home some Iñupiat poems. Her mom, she cried when Amka read them to us." He grunted. "You hear about teachers making a difference. But he was the only one who ever really tried. With either of my girls."

"Tried how?"

"Amka struggled in a few subjects. Mr. Willesdon took a real interest in her. He even used to take time to tutor her after school and on weekends. Sometimes he'd even send food home with her for us."

My heart sank listening to him. The more gratitude he expressed for the teacher, the more my suspicions hardened that the bastard must have seduced Amka, as well.

"All those whites who pretend to care about us," Tom continued. "It's lip service for most of them. There's only a few like Mr. Willesdon and maybe Dr. Harman who make any real effort."

His comment made it even worse. I was about to get up, when he said, "I would've told you when you came by the last time."

"Told me what, Mr. Obed?"

"That I shot him."

"Oh."

"Don't regret it. Don't care who knows. The only reason I didn't admit it then was 'cause I was worried about my wife."

"We'll look after her, Mr. Obed. I promise."

"That boy destroyed my Amka," Tom said, no longer even looking at me. "He got her into the drugs. He got her into trouble. And he threw her out of that boat. What he got, he deserved."

Maybe he did. I wasn't certain of much at this point.

Tom didn't move as I bid him goodbye and rose from my chair.

Kai was waiting outside the room. He didn't comment on the interview, even though I knew the room was monitored and he'd been listening.

"What now?" I asked Kai.

"Tom's already confessed," Kai said. "Hopefully, he will plead out with the state's attorney. With mitigating circumstances, maybe he'll only get ten years or less."

"Ten years," I muttered.

"He gunned down an unarmed man, Taylor."

"I suppose."

Kai looked at me shyly. "Have you got . . . er . . . dinner plans?"

"I do." I touched his arm. "Leftovers. And then half an episode—max—of my Netflix series in bed."

"Yeah, I'm on a similar program," he said casually, but I could see that he was putting on a brave face.

"Enjoy," I said, turning for the door. "Catch up tomorrow."

As I headed out to my truck, I wondered if I'd come across as too dismissive of his offer. But I wasn't about to start dating Kai. Or Evan. Much as I liked and respected them both as friends, I hadn't moved here to find a new partner. I'd come only to escape my previous life.

As I was opening the door to my truck, my phone rang again. When I saw "private caller" on the screen, I almost didn't answer. But just as it reached the fourth ring, the curiosity got the better of me.

"Hello, Taylor," Javier said in his silky tone. "I was just calling to say goodbye."

"You're still in Utqiagvik?"

"Not by choice. My flight had technical problems. Something to do with one of the cargo bay doors not closing. Trust me, I'd be happy to fly out of here with an open door, but apparently the pilot had misgivings."

"Can't blame him." I forced a laugh.

"Regardless, I have a tiny token of appreciation for you. For all you've done, especially for David. Why don't I just drop it off with you this evening?"

The last thing I wanted was to have Javier in my home. But I did want to speak to him. "Easier if I just come to you."

CHAPTER 32

At least there's a fire burning tonight, I thought as I joined Javier in front of the hotel's fireplace. Normally, I would've mustered a buoyant façade for him. Not today. Javier must've been aware of my frostiness from how I chose the chair farthest away from his, leaving an empty one between us. But he appeared as friendly as ever, greeting me with a warm hello and holding up a bagged gift.

I reluctantly accepted it and pulled out a weighty, mug-sized soapstone carving from inside. As I turned the smooth, dark sculpture over in my hand, I couldn't help but admire the craftsmanship. It captured a bear in mid-step, somehow conveying the sense of the animal in motion. I'd perused the local Indigenous art studios in town enough to know that a carving like this would have been expensive.

"This isn't necessary, Javier," I said.

"It's well deserved." He smiled. "If David were here, I'm sure he would've agreed."

I held my tongue and merely nodded.

"How are you managing, Taylor?" he asked, eyeing me with a look that he must have thought passed for genuine concern.

"I'm doing OK, thank you. And you?"

"Same." He sighed. "I miss my friend, though."

"And your patient, too."

"David was always my friend, first and foremost."

"Still, I imagine you must feel a lot of guilt."

Javier frowned. "Guilt?"

"For losing a patient that way," I said. "Especially when the antidepressant you prescribed him might've contributed to his death."

He viewed me silently for a few seconds. "Ketopram overdoses are not lethal, Taylor. It was the other drugs that killed him."

"But the Ketopram might've pushed him to overdose."

Javier closed his eyes and shook his head. "Didn't we already have this conversation?"

"We had *a* conversation about Ketopram."

"And I think I told you David had stopped taking his antidepressant."

"Yup. And I told you that his wife—also a psychiatrist—said it wouldn't have worn off in just a couple of days."

He tilted his head. "Is there something more you want to say, Taylor?"

"Guess who was the last person to ever to speak to David? At least over the phone."

Javier glanced skyward. "How could I know that?"

"The police do. They have the records."

"I'll play along. Who?"

"Dr. Avery Lincoln."

If Javier was surprised, he didn't show it. "I can only imagine what Avery and David discussed."

"Sounds like they spent most of their time discussing you. Dr. Lincoln told me as much himself."

"Did he?"

"He also told me about that study regarding the dangers of Ketopram." I paused, before adding, "The one you had buried."

"I didn't bury it," Javier said calmly. "The study's sponsor, Pierson Pharmaceuticals, did that."

"Oh, right," I said. "Was it also the drug company that called up Dr. Lincoln to blackmail him into keeping his mouth shut?"

"No." He looked me dead in the eyes. "That was me."

Neither of us said a word for a few taut seconds.

"You mind telling me why?" I asked.

"Primarily for David's sake."

"For David? Seriously?"

"The study in question had a single unexpected death when it was aborted. A suicide. In a patient who never should've been enrolled in the first place. I told David all of this. But he couldn't let it be. He tracked down Avery." Javier exhaled heavily. "To be frank, David had become paranoid about Ketopram. He kept seeing conspiracies and cover-ups everywhere that simply didn't exist."

"You're sure they didn't exist?" I asked.

"Beyond a doubt."

"So—as David's psychiatrist—you thought what? The best approach would be to call up a colleague and manipulate him into lying to David?"

"You're taking it all out of context," he snapped.

"Am I?"

"You have to understand," Javier said, staring down at his hands, which were tightly clasped together. "I could see David's depression was spiraling out of control. And his fixation on Ketopram was making him worse. Much worse. Avery had no right to tell David anything about that study. Legally or otherwise."

"This is all Dr. Lincoln's fault?"

"I called Avery, yes. And I tried to reason with him. But as always, he was so damn self-righteous. So yes, I threatened to dredge up the NDA to stop all this nonsense. To try to get Avery to help quell, not fuel, David's obsession with Ketopram. Because by that point, David was bordering on delusional."

Javier made it all sound so innocent. So believable. But I couldn't shake the sense that I was being played. "So this had nothing to do with you protecting your own interests in Ketopram and Pierson Pharmaceuticals?"

Javier's eyes narrowed. "My interests?"

"Aren't you financially invested in the success of this drug? Through paid appearances and shares and stuff?"

Javier broke off the eye contact. "Yes, well, I do have an educational stipend from Pierson," he said. "Once I saw how effective the medication was, of course I invested in the company. I saw huge potential in it. I would've been a fool not to put my money where my mouth was."

"You must have stood to lose a fortune if the news broke that the drug was dangerous."

"Not a fortune, no." He hesitated. "But not an insignificant amount either."

"Is that why you came to Utqiagvik, Javier?" Without even thinking about it, I shook a finger at him. "To protect your investment in Ketopram?"

"I came here because I was worried about my friend," he said evenly.

"OK, so maybe you came to kill two birds with one stone then?"

He glared at me. "That's a distasteful idiom to use in this case."

"But it's true, isn't it?"

"I have been studying this drug for three years, Taylor. I know it inside and out. I can't explain the recent cluster of deaths in this town. But I'm damn certain it's not because of some out-of-the-blue, brand-new side effect that only impacts people living in the Arctic!"

"You're that certain?"

"I would bet my life on it."

"Is yours the only life you'd be willing to bet?"

He gaped at me. "You're not suggesting . . ."

"What am I supposed to think?"

He folded his arms across his chest. "You think my modest investment in this medication would matter so much to me that I would forgo every ethical and legal responsibility I have as a doctor? As a human being, as well?"

"I have no fucking idea what to think!" The emotion overwhelmed me. I wanted to smash the sculpture he had given me into the fireplace. "Look at all the corpses piling up over this."

"David was my best friend. I'd do anything to get him back." His voice cracked. "But it doesn't mean there's some grand, tidy explanation for everything. Some pill to blame it all on."

He was the second doctor this evening to basically tell me the same. But I wasn't going to let him off so easily. "You tried to blackmail the very last person to call David. You were also the last person to see him alive. And when you did, he punched you in the face. And after his death, you've lingered here for days for no apparent reason. So many coincidences."

"This is irrational, Taylor. You're acting as paranoid as David did."

"Have you stuck around here to clean up the mess around Ketopram, Javier?"

"Totally irrational. A folie à deux! You're sharing his delusion."

"And was David's death part of that cleanup?"

CHAPTER 33

I woke up early, unexpectedly energized after the confrontation with Javier. I'd stormed out of the hotel with my unanswered accusation hanging thick in the air. I'd left as convinced as ever that Javier had come to town to protect his own interest in Ketopram. But I hadn't answered the one question that mattered most: Had Javier also intended to save David or to silence him?

Even my morning glass of kombucha and the most focused meditation session I'd managed in a week didn't bring clarity. But one thing I'd already decided was that I wasn't going to take the word of anyone else—not the chief, not Evan, and especially not Javier—that a suicide like David's couldn't be staged.

I dove into research on my laptop. The hits came fast and furious. I found numerous examples of murders that were made to look accidental through opioid overdoses. But most of those involved heroin or fentanyl, usually in known drug users, while the only opioid found in David's blood had been hydromorphone. Maybe it would've been impossible to spike a drink with that much hydromorphone, but reading on, I discovered it also came in an injectable form. Could Javier have surprised David by jabbing him with a needleful? No one had done an autopsy. Had anyone even checked David for needle marks?

But I cooled on that theory once I learned it would take a minimum of fifteen minutes for an injection of hydromorphone to reach its maximum effect. Instead, I turned my attention to GHB. I struggled with some of the online technical descriptions. But there was no mistaking the conclusion on one national toxicology website, which read: "Gamma-hydroxybutyrate or GHB, also known by the street name of liquid ecstasy, has been an elusive drug to detect in toxicology screening due to its rapid dissipation from blood and urine."

Other websites concluded the same: there was no reliable way to check for GHB in a person's system hours after exposure. Despite the negative toxicology screen, David still could have been drugged with it prior to his death.

The phone rang, and I answered it absentmindedly, while still scanning the website.

"This Taylor?" the woman asked.

I immediately recognized the gravelly voice of Brianna's aunt. "Good morning, Kerry," I said.

"You were looking for me?"

I snapped the lid shut on my laptop. "Yes, thanks for getting back to me. How are you doing?"

"Is it true about Dr. Spears?" she asked. "Did he really kill himself?"

In my mind, the jury was still out on that question. "He took an overdose, yes."

Kerry breathed noisily on the line. "I didn't like the way the last visit went with you two. Not at all. All those horrible suggestions about Gus and me . . ." She paused. "But I know Dr. Spears cared about Bree. I could see that, for sure. I'm sorry he's dead."

"Me, too. Thank you, Kerry." Sensing she had let down her guard a little, I didn't want to miss the opening. "I was calling to ask you about a teacher of Brianna's. A Mr. Willesdon. He taught English at the high school."

She coughed. "Yeah, if you two didn't get me so upset last time we spoke, I might've said more when Dr. Spears asked."

"More about Mr. Willesdon?"

"He was Bree's favorite teacher. She was devastated when he just up and left."

"Brianna spent a lot of time with Mr. Willesdon?"

"She signed up for all his classes. But Bree never talked too much about school. And as long she did her homework and her grades were OK, Gus and me, we gave her space. Kids that age, they need it." She wheezed. "Maybe too much space. If we'd known Dylan was going to knock her up . . ."

"Was Brianna already seeing Dylan by the time Mr. Willesdon left?" I asked, more to clarify the timeline for myself.

"Before then. Why are you so interested in Mr. Willesdon?" Suspicion crept into her tone. "Are you thinking something was going on . . . ?"

I chose my words carefully. "Mr. Willesdon seduced a girl in the grade below Brianna's. And we have reason to believe your niece was another one of his victims."

"Jesus Christ!"

"I'm sorry, Kerry."

"That . . . bastard."

"It would've been early in her pregnancy when Mr. Willesdon left, right?"

"Yeah, around then. I guess. Late in the winter of her senior year." Kerry paused to let out another rattling cough. "Hold on. You don't think he could've been Nevaeh's dad, do you?"

"I'm not sure, Kerry." I hesitated. "It's possible."

"When he left . . . that was right about the time I got worried about Bree. The depression and all."

"That must've been tough."

"Very. Especially on the night she ended up in the ER."

"The ER? Which night was that?"

"Early April of her senior year. She was about four months pregnant then."

"What happened, Kerry?"

"She overdosed on some pills," she said. "Just a handful of vitamins and Tylenol tablets. Bree swore she wasn't trying to kill herself. Just wanted to end the pregnancy. But Dr. Harman, he was wonderful. He pumped her stomach or what have you. And he kept a real close eye on her for the rest of the pregnancy."

"And Brianna improved after that?"

"A lot. She did well for a year or more. And then her mood got dark again. Real dark. Even before Dylan left. When Nevaeh was about six months or so."

I calculated the timing in my head, realizing the second depressive episode would've roughly coincided with when Brianna had sent Keefer that email. "Kerry, I spoke to Mr. Willesdon."

"You spoke to him?" The surprise launched another coughing fit.

"Yes. He's teaching in South Korea now."

"What did he have to say for himself?"

"He basically admitted to having seduced Brianna."

Kerry didn't say anything, but her breathing grew more ragged.

"He also told me Brianna emailed him after Nevaeh was born. He made it sound as if she was bargaining with him—"

"*Bargaining?*"

"Brianna thought Willesdon was trying to have the authorities take Nevaeh from her."

"Why? Bree was a good mom. Always!" Kerry cried. "Why would the son of a bitch threaten her like that?"

"That's the strangest part. Willesdon swears he didn't even know Brianna had a child."

"Then why did Bree think he was trying to have Nevaeh taken away?"

"No idea," I sighed. "But do you remember any kind of threat to her custody back then?"

"No," Kerry said. "Then again, you're making me feel like I didn't know anything that was going on in my niece's life."

"I don't mean to," I soothed. "I'm sure Brianna felt ashamed over what happened. Victims around that age usually do. That's why she hid it from you, I'm sure."

Kerry went silent for a few seconds. "Maybe Bree did mention something . . ."

I sat up in my chair. "About custody?"

"I do remember her asking me one time if a child could be taken from a single mother if the father demanded it. I told her Dylan would never dream of doing that."

"She didn't explain why she was asking?"

"No. She never brought it up again. And I never thought nothing of it."

I saw no point in terrorizing Kerry with more questions about Brianna and Keefer. So instead I asked, "How's Nevaeh doing?"

"All right, I suppose. But she's not the happy-go-lucky kid she used to be."

"It's going to take time, Kerry."

"And that child's imagination!"

"What about it?"

"She had a nightmare a few nights back. She keeps talking about it. Something to do with a bad man who was wrestling her mommy."

"Wrestling?"

"Yeah, wrestling. It really scared her, too. She's come into our room every night since. We've had to set up a little mattress for her beside our bed." Kerry wheezed a breath or two. "I'm no psychologist or nothing, but I think Nevaeh's looking for some kind of explanation for what happened to her mom."

"Is Nevaeh home now, Kerry?"

"No, she's at day care all morning. We send her there to be around other kids."

"Could I come see her this afternoon?"

"Yeah, all right. Not until after two."

"Perfect. I'll see you then."

As soon as I hung up, I scrolled through my recent calls until I found Dylan's number. He didn't pick up, so I texted him a message asking to call me.

I opened my laptop and glanced at the website on the screen. I thought about what Rick had told me about the prominent local who had a taste for GHB. Since I couldn't ask him, I decided to go to the next closest source.

I drove over to Eddie's house. I braced myself at the door for another confrontation, but his girlfriend answered. The bruise above her eye had yellowed but was no less prominent. "Hi, Rita. Is Eddie home?"

"Nah. He's hunting. Or fishing, maybe? Whatever." She looked skyward. "You know boys. They always wanna kill stuff."

"When will he be back?"

She snorted a laugh. "Like he'd tell me."

I motioned to her forehead. "Did Eddie do that to you?"

"I don't need no social worker interfering!" Rita said, and shut the door in my face.

I got back in my truck and drove to Manny's place. He answered his door wearing a shiny track suit and a welcoming grin. "Hello, Taylor." He waved me inside and guided me to the living room couch. "Word is they've arrested Rick's killer."

"Yeah."

"So how can I help today?" he asked with a chuckle. "You think maybe I kidnapped the Lindbergh baby?"

I didn't understand the reference, but I wasn't interested. "Tell me about GHB."

Manny scrunched his nose. "I don't recommend it. I think you'd have far more fun on molly."

"Rick told me there was a good supply in town."

Manny folded his arms, but his smile persisted. "Not sure what that would have to do with me. Even if I were in the illicit substance trade, I'd know better than to fraternize with members of Eddie's crew."

"How did Rick come to owe you money?"

"There you go again with that same bizarre theory," Manny said. "Who told you he owed me?"

"Eddie."

Manny only rolled his eyes.

"Rick didn't owe you money?"

"As if I would lend him . . . no, better not. It's never good to speak ill of the dead."

"The last time I saw Rick, he mentioned some local high roller who bought a lot of GHB," I said.

"Not sure how I can help you there." He shrugged. "Eddie doesn't exactly post his clientele list."

"Enough, Manny!" I snapped. "I'm not a cop. I'm not here to bust your balls about drug trafficking. I'm looking for someone specific."

"OK, OK! A high roller who likes GHB? That's not narrowing it down much."

"Why do you say that?"

"Who do you think buys most of the drugs in this town? Could be anybody. A politician, a professional, a judge, an exec with the oil company . . . Take your pick."

"All right. How hard would it be for someone from out of town to get their hands on GHB here?" I asked, thinking of Javier.

"Like a tourist?"

"Yeah, sort of."

"Not that hard." He frowned. "But why would they even bother to buy it here?"

"Where else would they get it?"

"Have you ever seen liquid ecstasy? It's a clear, odorless liquid. Undetectable. A single cc does the trick. Ten ccs gets you a party. And it's even more plentiful in Anchorage."

"What about getting it through TSA at airport security?"

He waved away my concern. "It would be as easy to carry up here as toothpaste. You could fill your contact lens container with enough of it to kill an elephant or two."

CHAPTER 34

Natan sat back behind his desk and folded his arms. "Just because GHB wasn't picked up on the tox screen doesn't mean that it was in David's system."

"I'm only saying it's possible," I said.

"And," Kai added from where he sat beside me, "just 'cause you don't want him to have taken his own life doesn't mean he didn't."

Kai hadn't made eye contact me with since I'd walked into the office. If I'd known he was going to take my turndown as personally as he had, I would've been gentler. Now it was too late to avoid the awkward tension between us.

"Isn't it worth asking the ME to double-check, Chief?" I persisted. "I read online that there are special lab tests that are better at detecting GHB, but they have to look specifically for the drug."

Natan studied me for a moment. "If I ask the ME to run this test—and who knows if he'll even agree to—then you'll let it go?"

"If it's negative." I brought a hand to my chest. "Promise."

"You did a good job exposing that teacher, Taylor." Natan sighed. "But we can't go down every rabbit hole that pops up. For one thing, we don't have the manpower."

"And there's only one detective on this force," Kai muttered, still refusing to look at me.

"Just the screen for GHB," I said as I stood up. "Then I'll leave it alone. I swear."

I left the station a lot less convinced than I had been on arrival. I wondered whether Javier truly had been gaslighting me or if I really was just going down a rabbit hole. Was I so desperate to give meaning to three random suicides that I was investing imaginary powers into one flawed pill?

I drove over to my office. Work was piling up, but I struggled to concentrate on it. I slogged through the inbox of my government email account, firing off brief responses without spell-checking them and probably committing a few grammatical war crimes along the way.

Once I'd sent the last email, I called the newest set of foster parents who had taken in the two Davidson children. I was relieved to hear that there were no new incidents and the kids were behaving, which I hoped also meant they were beginning to feel safe.

After I'd managed to catch up on my paperwork, I picked up my cell phone and clicked open my Instagram app to distract my dark thoughts. I hadn't checked my account in days, which was unusual for me. I didn't post much, if at all, but I enjoyed following updates from friends in California. It gave me a sense of connection to my past life. But even that link was growing tenuous as more and more wedding and baby photos popped up on the screen, distancing me even further from that world.

Today was no exception. Sarah, one of my best friends from college, had just posted shots of her still glistening newborn son. The one photo with her husband, Phil, leaning over her hospital bed and cradling the baby with the cheesiest grin on his bearded face almost made me tear up. Phil and Sarah embodied happiness. He'd been a classmate of Gabe's. We had set them up over a dinner party that we'd hosted for the sole purpose of introducing them. Sarah sent me a note every year on their anniversary to remind me. Last year, when she and Phil had a rare fight on that day, she'd written "thanks for nothing," and then added smiling and kissing emojis.

The memory of that dinner inspired me to open Gabe's page for the first time in months. The most recent photo showed Teresa and him, arms draped over shoulders, all smiles as they stood atop some trail I didn't recognize. I couldn't tell if I was imaging a slight baby bump through Teresa's T-shirt. Despite my pang of melancholy, I knew I could no better stomach the thought of Gabe feeding me or pushing me in a wheelchair now than I could on the day I'd learned of my mom's diagnosis. And if I had gone on to develop Huntington's disease, the physical disability would have been the least of our issues. Even worse would have been the aggressiveness, the dementia, and the slow withering of the soul—all of which I'd seen my mom through. Gabe would have stayed, no matter what. And the idea of that still seemed worse than anything.

In need of a distraction, I picked up the phone and tried Dylan again. He answered on the fourth ring. "Something wrong with Nevaeh?" was the first thing he asked.

"No. She's OK."

"What's up?"

"I have a couple more questions about Brianna."

"More?" he groaned. "What's the point?"

"It won't take long, Dylan. Some things have come to light that I'm just following up on."

"OK," he muttered warily.

"Remember when you told me about Brianna's depression? How she pushed you away and all?"

"Yeah."

"During that time, Dylan, did she ever seem worried about losing Nevaeh?"

"Like . . . during the pregnancy?"

"No. After Nevaeh was born. Was she ever worried about someone trying to take Nevaeh from her?"

He went quiet on the line for a moment. "Yeah."

"How so?"

"Just before I left . . . she went fucking mental on me. Told me
that if I ever tried to take Nevaeh, she would cut my nuts off."

"Were you threatening to take Nevaeh?"

"Take her where?" he said. "Once Bree booted me out, I didn't
have a roof over my head. I slept in my truck for a couple weeks
before I finally made way down to Prudhoe Bay."

"I wonder why she thought you planned to take Nevaeh."

"How should I know? That depression made Bree crazy."

"You don't think there could've been any other reason?" I asked.

"Like what?"

"Someone threatening her?"

"Threatening? Come on." But he paused a moment. "I'll say this,
she seemed fucking terrified. Like she really did believe she was
going to lose the baby."

"Maybe someone made her believe that?"

"I don't know."

"No one comes to mind?"

"Who? Bree stayed at home with Nevaeh twenty-four-seven
back then. Except maybe to see her aunt and uncle or go to the store
or appointments or whatever, she just never left."

"Not even to see friends like Amka?"

"No one. Bree just changed, OK? Didn't want anything to do
with me or anyone else. It was so weird . . ."

"How so, Dylan?"

"When we first started hanging out in junior year, it happened so
quick. Like she was pregnant the first week we hooked up. Almost,
the very first time we . . ."

Because she was already pregnant by Keefer. But I kept the
thought to myself. I wondered if Brianna anticipated the scandal

that would've followed if her affair with her teacher had come to light. Had she just hooked up with Dylan to silence any rumors and ensure she would be able to keep the child?

"Then, after the first couple months of the pregnancy, she got really sad," Dylan continued. "Especially after Mr. Willesdon left. But she got over it. She was doing good. Like we were a family. And then . . ." He uttered a noise that sounded like a gunshot. "The depression hit her again. She just locked herself and Nevaeh at home. She didn't even want me around."

"That must've been hard on you, Dylan."

"No shit," he said, sounding embarrassed. "What about Gus? He always creeped me out. Did you check him out?"

"We did," I said. "I don't think he was involved."

"You still think someone was abusing Bree?"

I didn't have the heart to tell Dylan about Brianna and her teacher. There didn't seem to be any point, since Keefer wasn't the person threatening to have her daughter taken away. "We're still working on that."

"Utqiagvik's a tiny town," he grunted. "If it's all true—the abuse and the threats to have Nevaeh taken away—then it was probably the same fucking person, right?"

CHAPTER 35

Kerry met me at her front door. "Gus is out at the shop," she announced, as if his absence needed an explanation.

We stood at the doorway in awkward silence for a few seconds before she cleared her throat and said, "Don't see how talking about her nightmare any more than Nevaeh already does will help the child."

"I get it, Kerry," I said. "But I used to work with traumatized kids back in California. Kids who lived through shootings and stuff. We found that talking it out through play often helped them."

"Helped them how?"

"Kind of like venting," I said. "Allows them to express their feelings. The theory is it will help prevent the trauma from festering."

"Some theory," Kerry said with a skeptical snort, but she turned away from the door and led me in.

I followed her into the living room. The cigarette stench was even stronger than on my previous visit. But aside from the pile of toys Nevaeh was playing with on the carpet in front of the couch, the place was otherwise immaculate. The girl was so absorbed in strapping her doll into the toy stroller that she didn't look up as I knelt beside her.

"Hi, Tiger," I said.

"I'm not a tiger," Nevaeh mumbled, fiddling with the straps on the stroller.

"A bear, then?" I held up my hands, hooked my fingers into claws, and made a roaring noise.

Nevaeh's lips flickered with a smile. "Not a bear."

"What kind of animal are you then?"

"A people kind," she said, satisfied her doll was strapped in.

I ran a finger over the straps. "She's all buckled in, safe and sound. Are we going to take her for a stroll?"

Nevaeh nodded.

"What's her name?" I asked.

"Kallik."

"That's pretty. How did you choose that name?"

"Auntie Amka gave her to me."

"It means lightning in Iñupiat, doesn't it, Nev?" Kerry said, exhaling smoke from where she sat at the kitchen counter with a cigarette in hand, watching us intently.

Nevaeh shrugged.

"That was nice of Amka," I said, with a pang of sadness.

Nevaeh picked up a toy milk bottle and carefully positioned its plastic nipple between the doll's open lips. Then she rested the bottle between the doll's movable arms. "Auntie Amka was going to take me fishing again."

"She took you before?"

"We caught a salmon. This big." Nevaeh held her hands wide apart. "Auntie said it was the biggest one she ever saw."

"Wow, Nevaeh! That's incredible. Maybe you'll be a fisher when you grow up?"

Nevaeh turned her attention back to her doll, wrapping a miniature blanket over the stroller. "Amka's with Mommy now," she said matter-of-factly.

"In heaven, right, Nev?" Kerry said.

Nevaeh nodded without looking at her.

"That's good." I forced a smile. "Your auntie and your mommy can keep each other company."

Nevaeh pulled the bottle from the doll's lips, whipped off the blanket, and unstrapped her from the stroller.

It made my heart ache to watch Nevaeh fidget—clearly the talk of her mother was upsetting her—but I also wanted to keep her engaged and trusting me. "Hey, are we going to take Kallik for that walk now?" I asked.

"She's hungry now," Nevaeh said as she reached for a plastic high chair and removed the attached tray.

"We'd better feed her then," I said. "What does she eat?"

Nevaeh reached for a small toy bowl full of fused plastic pasta. "She likes macaroni."

"Me, too. Do you?"

"Yup."

I watched silently as Nevaeh moved the doll into the high chair, clicked the tray over its lap, and put the bowl of pasta in front of her. She picked up a plastic spoon and began to feed her doll imaginary spoonfuls.

"You know what, Nevaeh?" I asked. "Sometimes, I get really bad dreams."

Nevaeh continued to feed the doll without looking at me.

"Your great-aunt Kerry told me you get dreams, too."

Nevaeh didn't acknowledge the remark.

"These dreams, they scare me." I could feel Kerry's eyes on me as I spoke. "I really don't like to be alone when I get one. Do you ever have dreams like that?"

"They're called nightmares," Nevaeh murmured.

"Exactly, Nevaeh. Do you get nightmares?"

"Sometimes."

"Can you tell me about your nightmares?"

She dropped the spoon on the tray and looked over to her great-aunt.

Kerry's lips broke into a grandmotherly smile. "You can tell the lady, Nev."

Nevaeh looked down at her hands. "It's . . . Mommy."

"Is something happening to your mom?"

"The man, he's wrestling with her."

"You've seen wrestling before, Nevaeh?" I asked.

"Gus likes to watch WWF sometimes," Kerry grumbled. "Last time he let her watch a bit of it with him. I warned him not to . . ."

"What happens next, Nevaeh?" I asked.

"Mommy yells at the man to let her go," she said. "But he stays on top of her. He won't let her off the bed."

"Bed, Nevaeh?" A chill rippled through me. "Do you mean a mat? Or maybe a wrestling ring?"

"The bed," Nevaeh said quietly. "In Mommy's room."

"And you're in the room, too?"

She shook her head. "I opened the door. I was thirsty. I wanted Mommy to get me a drink."

This nightmare was beginning to feel all too real. "And the man who's wrestling your mom, Nevaeh? Do you know who he is?"

She didn't say anything for several seconds. I was about to prompt her, when she said, "The man who gave me the lollipop."

My jaw almost fell open. "He gave you a lollipop?"

"After the shot. He said if I didn't cry when I got the needle, he'd give me a lollipop." Nevaeh looked up at me wide-eyed. "I didn't cry."

CHAPTER 36

I was still reeling as I stepped back inside my office. Could what Nevaeh had told me have been right? Was Evan really the man she'd seen? I'd heard shocking revelations before from other kids that hadn't proven reliable. It could've been just a dream. It was possible Nevaeh wasn't even talking about him. I wanted to believe there was another explanation.

But I didn't.

The only real question in my mind was when had the assault Nevaeh witnessed taken place? Was it the night Brianna died?

I'd phoned Kai as soon as I left Kerry's house, but he didn't pick up. Rather than leave an incendiary message on his voicemail, I texted instead. "Need to talk to you. It's important." But I hadn't heard back from him yet. I wondered if he still felt slighted by me. If so, what a terrible time for him to be sulking.

I thought of Evan's words to David that evening he had made us dinner: "Anyone who moves up here is running away from something."

As soon as I sat at my desk, I began to research Evan. I used my government access to search the national database for criminal records on him but didn't uncover so much as a misdemeanor. I also scanned the web pages for the state medical boards in Indiana and Alaska, but I couldn't find any disciplinary judgments against him.

I broadened my search and Googled his name. There were a bunch of reviews, almost all of them glowing, on websites that rated medical doctors. I found a few online articles, and even a newspaper piece titled "The Tireless Life of an Arctic MD." All of them cited his dedication and conscientiousness. None of them mentioned any dubious practices or allegations of inappropriateness with patients.

I stumbled onto an old website that listed him as one of the clinic doctors at a family practice in Indianapolis. On a whim, I tried the number listed. After I tapped through the phone tree, a friendly-sounding woman with a thick southern accent answered. "Apple-tree Family Medicine. Rosalee speaking. How can I help you?"

I hesitated, since I had not even considered what to say. "Oh, hello. Is this the clinic where Dr. Harman worked?"

"Dr. Harman?" Rosalee laughed. "Darlin', Dr. Harman hasn't worked here in the better part of a decade."

Scouring my brain, I remembered how, when I sat on the interview panel to hire a new nursing director at the local hospital, I'd had to call some of the applicants' references. "Rosalee, my name is . . . Candace." I blurted the first name that came to mind. "I'm a social worker in the town of Utqiagvik, Alaska. Dr. Harman has put his name forward for the . . . um . . . chief of staff position at the Samuel Simmonds Memorial Hospital here. And I'm calling to track down a reference."

"No problem, darlin'. You're looking for Howard, I expect?"

"Howard?"

"Dr. Greenstein. Howard and Evan worked here together."

"Is Dr. Greenstein free now?"

"Believe so. Let me check."

Rosalee put me on hold. After about a minute or so, a man's voice boomed over the line. "Dr. Howard Greenstein."

"Thanks for taking my call, Dr. Greenstein." And then I repeated the same lie I'd told Rosalee.

"Old Evan's really moving up in the world. Chief of staff for the Utqiagvik General, huh?"

I was too focused to take offense at the condescension in his tone. "Truth to be told, he's the only applicant," I embellished. "But we still have to go through the motions, such as reference checks."

"More than happy to help. Fire away."

Although relieved by his unquestioning attitude, I still had to strain to remember some of the questions from my last interview panel. "Would you describe Dr. Harman as a good communicator?" I asked.

"I'd call him world-class," Howard said without hesitation. "He's one of those doctors who's loved equally by colleagues and patients alike because he's such a good listener."

"Thank you, that's helpful." I went on to ask questions on the random topics that I could recall, including conflict resolution skills, leadership abilities, and deportment with other staff. All of Howard's answers about Evan were enthusiastically affirmative.

Wondering if I was wasting time for both of us, I changed tack. "Forgive me, Dr. Greenstein, but I'm required to ask: Are you aware of any criminal charges against Dr. Harman?"

He laughed. "Absolutely not."

"Any suspensions of his medical license or hospital privileges?"

"No."

"Any complaints with the state medical board against Dr. Harman?"

Howard paused. My heart skipped a beat. "No . . . not any in which the board found any fault with his care," he finally said.

"But you are aware of a complaint?"

"I'm not comfortable with this." Howard's tone sounded defensive. "I don't think you're allowed, legally, to ask me about unsubstantiated complaints, are you?"

"Please, Dr. Greenstein, I'm kind of in over my head." I adopted the most helpless voice I could muster. "Not sure what I'm supposed to do on these reference checks. Truth is, I like Evan. It's a small town. And he's a very popular doctor."

"Evan's a good guy."

"I agree. But for the sake of thoroughness, could you just tell me about this complaint? Totally off the record. And then I won't be caught off guard if any of the other references mention it to one of my colleagues."

Howard sighed. "Yes, all right. As long it's off the record."

"One hundred percent."

"There was this young woman about eleven or twelve years ago. A patient of Evan's. She had a lot of psychiatric issues. You know what a borderline personality disorder is?"

"Yes." I was all too aware of the psychiatric disorder that was characterized by a long-term pattern of unstable relationships, distorted sense of self, and excessive emotional responses. "I've dealt with a number of BPD patients in my career. They can be very challenging."

"Well, this particular patient had extreme BPD," Howard grunted. "I'd seen her a few times myself when I was covering for Evan."

"And she lodged a complaint about Dr. Harman?"

"Yes." He exhaled heavily. "She went to the board with all kinds of wild accusations."

"Wild in what sense, Dr. Greenstein?"

"In every sense. Not only did she claim that Evan and she were involved in a sexual relationship, she said that he coerced her into it and that . . ." His voice trailed off.

"Yes?"

"That he used to drug her."

My breath caught. "Drug?"

"You know? With meds like Valium and GHB."

I squeezed my phone so tightly that my fingers ached. "GHB? She said that?"

"It's known as a date rape drug."

"I've heard of it, yes," I said, trying to steady my breathing. "How old was this patient?"

"Twenty or so when she lodged the complaint. She'd been a patient of Evan's for years. He did so much for her, and she absolutely terrorized him." He sighed. "No good deed goes unpunished and all."

"And the board, they obviously dismissed the charges?"

"They would have, for sure."

"Would have?" I almost choked on the words. "Why didn't they?"

"Well . . . Marci . . ." He cleared his throat. "She was so impulsive. And so self-destructive . . ."

"What happened to her?"

He paused another moment. "She hung herself."

CHAPTER 37

I couldn't fight off the chill, despite the relatively warm evening, after I finally got home from the office. I even lit a fire, but it didn't help.

Three young women, practically still kids. All dead by suicide. All patients of Evan's. And he appeared to have sexually abused at least two of them.

Of all the revelations from my conversation with Dr. Greenstein, the one that shook me most was hearing that one of his patients had accused Evan of drugging her with GHB. My mind kept drifting back to the night I had slept over at his place. All those memory gaps, including the moment when I'd gone to bed with him. I had never drunk to the point of blacking out before. And I had woken the next morning to the worst hangover of my life.

Had Evan roofied me, too?

I fired off another text to Kai. "Call me! It's urgent!" Then I tried the chief's number, but it went straight to voicemail, too.

My mouth was dry with worry, and I opened the fridge to get a drink. I wished there was a bottle of pinot grigio waiting inside—

anything to calm my nerves—but all I found was a container of almond milk and the jug of kombucha. I poured myself a glass of the fermented tea and sat down on the couch.

I closed my eyes and tried to calm myself through meditation. But I couldn't tame the wild thoughts. No question, Evan had been preying on his young and vulnerable patients, all of whom shared mental health issues. But three suicides—four, if I included David— among his victims seemed beyond coincidental. Especially when I considered that Brianna had tried to take Nevaeh—the one potential witness to her mom's assault—to her grave with her.

What if they weren't suicides?

I thought of Javier's adamance that Ketopram couldn't be linked to these deaths since nowhere else in the world had reported an association between the antidepressant and suicide. *Maybe it was because Ketopram had nothing to do with them?*

It blew my mind to consider that I'd woken up this morning suspecting Javier might have staged David's death, and now I was wondering if Evan had orchestrated all of them.

The stresses of the day and the terrifying revelations I'd heard were catching up to me. My head was spinning, and I was starting to feel woozy. Fatigue draped over me like a curtain. I could barely keep my eyes open. I flopped over to lie on my side. I reached for my phone, determined to try Kai one more time.

I heard shuffling behind me.

A warning sounded like a siren inside my skull. But I didn't have the energy to even turn my head to see who it was. I tried to raise my phone to call Kai, but my arm wouldn't cooperate. My mouth wouldn't open to cry out for help.

What is happening to me?

"I don't bother to lock my door in this town, either."

Evan!

I was too exhausted for fear to take hold. But I fought to stay conscious and struggled to shift my gaze toward the source of his voice. When my eyes finally did comply, I saw two of Evan's faces hovering above me.

"Kombucha. Gross. Don't know how you drink so much of that slimy new-age crap. You probably didn't notice, but I added a little kick to it. The almond milk, too, just in case."

I tried to tell him it was too late to cover up what he had done. That there was no point in hurting me. But my lips only quivered uselessly.

"Must admit, I was kind of surprised to get a text from my obnoxious old pal Howard this afternoon," Evan said. "Even more surprised to find out that I'd been applying for the hospital chief of staff job that I already have."

It was all I could do to keep my eyelids open.

His eyes pierced through me, and that smile—which I'd mistaken for so long as empathetic and caring—chilled me. I had to close my eyes.

"It's time to go, Taylor."

And then, for the first time in months, the Arctic went dark as night for me.

CHAPTER 38

My whole body shook. My head throbbed. But I felt wide awake, as if someone had roused me from sleep with a dousing of ice water. Afraid to move my head or make a peep, I absorbed my surroundings with a sweep of my eyes. I lay on a flimsy mattress. A skinny table with a padded bench attached stood beside me. Across the narrow space, a galley kitchen lined the opposite wall. I suddenly recognized I was riding inside an RV as it rattled along what must have been a very uneven dirt road. Through the nearest window, all I could see was the hazy light of the deep dusk.

With rising anxiety, I tried to spread my arms apart, but they wouldn't budge. I glanced down and saw padded leather restraints around my wrists. I struggled harder to free my arms, but the binding held tight. I could feel a similar kind of pressure encircling my ankles.

"Hello, Sleeping Beauty," I heard Evan say.

I turned and saw the back of his head rising above the vehicle's driver's seat. His familiar and yet now somehow foreign eyes stared back at me in the rearview mirror.

"Where are we?" I asked, surprised by how strong and clear my voice sounded.

"Thought we'd go for a drive," he said pleasantly. "Sorry about the bumps, Taylor. These old oil company roads can be rough. Worth it when you get there, though."

"You drugged me," I said, as the recent events congealed in my consciousness.

"I'm sorry." His tone was remorseless. "But did I ask you to pry into my personal life?"

My chest pounded. "What's the point of this, Evan? They already know."

"Who does?"

"Kai and the chief."

"They do? Then why didn't they come to your place to get me this evening? Between there and the RV, we were in town for hours before we left."

"What time is it?"

"About midnight," Evan said. "You slept well after your kombucha."

"Your GHB."

"Either way, no one suspects me, Taylor."

"I texted Kai. I told him everything."

"Except you didn't. I have your phone. Not now, of course. Had to leave it behind. Don't want us to be tracked." He chuckled. "I unlocked it using that angelic face of yours while you slept, and then I read through your texts. All you told Kai was that you needed to speak to him, you didn't say anything about me."

"I called him," I croaked, desperate to bluff my way out. I kept pulling at the restraints.

"I saw your calls, too. Three of them that lasted no more than eleven seconds. I'm thinking they went straight through to voicemail and that you just hung up."

The futility of my predicament was growing clearer by the second. I was in the middle of nowhere with a homicidal sociopath. I fought back panic. "Why, Evan?" I asked, frantic to engage him somehow, to distract him from whatever he planned to do with me, aware that wherever he was taking me would likely be the last place I ever saw.

"I told you. You meddled into my—"

"Not that," I cut him off. "Brianna, Amka, David . . . and Marci."

"Marci," he sighed. "The woman who unraveled my life. I wish Howard hadn't mentioned her to you. That big mouth of his opened up a whole can of worms."

"What happened to her?" I wanted to do anything I could to keep him talking, to keep him distracted, as I struggled to get free.

"She was batshit crazy. A borderline personality of the highest order. As manipulative as she was destructive. But, oh my god, was she seductive." He went quiet for a few seconds as the vehicle shimmied along the broken road. "She had me convinced I was her savior. She was the one who introduced me to GHB. Showed me how in the right dose it could heighten our pleasure. Ecstasy. But in the wrong dose . . ."

"What happened to her?" I repeated.

"Marci went too far. Way too far. She began to blackmail me. When I finally drew the line, she went straight to the Indiana State Medical Board. That bitch intended to ruin my life and my career. She was laughing when she told me what she'd done." He scoffed. "That's when I realized how useful GHB could be in a pinch."

"You drugged her? And then staged her suicide by hanging?"

"You make it sound so simple. Thin as she was, Marci was still a deadweight once unconscious. I almost put my back out getting her head through that noose."

I shuddered at how matter-of-fact he sounded.

"I didn't want to hurt her, Taylor. But what choice did I have? Do you know what they would've done to me if she could've proved a tenth of her allegations? It was about self-preservation. And I paid dearly for it." He motioned to the window. "Look at where the hell

I've ended up. I had to come to this frozen shithole to salvage the remnants of my career."

"How about Brianna?" I felt almost as nauseated by his murderous self-pity as I did from the jerky ride. "What did she do to deserve it?"

"Brianna. Oh, she was different." His tone softened. "She broke my heart. I've never been so in love. Those magnetic eyes. Those exquisite lips." He sighed. "Bree was such a hot mess when she first came to me that night in the ER—four months pregnant and 'overdosed' on a harmless amount of medication. But I put her back together. Never said a word as she continued to live with that fucking little moron Dylan, who actually believed he was Nevaeh's dad."

"You knew about Keefer?" I asked.

"She told me all about the manipulative prick that first night in the ER." Evan glared at me through the rearview mirror, and I froze. "Bree loved me. Me! We were biding our time until we could be together. I didn't even touch her . . . not that way . . . until four or five months after Nevaeh was born." He shook his head. "But who knew she'd react the way she did?"

I couldn't believe I'd once considered Evan a good man, a friend even. *Keep him talking, Taylor, it's your only chance.* "How did she react, Evan?"

"I thought GHB would make it easier . . . break the ice, as it were. It worked, too. It got better after the first couple times. But then Bree sank back into the bottomless pit of depression. She didn't want anything to do with anyone, including me. I had to threaten her with Nevaeh—that I'd convince the real father to claim custody—just to get her to see me. I even worried Bree might go the same route as Marci did and report me. But I never once stopped loving her." He paused again as we slowed to a crawl and the road became even more jolting. "But man, how she resented me. Me. The person who loved and supported her most in this world."

"Supported her?" I blurted.

"Yes, Taylor. Supported." He eyed me stonily through the rearview mirror. "Despite her bitterness, her ungratefulness, I wanted Bree to get better. To be whole again. Three years of mainly lows, I never wavered. I even referred her to David for help. What a mistake that was! But I was desperate for things to be back to the way they'd been between us. Three goddamn years I had to wait for her to emerge from that darkness! But it was so worth it when she finally did with the help of Ketopram. Things were good between Bree and me for a while. Very good. We were going to be together. A family. And then—out of nowhere—she decides to leave Utqiagvik. Without me."

"She told you that?"

"No." He snorted. "Amka did. At one of her appointments. Can you believe it?"

"Were you and Amka . . ."

"Of course not! She was my patient," Evan said without a trace of irony. "But she was the one who let it slip that Bree was planning to leave. To go to Fairbanks to track down Dylan. That useless little twerp."

"Did Amka know about you and Brianna?"

"Only at the very end. And I didn't find out until the night Amka died. Bree hadn't told anyone up till that point. That was our deal. Same reason I felt safe in letting her talk to David. Bree knew I could have Nevaeh taken away at a moment's notice." He laughed. "You of all people know how it is. An unstable single mother with mental health issues? Sometimes, it's just best for the child to be removed from the home."

As frightened as I felt, the heinousness of his cruelty outraged me. I wriggled harder against the bindings. "That's why you killed Brianna?" I asked. "Because she was leaving you?"

"It wasn't that simple. The night she died, what a clusterfuck! Nevaeh was supposed to be staying with Kerry and Gus." He heaved a sigh. "It started off well enough. Bree and I were talking. I told her I forgave her for betraying me, for planning to abandon me. That we could still work it out. I meant it, too. We even ended up in bed. The sex got kind of rough, but that's how she liked it. And then—of all nights—Nevaeh has to get up and walk right in on us."

The mental image disgusted me, but I needed to keep him talking. "What did you do?"

"Initially, Bree seemed OK with it. I even gave Nevaeh a half dose of liquid Dramamine. But the moment the kid was back in bed, Bree absolutely lost it. Freaked out like I've never seen. She swore she was going to tell Gus. Go to the police. She threatened to share all the emails and texts I'd ever sent her over the years. I swear, it was like with Marci all over again. But worse.

"I managed to calm Bree, finally," Evan continued, talking in a stream of consciousness, as if eager to unload his secrets. "But I knew that I'd lost her. That she'd turned against me. It was only a matter of time until she turned me in. And what was I going to do then? Go farther north? To the North Pole?"

"So you drugged Brianna and set her up in the running car in her garage?"

"It was her or me."

"And Nevaeh?"

"The kid saw us! She knew who I was. What was I supposed to do?" he asked, as though that should have been obvious to me. "Trust me, Taylor. I got choked up carrying the kid out to the car. In a way, I'm relieved I only gave Nevaeh a half a dose of Dramamine. I'm kind of glad she made it out, despite the added complications."

As awake as I felt, I still wondered if it was all a nightmare. I couldn't imagine a more twisted conversation.

"At first, it was all manageable," Evan said. "Don't get me wrong. I was crushed to lose Bree, of course, but life went on. Nevaeh got a new home. No one was the wiser. But then that loser Rick had to go and steal from his own boss, that piece of shit drug dealer Eddie."

"What did Rick have to do with it?"

"He went on the run and took his cokehead girlfriend with him.

But the moment Amka disappeared, David had to ride into town on his white steed, determined to compensate for his guilt over Brianna's death by tracking down Amka. Jesus! And then he had to dig into Bree's past, too. I desperately tried to warn him off, I really did."

It suddenly hit me. "David's beating? You were behind that, weren't you?"

"That clown, Cupun Meelak, is a patient of mine. The kid has a little opioid issue. I paid him in pills to go discourage David. But his steroid-addled beefcake of a buddy overdid it. He collapsed David's lung so he couldn't fly. Those idiots grounded David in the very last place I wanted him to be." Evan stopped talking for a minute. When he began again, his voice was noticeably calmer. "I still thought it would be OK. But David kept poking deeper into Bree's past. Then Rick brought Amka back into town. And she took off and showed up on my doorstep at two in the morning, coked out of her mind, screaming all kinds of craziness."

"Like what?" I asked, stilling my wrists as the fight seeped out of me.

"Listening to her rave on, you would've thought I was responsible for global warming or something. Apparently, Bree had told her about us the last time they saw each other. Not everything, but enough. And Amka—stoned as she was—had somehow decided I'd driven Bree to suicide." He glanced over his shoulder at me. "I had no intention of touching Amka, but there was no reasoning with her. You know how it is with cokeheads? Impossible! It was clear that what was best—for both of us, really—was for Amka to follow the same path her sister had." He nodded to himself, as if his rationale was airtight. "It was so easy. Amka fell into a deep sleep within a couple of sips of the spiked drink I finally convinced her to have. For what it's worth, she didn't suffer. She didn't even wake up when she hit the water."

Is that to be my fate, too? "And David?" I croaked.

The RV sped up again. "After Amka's death, David was on a

total crusade. He told me he wasn't going to stop until he found Brianna's abuser. I'll admit it, Taylor. I panicked. I could've maybe blamed it all on Keefer. After all, the son of a bitch had seduced both Amka and Brianna while they were his students. Just kids." He snorted his disgust, oblivious to how much worse he was than even the teacher. "But there I was, alone with David in his hotel room, pouring him a scotch. The solution in my hand. All I had to do was add a couple drops of GHB."

"How did you get him to overdose on all the other pills then?"

"That part was kind of ingenious," he said smugly. "After David passed out, I went back to the hospital and helped myself to a feeding tube and a few other supplies. I snuck back in up the fire escape. With David unconscious, I crushed up the pills, dissolved them in whiskey, and fed them down with a big syringe."

"Jesus," I murmured. Though I had suspected Evan of being involved in the deaths, to hear him walk me through the specifics of each murder was horrifying. I tugged again at the restraints.

"I liked David," Evan said wistfully. "I really did. I wished it hadn't come to that. But the truth is, after he was gone, everything was so much tidier. It really only left one loose end."

"Me?"

"No. Well, now obviously," he said. "Until today, when you called Howard, I didn't expect you to be involved. God, I wish he hadn't mentioned Marci." Evan sighed again. "No, I meant Rick. For all I knew, Amka had told that loose cannon of a boyfriend about Bree and me, too."

"But Amka's dad shot Rick."

"And why do you think Tom did that?" Evan asked. "I convinced him Rick pushed Amka out of the boat that night. Then, after Sonya broke her hip, I let Tom know exactly when the cops would be taking Rick to visit his grandma. Christ, I might as well have pulled the trigger on the rifle, too." He sounded proud of himself.

"So many dead," I said. "Do you really think you can sell a fourth suicide, Evan? As if the whole town has turned into some kind of death cult? You don't think the chief and Kai will see right through it?"

"It will seem a lot more believable after I publish a note on your Instagram account."

"A suicide note? What am I going to say?" I uttered a bitter laugh. "I just wanted to join the club?"

"No. You're going to say that you couldn't live any longer with the specter of Huntington's disease hanging over your head."

Even after all that had come before, those last words of his still rocked me. "How . . . how did you know?"

"Remember, Taylor? Everyone comes here to escape something. Besides, you think you're the only person who can do an online search? I found your mom's obituary soon after you got here. And then that night you and I had drinks and our little fun—"

"The night you roofied me!"

"I don't even think it was necessary. I'm pretty sure you would have fucked me, anyway. Regardless, you were very chatty. You went on and on about how tormented you were over the Huntington's. How you couldn't bear the idea of dying the same slow, horrible death as your mom did." He snorted. "Have to tell you, you've got a weird approach to foreplay."

The tears came out of nowhere.

"It was just fun, you know, Taylor? Nothing personal. There have been others like you along the way. But my heart always stayed true to Bree."

"You bastard," I sobbed.

"Look at this way, Taylor. You won't have to stress anymore. Worrying that every time you spill a drop or struggle to find a name that the Huntington's is about to set in. The incapacity, the helplessness, the indignity . . . Now none of that will ever happen to you." The RV slowed to a stop. Evan looked over his shoulder at me with a cruel grin. "How about that? Perfect timing. We're here."

CHAPTER 39

"I'll be back in a minute. Don't go anywhere," Evan said with a laugh as he climbed out of the driver's seat.

I jerked my head around, frantically searching for something to grab between my hands as a weapon. But it was hopeless. Even if my arms weren't bound, there was nothing nearby that wasn't fixed to the walls or the floor. Seconds crawled by as I fluctuated between resignation and despair. I thought of my mom. My brothers. And of course, Gabe. Why did I ever leave California? Only to wind up here, to die in the most desolate place on earth.

About five minutes later, the back door to the RV slid open, and Evan stepped inside. My heart thudded harder when I saw that he was wearing rubber boots over waterproof waders that disappeared under his nylon jacket.

He stood above me, close enough that I got a whiff of his spearmint gum. He pointed to my ankle restraints. "I'm going to loosen those now, Taylor. Will be best for both of us if you cooperate."

I didn't say a word or move a muscle as Evan knelt beside my legs and began to loosen the straps. The second I felt them fall free,

I swung my hip out and kicked wildly. My heel smashed into his thigh just above his knee. He yelped and fell back against the side of the RV.

With my arms still restrained in front of me, I tensed my abdomen to sit myself up. Before I could swing my legs off the mattress, Evan threw himself on top of me, pinning me back down to the bench.

"You bitch!" His spittle sprayed my eyes, and his nauseatingly minty breath filled my nostrils. "You're going to wish you didn't do that."

"I should just let you kill me?"

Instead of answering, he got to his feet, freeing my legs again. But before I could get up again, he grabbed me by the armpits and jerked me painfully to my feet.

"Move!" he barked, shoving me forward.

I shuffled along to the open door and then onto the steps of the RV into the near twilight outside. I lost my footing on the last step, and Evan grabbed me roughly by the shoulder to steady me.

Without a jacket, I shivered in the chilly air. My eyes darted everywhere, trying to recognize my surroundings. We were at a beach, close to one end of a protected cove, but beyond that I had no idea where I was. All I could see was tundra beside us and black water ahead.

"Goddamn charley horse." Evan bent over to rub his thigh. "You'll regret that."

"I hope it hurts."

He pushed me toward the water. "The currents are good here. The fishermen like this cove. You're sure to be found."

I gritted my teeth. "Another suicide by drowning?"

"No time to be any more creative."

I dug my feet into the ground, trying to resist.

"The water's no more than forty-five degrees." He shoved harder. "It'll be quick. Better than you deserve."

A surging sense of defiance was edging out my fear. I allowed him to push me to within a couple yards of the water. "No!" I screamed, as I wriggled free of his grip and bolted along the beach.

I only got about seven or eight strides, before I tripped over a divot and toppled onto the hard sand, hitting my forehead against a sharp rock.

"Get up!" Evan snapped from somewhere behind me.

"Fuck you!" I said, as I felt blood trickle into my eye. I thought I heard a buzzing sound over the lapping of the ocean. I wondered if I was concussed.

"All right, we'll do it your way," Evan said.

He grabbed my shoulder and rolled me roughly over onto my back. As I stared up into his face, I couldn't believe he'd ever managed to mask the fury and heartlessness that filled those dark eyes.

He seized me by the armpits and yanked backward. With my wrists bound, there was no way to wriggle free of his crushing grip. Ignoring the pain, I fought to dig my heels into the sand as he dragged me toward the water. My legs thrashed, unable to resist the backward motion.

"Let go," I screamed.

The icy water hit my neck like the slap of a frozen hand.

"Stop, Evan!"

But he kept dragging me out, and soon my entire body was immersed.

The buzzing grew louder. The freezing water soaked my hair and enveloped my ears and jaw.

"Evan, let me—" But the water filled my mouth and nostrils and choked off the rest of my pleas.

He shoved my head down until it was submerged. I struggled, but the world closed in on me. Out of nowhere, I had a panicky flashback to second grade when a gang of kids dogpiled on top of me until I couldn't breathe.

Suddenly, he relaxed his grip and my face broke through the

water again. I sputtered and hungrily gulped at the cold air. But a new terror gripped me. Was Evan planning to play with me like a cat with its prey? To torture me with repeated dunks until he got bored enough to just let me die?

The water dripped out of my ears, and I slowed my thrashing. The buzzing had quieted. I thought I heard him say something. But then I realized it wasn't Evan who was speaking.

I rotated my head toward the horizon, from where the voice floated across the water. I made out the faint hull of a boat. I had to strain my eyes in the weak light to see the figures standing on the bow. Two of them were in uniform. A third man held a bullhorn to his mouth. And the fourth held a rifle.

"Let her go!" the chief's voice barked over the bullhorn.

I looked over to Evan, who was still gripping my hair, as he squinted at the police boat.

"It's over, Evan!" Natan called.

"Don't be so goddamn sure!" Evan shouted back.

"Let her go! Now."

Several horrible seconds passed where no one spoke, and I fought to keep my face above water.

"Not this bitch," he grumbled, loud enough only for me to hear.

My head was shoved under again. With hope so close, I thrashed even harder, but the sense of suffocation was overwhelming. I felt dizzy. My vision tunneled. I fought to stay conscious.

I heard two thuds.

Evan's grip loosened on my hair, then was gone. I frantically flexed my neck, straining to pull my face out of the water.

I managed to inhale two quick breaths of air, but as I drifted free, with my arms still bound, I couldn't stop myself from sinking. To my horror, my head dipped below the water again.

Kicking as hard I could I bumped into something that floated beside me. I realized it had to be Evan.

The dizziness intensified. Pressure formed on my chest. I could feel myself drifting in and out of consciousness. Was I really going to die this close to being rescued?

Then I felt something reach under my back and scoop me out of the water with ease. It took me a moment to realize I was enveloped in Kai's thick arms as he carried me to the shore.

"You're safe now, Taylor. Just breathe. You're gonna be OK."

CHAPTER 40

After Kai found me a clean, oversize uniform to slip into, he wrapped three blankets around me while the chief served me hot coffee from a thermos. I didn't need the caffeine, but the warmth down my throat was exquisite and helped to settle my chattering teeth.

One of the junior officers stayed ashore to watch over Evan's body. The other one—who was trained in first aid and seemed eager to apply it—insisted on bandaging the cut on my forehead, before he sat down at the helm and turned the boat back toward town.

I had no doubt the terror of the past few hours would come back to haunt me, but at that moment, sitting with Kai and the chief in the bow, I felt giddy with relief and almost euphoric over the second chance I'd been given. I was also immensely curious. As soon as I finished summarizing Evan's informal confession, I looked from Kai to Natan and back and said, "Now your turn."

"Gus," said Natan.

I gaped at them. "How the hell did Gus know where I was?"

"When he got home from the shop, Kerry was a mess." Natan said. "When she told Gus what Nevaeh had said about the nightmares, Gus was furious. He was convinced she had witnessed Evan rape Brianna. He called me straightaway."

"Between Gus's call and the urgent messages you left . . ." Kai shook his head. "When you didn't answer any of our calls or texts, we figured you had to be with Evan."

"But how did you track us down?" I asked.

"We couldn't trace your phone," Natan said. "It was offline, which made no sense."

"So we focused on Evan's instead," Kai said. "When we tracked his weak signal—off-road and heading for a desolate cove in the middle of the night—it set off alarm bells. We knew the only way to catch up to him was by sea."

"Brilliant. Thank you." I reached over and patted Kai's arm. "You weren't answering any of my messages, I assumed—"

"No, Taylor." Kai broke into a shy smile. "Wasn't like that."

"You picked a terrible time to get yourself abducted," Natan said, leaning forward and refilling my cup.

"And why's that?" I said, trying to steady the cup in my still trembling hand.

"We were already out on this very same boat making the single biggest drug bust of the past six years in Northern Alaska."

"What kind of bust?"

"Eddie was trafficking a couple kilos of coke, a brick of fentanyl, and about a thousand tablets of MDMA on a fishing boat out to the rigs at Prudhoe Bay," the chief said. "We cut them off at Admiralty Bay."

"Congratulations!" I said. "How did you find out?"

Kai and the chief shared a glance. "We got an anonymous tip just as that boat was leaving harbor," Natan said.

"Anonymous?" I said.

Kai nodded. "But I'd bet you a grand right now that the guy who called in the tip was on a spin bike at the time."

"Manny?" I laughed, feeling oddly pleased at the idea.

"Looks like maybe Manny got revenge for his stabbing after all," Kai said. "The crew on the fishing boat were eager to roll on Eddie. We've already picked him up."

"But we lost cell reception out on the water and didn't have a chance to check our messages until we got back," Natan said. "That's when we found out you were missing."

I slumped back in my seat, the effects of the night catching up with me. "Well, I'm glad you kept looking for me."

"I still can't believe it," Natan said. "All those murders dressed up as suicides. Evan even engineered Rick's shooting. Almost ten years I knew the guy. Never once did it cross my mind." He sighed. "I must be losing my touch. First the teacher, and now the doctor."

"No one suspected, Chief," I said. "Sociopaths are always the most convincing. Lying for them is like breathing for the rest of us."

Natan rubbed his face. "Those poor girls."

"And poor David, too," Kai added. "All he wanted was to help Amka. Doc was a stand-up guy."

I leaned forward and grabbed both of their hands in mine, overwhelmed with gratitude. "Five more minutes and you could've added me to that list."

Kai squeezed my hand. "Doctors are replaceable. You're not."

I smiled at him. Soon I would find the right time and way to tell him how much I cared for him, even though those feelings weren't romantic. In the meantime, I just held on to his hand.

All I wanted was to go home. And that home was far away from Utqiagvik.

CHAPTER 41

Nearly three weeks had passed since Evan tried to drown me. I'd had two terrible nightmares—from one of them, I woke up screaming—but otherwise I avoided thinking about him. The women he had killed were a different story. I couldn't stop thinking about them. The hell he must have put Brianna through all those years before finally killing her. And as if Amka's murder weren't devastation enough for the Obed family, Evan had ensured they suffered even more. Amka's father was in jail awaiting trial for killing Rick, although I heard the state's attorney was considering leniency. And we'd had to move his wife to an assisted living facility, because she was in too much pain and too lonely to live by herself.

But of all Evan's victims, I dwelled most on David. Kai was right: he'd only come to town to help. It broke my heart to realize that, as blameless as David was in the girls' deaths, he carried the weight of responsibility for them right into the grave Evan had dug for him.

One of the first calls I'd made after my rescue was to David's ex-wife. Beth had already heard from the Medical Examiner's Office, but she still got choked up on the phone discussing his murder. "Ali is too devastated to see it," she said. "But once she gets over the worst of the shock, it will make a difference. To know that her father didn't abandon her . . . That will mean something one day."

I believed it, too.

I had my own bridges to mend. I'd been trying for days to arrange a videoconference with Javier, who was back in Anchorage. And now that the time had come, my palms were sweaty as I clicked the icon on my laptop to initiate the call.

I couldn't help but smile when I saw Javier on the screen, dressed in a camel hair blazer paired with a pale blue shirt. His hair was perfect, as always. All he was missing was an ascot to make the outfit complete in my mind. But despite his affable grin, something was a bit off. He looked a little older, a little less radiant.

"Hello, Taylor," he said, his voice as warm as ever.

"Hi, Javier. Thanks for taking the time."

"For you, always."

I wondered if such flattery came to him out of reflex. "Can I start by apologizing?" I asked.

He brushed it away with a flick of his fingers. "No need."

"There's a huge need, Javier. I accused you of terrible things. I'm surprised you haven't sued me."

Javier shrugged. "I don't want your house. Matter of fact, I don't want any house in that town. So what would be the point?"

I laughed. "I really am sorry, Javier."

"You don't need to be, Taylor. You reached the same conclusion David had. And you both had good reason to believe it. How were any of us to know there was a sociopath behind it all, pulling the strings?"

"Thank you." I touched my palms together and held up my hands. "How are you doing?"

"I miss David."

There was something so moving in the quiet way he said it that I had to swallow away a lump in my throat. "I do, too. And I knew him only a fraction as well you did."

"He just wanted to do right by his patients. You can't ask more of a doctor."

"He almost cared too much, if that's a thing."

"This whole . . . ordeal . . . has given me pause."

"How so?"

"You may not believe this, Taylor, but I'm not the most humble man alive," he said with a small wink. "What happened in Utqiagvik really made me question myself and my motives. Of course, it turns out that Ketopram had nothing to do with those senseless deaths. But at the time, I began to believe it could have been linked. Out of pride—and yes—self-interest, I rationalized it all away. I justified it to myself, too. I lost my priorities. I should've put my friend and patient first."

"Wow, Javier, that's incredibly self-aware of you. *And* humble."

He waved his hand again. "Ah, it was only temporary. Turns out I was right all along. And I'm as infallible and insightful as I always believed myself to be."

I laughed. "You're something, Javier, you know that?"

"Ha! Tell that to my first three wives."

"Speaking of ex-wives, I spoke to Beth a couple weeks ago. But I haven't had any contact since. How's the family coping?"

"Poor Ali," he sighed. "I wish David could've heard her at the funeral. She spoke beautifully. He would've been so proud. She really, really loved her dad."

"I can't even imagine."

"And you?" Javier raised an eyebrow. "I heard about the . . . attempt on your life. That must've been terrifying, Taylor. How are you managing?"

"I'm all right." I saw no point in going into the details. "Still processing it, I suppose."

"You will be for a while, no doubt," he said. "I know several excellent trauma counselors here in Anchorage. If you need me to connect—"

"Thanks, Javier. I have enough support for now." That wasn't necessarily true, but I wasn't ready to involve Javier or trauma counselors.

He nodded his understanding. "So what's next for Taylor Holmes?"

"I'm leaving Utqiagvik."

"Really? Why would anyone leave that charming little homicidal town?"

I laughed. "It's really not so bad. There's a desolate beauty to the place. And a surprisingly strong sense of community."

"To each her own, I suppose. So where will you go?"

"Back to San Diego. There's a job waiting for me there. But I won't leave here until they've found a replacement for me."

"Are you really going to be OK?"

"I am. Thank you."

"Excellent. You're good people, Taylor. I hope you realize that."

"You, too, Javier. You, too."

I closed the chat window with a click of my mouse and stared at the email inbox that popped up in its place, uninspired to tackle my list of new messages. I'd already handed in my resignation, although it wasn't clear how long it would take to replace me. It didn't matter. The job in San Diego had an open-ended start date. While it was my friends and family who drew me home, I had thought about reaching out to Gabe. But I wasn't going to. It would've been too selfish. He had a new life, and I had no right to interfere with it.

But one thing was clear to me. It was time to stop hiding.

I opened my drawer and extracted the envelope from the state lab. I had taken the blood test for Huntington's disease the day after my abduction, and I only received the results yesterday. I still hadn't opened the envelope. I wasn't sure when I would. But I was determined not to let the threat of Huntington's control my life any longer.

That night on the beach, as I'd thrashed in the freezing water, as my vision tunneled and I felt my life slipping away, all I begged for was another chance. I'd been given that much. And regardless of the test results, I wasn't about to waste it.

ACKNOWLEDGMENTS

I am blessed to have many friends, colleagues, and professionals available and willing to bounce ideas off, from the first inkling of a story right through to the final draft. Never more has this been true than in writing *The Darkness in the Light*. As usual, there are too many people to acknowledge individually, and the risk of inadvertently missing someone runs too high. But there are a few people I must single out for going above and beyond.

This novel delves into the world of virtual medicine and psychiatry. And while the story is fictional, I was determined to capture those aspects as accurately as I could. And I am thankful for the feedback from Dr. Anna Nazif, a superb psychiatrist who helped me do it.

I am so lucky to work with Kit Schindell, a friend and a supremely talented freelance editor. After all these years of partnering over many manuscripts, we have found the perfect cadence for real-time improvements to the stories. I also rely on another close friend, Mariko Miller, a first-pass reader who is full of wonderful insights. And it was a particular joy to get early input from my daughters, Chelsea and Ashley, on the story. I'm also thankful for the guidance of my agents, Henry Morrison and Danny Baror.

Of course, you would not be reading this were it not for the support of my publishing house. I'm delighted to continue my partnership with Simon & Schuster Canada, including (publicist extraordinaire) Jillian Levick, Nita Pronovost, Gregory Tilney, David Millar, Felicia Quon, and Kevin Hanson, a publisher with a big heart. And I am particularly grateful for the insights, ideas, and collaboration of my talented editor, Laurie Grassi, who always brings out the best in my writing.

Finally, this novel deals with a very sensitive theme in the form of suicidality. It is an issue I confront far too often in the Emergency Department. I have seen more damage and suffering as a direct or indirect consequence of attempted and completed suicides than from almost any other form of emergency. I am acutely aware of the prevalence and insidiousness of suicidality, which, like all other mental health issues, has only intensified since COVID. I understand how taboo the topic can be, but I am also of the belief that talking about it is one way to help prevent it. And I hope this story helps to raise awareness in a respectful way about another deadly, although potentially silent, epidemic.

ABOUT THE AUTHOR

©Michael Bednar Photography

Daniel Kalla is an internationally bestselling author of novels, including *Lost Immunity*, *The Last High*, and *We All Fall Down*. Kalla practices emergency medicine in Vancouver, British Columbia. Visit him at **DanielKalla.com** or follow him on Twitter **@DanielKalla**.

> "Kalla has long had his stethoscope on the heartbeat of his times."
> *Toronto Star*

Also by DANIEL KALLA
Globe and Mail and *Toronto Star* bestsellers

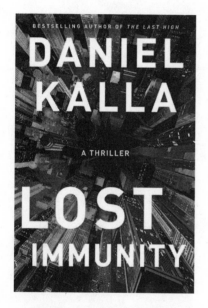

> "Kalla . . . has a knack for writing eerily prescient thrillers."
> **CBC Books**

> "A thrilling, front-line drama about the opioid crisis."
> **KATHY REICHS**

SIMON &
SCHUSTER
CANADA